SANCTITY OF FREEDOM

AN INSPECTOR WILLIAM FOX SERIES

PETER THOMAS PONTSA

Iconic Scribes Press Inc.

Reviews

This sequel offered great pacing and intensity, complete with some nice twists along the way. The characters and their relationships are believable, and the intricacies of foreign affairs have been incredibly well researched. I felt as though I had been thrust into the underworlds of China, North Korea and South Korea.

MIKE MADILL, AUTHOR

For Angela, my best friend, my confidante, and my love.

Quotes

"Freedom lies in being bold."

Robert Frost

"Freedom is not worth having if it does not connote freedom to err and even sin."

Mahatma Gandi

"From every mountain side, let freedom ring."

Martin Luther King.

Contents

One

The Note

May 2019

The ship's shadow shimmered against the sun-bleached skyline of the distant city. For once, Do Yun Cho had made the right choice. The price he would pay could very well be his life. He took a drag of the cigarette, exhaled and flicked the remainder over the stern. Little did he know it would be the last one he ever smoked.

He turned toward the approaching footsteps and stared into the face of trouble. After thirteen days at sea, the North Korean agent demanded his answer. "Are you coming back?"

"No, I made a promise never to go back."

"You, stupid man," he said. "You must return!" he yelled shaking with fury.

"Never!" said the other.

"This was your last warning," he shouted. He stomped and grabbed Cho's windbreaker. Cho struggled, pushing away from the aggressor.

"No," he repeated as the glint of polished steel, followed by searing pain, felled him to his knees. He grabbed at his gut, now perforated with multiple stab wounds. The blade's final slash severed the trachea. The killer threw the body over the aft rail, the splash imperceptible, lost in the turbulence that washed it away. The activity drew seagulls and cormorants soaring toward the void that disappeared as fast as it had appeared. The killer wiped the blade and his blood-splattered hands with his bandana, then replaced the knife back in its sheath. He released the bandana into the light wind and watched it flutter to the river. His eyes swept along the deck. It was empty. Relieved, he placed both hands on the aft rail and peered into the propeller wash. Reassured, he found his phone and cupped the device as a gust tousled his hair.

"Is it done?" asked the grit-laden voice.

"It was quick. He refused to obey," the killer uttered in harsh Korean.

He retreated from the stern and paced to the galley for his shift. His assignment, set by his superiors in North Korea, had been completed to the letter.

He had anticipated a small degree of remorse from the defector and made provisions to bring him back. This awkward execution was right on Canada's doorstep. He tried reasoning with the stubborn man to no avail. His orders were clear: bring him back or dispatch the traitor. The Reconnaissance General Bureau (RGB), North Korea's Intelligence Organization, had trained him to be an artful killer. He had performed his duty. There was nothing else he could have done.

The ship carrying Japanese manufactured electrical machinery would be delivered at De Port-de-Montréal this afternoon at Terminal Tremont Fifty-Two. He planned to disembark and meet an accomplice, be driven to the airport and flown out of Canada before the authorities pieced it together.

His mission and escape route were planned with little leeway for mistakes. There was a high probability of being apprehended if his associate missed their rendezvous. It was essential he cut and run to the safety of North Korea.

***

The spring weather's ice melt cleared the St. Lawrence River. Freighters and cargo ships moved freely along the seaway. Much-needed materials arrived and resupplied the country, because of its explosive economy.

Blessed with a balmy day in May, William Fox and Tracy Jordon arrived at the marina for the pre-opening of boating season.

William took a weekend off. As an inspector at RCMP Montréal's C Division his busy schedule allowed little time for fun, so he was looking forward to some downtime with Tracy.

A few enthusiastic boaters primed for a glorious Sunday morning milled about the docks. The marina owner making his rounds waved to William who towered above the rest.

"Make sure you bring your vest," he said, nudging his friend beside him.

"Got it," said William holding up his life jacket gripped in his well-developed arm.

"Not that one, the bulletproof one," he replied as both men chuckled. William extended his middle finger hiding it along his thigh.

"I saw that," said Tracy. "Just smile and wave back."

"He's an asshole," said William waggling his hand.

"I know. Just ignore him," Tracy said, tossing a microfiber cloth at William. "Let's get started."

Last year while on patrol, William and officer Philip White were ambushed, on the seaway. The gangsters shot up and damaged his cruiser the *Midnight Fox*. A near death experience William would like to forget.

Tracy stood mid-height with blonde hair and steel-blue eyes and resembled Scarlett Johansson. An outspoken and strong-willed woman, she had led an expedition for Chinese artifacts. She reunited with William after he rescued her from Triad kidnappers intent on stealing the treasure. Like today, she often kept him in line when he got antsy.

William wore torn jeans and a beat-up sweatshirt with McGill embossed on the front. Tracy dressed in dingy leggings and a perforated t-shirt. They spent the better part of the morning cleaning the vessel for a shakedown run. The marina had dry-docked the boat for the winter and now it required attention.

William's brown eyes swept across the sleek sharp bow. His soft circular pressure with Carnauba wax made its surface glisten. A lax river breeze tussled Tracy's blonde hair. She rubbed her microfiber cloth over the *Midnight Fox's* hand painted cursive. Overlaid beside it a red stripe split the length of the stealthy hull. William strode ten paces to the stern and removed the engine cover. He checked the fluids and assessed the boat's running gear.

In preseason, an opportunity opened for boaters to carry out early safety maintenance. William, an experienced skipper, expected to be on the water sooner by taking precautions. Most issues could be remedied during pre-inspection and a shakedown run.

William started the twin Mercury Engines and released the bow while Tracy freed the aft lines. They leaped into the cockpit as the boat drifted away. William slid the throttles forward and the cruiser's bow lifted. He guided the boat out of the marina, headed into the channel and coxswained toward the Jacque Cartier bridge. Tracy shook her head in the gust, and it tangled her lustrous locks. She smiled face-first into the breeze, enjoying the cool crispness of freedom. William braced himself as he shoved the twin levers forward in the gate.

"Let's see what this baby can do," said William, grinning.

William freewheeled across the channel, checking his gauges while listening to the sterndrive for issues. The police scanner crackled.

Frowning, he reduced the engine speed and slowed to a crawl, listening to the dispatch. The Longueuil Agglomeration Police Services (SPAL) was attending a homicide scene at Parc de l'lle Charron near Terrasse-Charbonneau. The Coast Guard was on location along with the investigating officers. A body had been discovered on the municipal beach on Charron Island and the media was already on scene. Grasping the severity of the situation curiosity got the best of him.

"Tracy, we're not far. I'd like to check it out."

"Oh, my God. When are you going to stop? This was supposed to be our day together!"

"Just for a few minutes, Tracy. I need to see what's going on. They may need my help."

"All right. But we have to get back, and soon," she said, rolling her eyes.

William knew the better idea was to forget the call rather than get entangled. *But a dead body on a public beach concerned all police departments.* His curiosity already had annoyed Tracy, and it might get worse the more he immersed himself.

His main concern dealt with national security. If the deceased had an international connection, part of his mandate, set down by the Ministry of Public Safety, and the Federal Police Commissioner, included connecting homicides with terrorist activities.

He arrived at the scene only to be waved off. William extended his badge, and the officer gestured him back to the dock. Two uniformed police officers helped secure his cruiser.

"Bonjour gentlemen. I'm Inspector William Fox."

"Bonjour Inspector. What brings you here?" said the officer.

"Just professional interest. Perhaps the RCMP can help."

"We have a homicide investigator on the scene," said the officer pointing toward the orange security tape.

"Tracy, wait here. I'll be back in a minute."

Tracy slapped the vinyl seat, scowling. Her date with William had taken a turn for the worse. She nearly exploded in fury, bouncing in the seat.

William walked past the large mobile command center; a high-tech vehicle capable of data processing. He lifted the perimeter tape, glanced over at the still body under the protective canopy. William saw an officer near the crime scene, appearing to be the person in charge, and waved at him to get his attention.

Montréal Gazette journalists rushed the orange tape in anticipation of a statement from the new arrival while constables held them off.

The investigator rubbed his forehead and stepped forward in comfortable rubber-soled boots. A snug, grayish windbreaker hugged his solid frame, along with his slim fit charcoal chinos, his grizzled hair and his beard neatly trimmed. He turned to William, holding a clipboard and wearing blue micro flex gloves. A pen in his left hand publicized his south paw, a liability to unsuspecting challengers. William approached and exposed his belt badge to him.

"Bonjour, je suis l'inspecteur Fox."

"Ton français est rouillé. Peut-être que l'anglais sera meilleur. I'm Detective Guy Allard by the way," he said, launching an automated smile.

"Pleased to meet you," said William.

"Inspector Fox, your French ... a bit rusty, yes? Perhaps you'd prefer English?"

"English would be preferred. May I speak with you about this homicide?"

Guy handed over the pen and said, "Sign in."

William's eyes darted along the sheet as he signed.

"How may I help the Inspector?"

"I'd like to take a look at the body."

Investigator Allard looked up from his sign-in sheet, wrinkling his brow.

William caught the annoyance and realized Guy Allard was formidable. As tough cops went, he resembled a pillar of hardened flint. The kind of guy who went by the book and dished it out as good as he got. The sort of professional William respected.

"Why?" asked Guy.

"This is not protocol, but the victim may be of interest to my department. I'd like to take a few photographs," said William. "We'll run them through our system."

Guy removed his shades, gave William a cold disapproving glare, and slapped his clipboard on his thigh.

"Okay, your database may be useful."

The coroner paused and waved over the gurney that would transport the body to the pathology lab.

"Pardon, Monsieur. I am with the RCMP. Detective Allard gave me permission for a peek," said William.

Guy said to the coroner, "It's okay. He can take a look."

The coroner unzipped the bag. William took a facial photograph first. The slash through the neck was grave. William noticed scrapes and bruises indicative of a desperate struggle.

William retrieved his cell and located his Mobile Biometric Check, a digital fingerprinting application. He asked the coroner to rotate the arm and focused the camera lens at the digits of the sodden hand, then repeated the process with the other hand. Satisfied with the image results he hoisted himself up and stood beside Detective Allard and shook his head.

"His prints are not in the system."

"He may be a foreign national," said Guy. "It's amazing how fast the Biometric system check works. Far cry from the old days."

"True."

Guy brought the clipboard to his chest.

"We discovered a temporary Canadian passport. His name was Do Yun Cho." Guy held up an evidence bag containing a white official document. "As well as this," Allard added. He held up another baggie with waterlogged note paper.

The address was bleeding but readable. William's eyes twitched and his stomach lurched as he recognized the location.

"Thank you … Detective Allard."

"Are you feeling well, sir?"

William did his utmost to compose himself and said, "Yeah, I'm okay. Who found the body?"

"Over there. The young boy."

William heaved a sigh, turned, and ambled over to the boy who appeared to be in his mid-teens. A police officer was consoling the young man as William approached.

"Excuse me, officer, may I speak to the witness?" said William.

The officer moved away as William smiled at the young man. The boy's face was ashen, and his eyes blinked frequently. William registered the signs of shock, something he saw all too frequently.

"Hello, my name is William. I'm an RCMP inspector. I heard you're the one who found the body?"

"Yes. I … I found it," he replied.

"The policeman told me you are Anthony Fabergé," said William.

"Yes," said Anthony.

"Can you tell me what you saw?"

"I was fishing, and I hooked a massive fish. I pulled it over to the shore. Except it wasn't a fish," his adam's apple bobbed up and down. "The man didn't move, and I wasn't sure what to do," said Anthony. "So, I ran over to the bait shop."

"And he's the one who called the police?" asked William.

"Yes, the guy at the bait shop did."

Tracy slipped out of the boat and made her way over to them.

"Hi, I'm Tracy,"

"This is Anthony, our witness," said William.

"How are you feeling?" said Tracy.

"I never saw a dead body before," he said.

"You have been brave. Is someone coming to get you?"

"Yeah, my parents will be here soon. We live nearby." He swallowed, "They say we have to go to the station first for a statement. My mom and dad have to come with me."

"They will have someone there for you to talk to," said William.

"Why would someone kill him?" said Anthony, his nostrils flaring.

"That's an interesting question. I don't know the answer. But Detective Allard will find out. Here, take my card. Call me if you remember anything," said William.

"He's too traumatized right now," said Tracy, whispering in his ear. William placed his hand on her shoulder.

"Can I go for a ride in your boat someday?" said Anthony. "I saw you come to shore in it."

William smiled and took a sideways glance at his cruiser.

"Why not? But get your parent's permission. Okay?"

"Okay," said Anthony.

William's chest tightened as he exhaled. Stepping onto the cigarette boat, a sense of dread lingered. He sensed the address on the note was about to change his life.

Tracy and William waved goodbye to Anthony and powered up the boat. Traveling back to the marina, it was a Sunday that neither had envisioned.

On Monday, he planned to liaison with the Canadian Security Intelligence Service (CSIS) in case they could provide further intelligence data. Their vast database updated information every second. Alongside his department's resources, the combination would furnish leads necessary to help the police in Longueuil.

William's response to the note's washed-out address upset his stomach. He chewed a couple of antacids to relieve the distress. The familiar address belonged to Mr. Kim's Taekwondo Dojang. If the dead man was a student, William had never seen him. Had he studied taekwondo in South Korea? If so, Mr. Kim had never introduced him. Could it be someone from Mr. Kim's past? A policeman or a military man? Did he come for help or for some other nefarious reason?

Just who was Do Yun Cho? And, would this homicide case test his friendship with his mentor, Mr. Kim?

Many questions and dubious explanations led to nothing. Perplexed, his mind was automatically engaging in this exercise of deduction before the issues became difficulties. In normal circumstances the sequence would follow a logical progression of thought. Not now, not today. He knew it was already too late the moment he realized whose address was smeared across the note.

"Tracy. I apologize for today," said William.

"I know. You just can't help yourself. That's why I love you," said Tracy. "But I was still disappointed."

"At least we know the cruiser is seaworthy," said William raising his voice against the wind speed.

"Yeah, I guess that's one thing." Tracy brushed back her hair while William slipped the boat around. "I'll make dinner and you're washing dishes," she said in a coquettish manner.

William made an evasive expression, his eyes rolling and wandering away. He had to see Mr. Kim about that note.

Two

The Cadaver

May 2019

William berthed his cigarette boat and managed to tie her up. Attaching the bow line to the cleat was difficult with trembling fingers. All he could think of was Mr. Kim and whether he was in trouble. Stepping onto the dock, his deck shoe twisted on craggy boards, almost tipping him off the dock. Regaining his balance he smiled with relief, having evaded the oily, fishy, ice-cold water. He checked with Tracy as she finished tying off the aft.

"Tracy, I've got something urgent to discuss with Mr. Kim."

She sighed and slung her shoulder bag over her arm.

"Whenever you two get together, it's time for the girls to clear out," she said.

Giving him a sideways glance she pulled out her phone. "I'll go home on my own." She trekked to the marina clubhouse while speaking to a cab dispatcher. Her chin quivered in anger, and her breath became short from walking so fast. She reached for her inhaler.

***

On the way home, Tracy sat fuming in the back seat. In front of the duplex, she slammed the cab's rear door. The driver turned around in shock. The day she had planned with William had gone awry. It was their last day together before she would fly back to Sydney, Nova Scotia to join her father Jeffrey and continue cataloging Admiral Zheng He's treasure.

The invitation to clean the boat was last minute. She agreed, knowing her laundry could wait. Visiting a murder scene and disrupting her agenda made her furious.

Regaining her composure, she threw the soiled clothes into the washer. She retreated to the kitchen for a cup of tea while the machine was running. She wanted to rest and have fresh clothes before flying out early the next morning. Strapped for time, she decided to order a pizza instead of making dinner.

The Toronto trip to meet William's mother and disabled brother Jamey had been an enjoyable experience. It was only last summer that the four of them connected. That weekend of jubilation and reminiscing slid by faster than anyone thought. They promised to keep in touch.

A musical jingle from the clothes washer told Tracy her cleaning was ready. She tossed the damp clothing into the dryer. Moving into the living room she sat on the sofa, sipped her tepid green tea, and waited for William to arrive for dinner.

He was supposed to be here by now.

Tracy hit the dial button and texted William.

> I'm taking a bubble bath, where are you?

*****

William glanced at Tracy's text message, pocketed his phone without replying, put on his helmet, and mounted the Triumph Rocket opposite to the kickstand side, easing his left leg over the seat. The maneuver allowed him access to his sidearm should a precarious situation arise. It was a tip from the motorcycle traffic service unit in Saskatchewan.

William drove to Mr. Kim's modest semi-detached brick bungalow in Montréal-Est. He needed to know Mr. Kim's relationship with the homicide victim, if any. Arriving on the porch enclosure William heard the familiar sound of a Korean TV game show through the door. Knocking firmly, the door opened to the smiling martial arts master.

"William, this is a surprise. Sundays are for family,' said Kim.

"My humble apologies. I need your help," said William. The fragrance of Korean food was heavy and reminded William that he hadn't yet eaten.

Kim stepped back and motioned William into the entrance hall. He unzipped his boots, placed them on the mat by the door, closed it, and followed Kim into the sitting room.

"Take a seat. Beer?" said Kim as he removed a throw blanket, folded it, then draped it on the sectional. William felt cozy listening to Korean TV streaming into the room and reminded him of his teenage years growing up in Seoul. Kim returned with the remote in hand and two Labatt's Blue. He shut down the TV and handed a bottle to William. Kim took his place opposite and snuggled into a chair.

"You look grim," said Kim.

"Yes, there is a development you should know about," said William.

Kim tilted his head to the side and said, "What sort of development?"

William set the beer down, shifted forward, and with an edge to his voice said, "The Longueuil Police are investigating a homicide on Isle Charron."

Kim's eyes flickered as he raised his head in anticipation.

"Is this victim Korean?"

William's forehead glistened with sweat. He wiped it away with the back of his hand.

"Yes, he is. Do you know someone called Do Yun Cho?" said William.

Kim shifted, raised his eyebrows, and sipped his beer.

"No. Just how was he killed?"

"Multiple stab wounds to the abdomen, before a deep and vicious throat cut," said William.

Kim touched his bowed forehead.

"This is terrible news. But how does this affect me?"

William cleared his throat.

"The police found a note on the deceased. It had the address of your taekwondo dojang."

Kim's lips sagged and his eyes opened further.

"I took a picture," said William, extending his phone, so that Kim could view the screen.

Taking the phone, Kim's eyes narrowed, trying to recall the face. "I don't know him," said Kim.

"We have a problem. This man was on his way to you. Perhaps with a message. Perhaps to threaten you. Perhaps he wanted to kill you. You are lucky he didn't get this far," said William.

Kim rose abruptly and paced the floor.

"What are you going to do?" asked Kim.

"I know about the significance of the note. But there will be police following up probably tomorrow."

"I can't tell them anything I don't know."

"All the same. I think you should remain discreet because when the police arrive, they will escort you to the morgue for identification. You will be badgered with questions about him. His relationship to you or any other information to help their case. Remain careful and leave the rest to me," said William.

"I think I should try to find out as much as I can," said Kim. "Perhaps someone in the Korean community knows about this man."

"It's a possibility we should explore. I will run the photo through Interpol's international data files. When you're finished, we can talk later at the dojang."

"Okay," said Kim. A weariness weighed him down as he escorted William to the door.

***

William started up his motorcycle and headed home. He took advantage by gliding past traffic with smooth lane changes.

The current situation took up his thoughts. William had been Mr. Kim's taekwondo student for many years and understood the man. At Kim's home, he had perceived a deception of sorts. Over the years he had learned whether Mr. Kim was being truthful with him or not. What could it be? What was he hiding?

This homicide was like a time bomb ready to go off and he needed Mr. Kim to trust him. Maybe he would come forward after he'd talked to the police. Otherwise, William would be forced to pressure Mr. Kim to answer his suspicions.

William arrived home to a cold pizza dinner and a wilted Caesar salad. Tracy had packed, ready to leave in the morning for Nova Scotia.

"Did you get my text at all?" said Tracy.

"No, I haven't even checked my phone," said William, averting his gaze. "Sorry, dear."

"How is Mr. Kim?"

"Great. He wants to get together at the dojang."

"Were you happy with the *Midnight Fox's* performance today?" said Tracy, changing the subject.

"Flawless. She's fast, beautiful, and flies like a dolphin."

"Ahem! Really that good huh?"

"A little like you," said William as he chewed a pepperoni slice.

Tracy's cheeks flashed pink.

"Wanna beer?"

"Sure. Heineken zero will do," said William. "I've got an early start."

"Me, too. I have to be at the airport first thing tomorrow morning."

After their late dinner, Tracy cleared the dishes away as William washed and dried them. Then she took William by his hand and guided him into the bedroom. She pulled the curtains closed over the windows and pushed him onto the bed. William grinned as he ran his finger along her nose to her lips. He wrapped his arms around her and kissed her. Tracy rolled onto her back and pulled him closer.

***

As predicted, on Monday morning Kim's studio doors opened and two homicide investigators from The Longueuil Agglomeration Police Services entered the dojang.

"Good morning, Mr. Kim, My name is Guy Allard." He flashed his badge. "May I have a word?" The other cop followed in silence.

Guy briefly explained his homicide case, and asked "Would you be able to come down to the station to identify the body?"

"Sure. I'll meet you down there." He turned toward one of his blackbelts and said, "You take over the class."

***

At the morgue, Kim examined the cadaver and behaved as if he'd never seen this man.

"No, I don't recognize him," said Kim.

"Why does he have your address?"

"I have no damn idea!" said Kim, stiffening into a rigid posture.

Guy looked crestfallen. There was no easy solution here or a new lead to the next inquiry.

"Could you ask within the Korean community?"

"Okay," said Kim. "But I already told you, if there was something, I would have already said so."

All of Guy's attempt were fruitless. The drawer with the cadaver slid back in place. He dismissed the pathologist and waved over to Mr. Kim.

"I'll be in touch," said Guy, with an edge to his voice.

Three

The Favor

<hr>

May 2019

Mr. Kim sat in his dojang office, looking at an old black-and-white photo of two children, posing in front of a run-down shack. A lonely tear traveled down his cheek. He hadn't seen the girl in a long time. Was she still alive and was Do Yun Cho her messenger? Was it time to go look for her?

In South Korea, during his youth, there were hundreds of thousands of villages. A typical village had a communal well and an area for washing clothes, often a riverbank, and a granary for threshing grain. Shaman or healers took care of the people's health. There was always somebody in the village who sold cigarettes, sugar, and cooking fuel out of their house. For sanitation, they used the bush or the outhouse.

Some of the villages were remote, reached only by paths or rutted cart tracks. Kim's village was such a place, not much more than a hamlet. It existed beyond the fork of two roads leading from the county toward the border province of Gyeonggi-do. The roads converged and went around the opposite side of the mountain into a worn track. A small river flowed along the valley floor.

There was a market town a few kilometers away that was built under Japanese colonial rule in the early part of the nineteenth century. The invaders created all sorts of systems that were still in use after the two Korean Wars.

The Kims, Parks and other families had built homes in the hamlet. The dwellings' mud walls were protected inside by plastered newspaper and posters. Heavy wooden pillars were used for the roof structures then covered in thatch. Whenever it rained the walls eroded and it kept the villagers frustrated with constant repairs. His father Kim Han was mixing a pot of clay and straw to patch yet another hole when his children arrived home from school.

The afternoon sun retreated over the mountains and cooled the evening as the trio sat together. The children were seated around their father Han. He let the mud mixture stiffen, and his resolve firmed as well.

Kim Min Su was seven and the eldest son. His youthful energy and excitement kept him shifting about, rubbing his toes in the dirt. His younger sister, Mi Cha, was four. She sat, chin on her hands, with her elbows resting on her knees. She dreamed of butterflies and bees.

"This is the final time I warn you both about using the old bridge," said Han.

"But Appa, it's the easiest way to go to school," said Min Su.

"The government built the Amjeong-gyo Bridge in nineteen-seventeen," said Han. He shifted his rear from one cheek to the other. "It's old and worn out now. During the First Korean War, the Guamgang Mountain Railway stopped using it to deliver produce from the North."

"So that was a long time ago," said Mi Cha.

"Yes, the concrete is crumbling and it's dangerous. So, use the new bridge," said Han. "The war was around here. That means booby traps could be near the old paths," Han added.

"Appa, what's a booby trap?" said Min Su.

"Punji sticks are sharpened bamboo spikes made to impale a victim. They put them in holes and cover them up." He scratched the hairline above his ear.

"That's scary, Father. We have been lucky," said Min Su.

The sun disappeared and it was turning cooler. The children shivered and crowded a little closer to their father.

"Would you like to hear how I met your Omma?" said Han.

"Yes, Appa!" they both yelled out.

"Don't repeat this to your mother."

Min Su and Mi Cha said, "We won't, Appa."

"During the Second Korean War, the entire area around here was in a fierce battle. There were snipers stationed up along a ridge." He pointed over his shoulder. Eager eyes followed his finger like it was a birthday balloon drifting away. "The old bridge was used by both sides for attacks and retreats."

The boards rattled as the gate was slammed up against the wooden fence. Binna stepped through. She had long black hair in a chignon secured with a bun stick. She carried a basket with vegetables and stopped for a moment, taking in the assembly. Her eyes flicked, adjusting to the trio hidden in the dusk. Below the blushed wide cheeks, a pert smile erupted over a soft pointed chin.

"I'm making dinner soon. You should all get washed up," she said.

She turned and shuffled her naked feet along the ground. They swooshed in the dirt as she padded toward the door of the shack.

Han looked toward the children. He had their attention.

"I was a soldier and was ordered to patrol the valley around the bridge. I got wounded," said Han.

"Did it hurt? Do you have a scar?" said Mi Cha impulsively.

"Later, little one. The medical helicopter only took the seriously injured. But the doctor took the bullet out and a pretty nurse took care of me. We fell in love. She is your mother. When I recovered and the war was over, I stayed here to build my life."

"Our mother is so pretty," said Mi Cha.

"Yes, she is," Han smiled in contentment. "So, there you have it children. That's the history of our family. Now, let's wash up for dinner. And one more reminder. Let's use the new bridge to go back and forth. Okay?"

"Okay, I will," said Min Su.

"Me too," said Mi Cha.

Kim brushed the moisture away with the back of his hand and returned the cracked and worn photo to his wallet. He rubbed the knots from his temple. It was time to ask his close friend for a favor.

He texted William.

Talked with Allard. Come to the dojang.

Four

The Courier

April 2019

Brian Pendergast was a diplomat for Global Affairs Canada and worked at the Canadian Embassy in Seoul. He was running late for a lunch meeting. He thumbed the elevator button and looked at his watch. Concerned he may offend his date, he punched the button again. He was frustrated with the numbers displayed on the floors. Finally, it reached his level, and he entered the empty car. A faint hint of English Leather lingered. He had just missed the ambassador in the elevator. Pleased he didn't have to interact with the overbearing man, he headed to the lobby as fast as he could, skirting through security. A cab waited for him.

Brian jumped in the back seat as the young fresh-faced driver turned to him and said, "Where to, sir?"

"Gwangjang Market. Can you move it?" said Brian.

"Right away, sir."

Ten minutes later, Brian said, "Stop here."

"Sir, this is not the gate," said the cabby.

"Don't worry about it." Brian handed a generous wad of Korean Won to the surprised driver.

"But sir, this is too much—"

Brian had already slammed the back door of the cab, walked past the pharmacy and turned into the alley. There in front of him was the rear entrance to the market. The aroma of seafood and fried food flooded the market and enfolded him in a culinary embrace. He grasped his midsection as it growled in anticipation.

Brian was tall, chiseled, and assertive. He was thirty-four and grounded. Women appreciated his good looks and charming nature. He rushed through the local lunch crowd and obvious tourists, scanned the market for his lover Ava Ryan and waited for her at their favorite food vendor.

His memory of the first time they met, at the same food vendor, about a year ago, was unadulterated and still meaningful. He had just ordered kimbap, the Korean sushi wrapped in seaweed. Her behavior had been curious as she stood beside him. She was reserved yet retained eye contact. His manner attracted self-assured women. He had run open fingers through his brown hair. She had run her fingers through hers. To his delight, that's how it had started, by mirroring him. Waiting for the meal, he sensed a beguilement emanating from her.

"I'd like kimbap, too," she said in an Australian accent.

He looked over at the curvaceous blond and her alluring eyes. She smiled and flipped back her hair. A flirtatious signal he returned with a smile and excited eyes. Brian took her in, astounded at the attractive and well-dressed woman. She was out of place wearing an evening dress.

He led off by asking her "You have good taste in food. How long have you been in Seoul?"

"A few years," she said. Their eyes connected, speaking a silent language.

"My name's Brian," he said, taking his order and handing it to her.

"Thanks, I'm starving," she took a bite of the kimbap. "Delicious." She wiped her right hand on her napkin and shook his, and said, "I'm Ava."

After they had finished their meal, Brian asked, "Like to try something else?"

"Sure, I feel adventurous." She was taken with him and had touched his arm. Brian shivered with a jolt of anticipation.

"Let's go," he said. She had followed him through the food court. They tried every conceivable delicacy. The time went faster than expected. In the late evening, with drinks in the suite of the Four Seasons Hotel, they became lovers.

After months of lunches and dinners, Ava started asking probing questions. Brian recognized a *Kompromat* and became troubled. Falling into a romantic relationship with a foreign intelligence officer is treason.

"You played me," he had said, frowning in disappointment. He had become fond of her and she of him. He had to admit that both their governments were better for the exchange of certain facts. And on occasion, some delicate matters were taken care of discreetly.

As he got to know Ava, he had learned that she was an intelligence agent with the Australian government. Her ancestors were from the Wiradjuri tribe in Central New South Wales. Her Irish father and his dominant genes had left her a legacy of racial distrust until she had blossomed and developed her special skills as an agent.

Brian was intrigued by her call that morning to meet her for lunch at the Gwangjang Market.

***

Ava navigated the crowd and breached a long queue at a popular stall. She spotted Brian a few meters away.

"Hey," he said waving. Ava wore a khaki cotton loungewear set. Her greenish-blue eyes shone. The thirty-something blond layered deep pink balm across her lips. Brian didn't care if she spied for living. He liked her spontaneity, playfulness and her quick wit. He loved the way she kissed.

"Been waiting long?" she said.

"No. You look ravishing," he said. Ava tapped his arm and pecked his cheek.

"What shall we eat?" said Ava.

"How about steak tartare? Or better yet, baby octopus?" said Brian.

Ava stuck her tongue out. "Disgusting. Let's have calamari," she said wrinkling her nose.

"Very funny. Kimbap and Kalguksu it is," said Brian. He gripped her hand and drew her along to the eatery.

They found a booth in a narrow food mart, slid in, and ordered from the wall-mounted digital menu.

"What's so important? said Brian.

"Well, it's sensitive. A person's life is at risk," said Ava.

"All right. Let's have the short version."

"It involves an undercover operative."

"What's my part in this?"

"We need a temporary passport. To move my informant to Canada."

"I will be facing a lot of criticism," said Brian. He stroked both temples with his index fingers.

"He is willing to share sensitive information with our government and yours. But we must get him out of North Korea. Before the Reconnaissance General Bureau agents catch up with him?" said Ava. Her head tilted and she grimaced.

"Anything else? Because there's a limit on how much I can help," said Brian.

"Yeah, I get it," Ava expended a slow deliberate breath.

"He will give me a thumb drive. It must get to our agents," she said.

"When am I supposed to do this?" said Brian. "And where?"

"Passport first, I'll tell you where and when to meet," said Ava. "But it will be in Dandong."

A childlike server with a short bob and red apron brought their orders and muttered through a surgical mask, "Anything else?"

Ava waved her away.

"Are you going to dig in or not? said Brian.

"Delicious," she said, as she dove in with her chopsticks.

He wasn't sure whether to eat or to leave. There was a time when he could have. But now he was in deep and didn't dare say no. And he didn't want to be compromised by an agent, even if she represented one of the Five Eyes. The clandestine community was an alliance comprising Australia, Canada, New Zealand, the United Kingdom and the United States.

His fate was sealed and their enjoyable rendezvous didn't cut it anymore. His position as a Global Security Reporting Program officer collecting information for Global Affairs Canada was getting severely fucked up. And now she expected him to succeed at fooling the Chinese and the North Koreans and make it safely out of Dandong, China.

***

Brian's misgivings about helping Ava almost destroyed their relationship. But love and loyalty won over. The passport for Do Yun Cho passed through channels on his recommendations. But, lying to the ambassador about flying to Dandong, China became difficult to manage. He overcame his fear and basic instinct to be a good patriot. The incredible attraction to Ava superseded his normally sound thinking.

The city of Sinuiju was in North Korea, situated across the Yalu River from Dandong. The Australian Intelligence analyst report broke down the reality of the border towns. The Chinese had no intention of letting the North Korean economy collapse.

Before he arrived, Ava had said to him, "There is a hole in Pyongyang's government's sanctions, big enough for coal, oil, you name it to slip through."

"How big?" Brian asked at their last encounter.

"Every day there are legions of trucks passing across the Friendship Bridge," said Ava. "With little inspection, making illegal entry easy," she added.

"How is your guy getting over?"

"In the back of a truck. The driver's a meth dealer and bribes the guards."

"How will I recognize him?"

"He'll be wearing a Nike fleece tracksuit and a woven friendship bracelet."

"Where do I pick him up?"

"There's a used piano store on a side street. You can meet him there."

"I'll give him the passport," said Brian. "Then get him on a plane."

"Good," she said. "Later you'll meet my team for the flash drive handoff."

"I'm not used to this covert stuff," he said. "I'm sticking my neck out because I love you."

"I'm grateful," she replied. "I care about you, too."

***

On the drive from the Hilton Garden Inn to the piano shop, the downtown streets were wet after the recent rainfall. People were milling around outdoor food stalls, eating peanuts and drinking beer. Chinese lanterns hung from lines stretched across from one building to another. Along the perimeter were overflowing waste containers. Small food shops, in lengthy rows, made dining selection a daunting decision.

Brian crossed the street, snaking around scooters and cars toward the piano shop.

"Get him on an airplane and get him out of China," Ava had said.

As he opened the shop door, a bell jingled overhead, summoning the owner from the back.

As the man approached, Brian could hear the *plink-plink* of someone tuning a piano. Brian met the man halfway along the row of aging pianos. The shop owner gestured toward the back.

"He's waiting."

The man in a Nike tracksuit smiled as they recognized one another.

He was an average man, with dilated irises, a dark complexion, drooping eyelids and inflamed nostrils. He wore a hoodie and a silver linked chain draped mid-chest.

"Are you ready?" said Brian glancing at the man's bracelet.

"Ava must trust us. A tough position this, eh Boss?" said Do Yun Cho.

His accent and border slang referring to Brian as *Boss* annoyed him.

"Don't call me that," said Brian.

"Out back. There's a car and driver," said Do Yun Cho.

"Are we clear?" said Brian.

"Were you followed? Cuz I wasn't," said Do Yun Cho.

"No. I'm good."

The back alley was empty except for the driver in the car. They both got in and Brian said, "Get us to the airport."

The driver pulled forward and immediately braked. A black sedan closed off the access to the street. Two shabbily dressed males, both small, gaunt, and with eyes black as coals stepped out, automatic pistols raised.

"What the fuck?" said Do Yun Cho.

"North Korean agents," said Brian. "Get down!"

The Reconnaissance General Bureau agents shot at the driver. The windscreen glass shattered, and the driver slumped.

"Move it," shouted Brian. He pulled Do Yun Cho from the rear of the car. Slugs pinged off the car and chipped the brick wall. He yanked the shop's back door open and rammed Do Yun Cho back inside. They lurched haphazardly through the row of pianos and out the front.

"Can you ride a scooter?" said Brian.

"Yeah," said Do Yun Cho. He stepped in front of one and forced the man off, propelling the rider onto the roadway. Brian and Do Yun Cho stepped on, spinning off into the crowd of motorcycles, scooters, and cars.

The RGB had a reputation for its kidnapping abilities. This time they had been outsmarted and thwarted by a Canadian diplomat. Brian shouldn't have even been put in this position.

They raced to the airport and Brian was true to his word. He purchased a roller case and new clothes for Do Yun Cho and helped Cho to security. With concerns of the North Korean Intelligence agency after Cho, he arranged for his charge to travel from Dandong to Shanghai, Paris, and then onto Montréal. The rest was up to Cho and Brian hoped there would be someone in Canada equally generous with their help.

He summoned a cab back to the hotel. His assisgnment wasn't finished yet, since Ava had instructed him that she would give him the thumb drive in Seoul. He wasn't a spy. Remaining in his hotel room until his flight for Seoul was his best option to evade the North Korean agents.

***

After Do Yun Cho arrived in Paris a new team of the RGB discovered him. His airline had a long delay for his connecting flight. His street-smarts saved him by dodging his abductors or assassins. He acquired a beat-up Renault, drove to Marseilles and embarked on a ship bound for Montréal. Bluffing the captain and working in the kitchen would take longer, but it was safer.

His North Korean handler, Park Ho Jin, had promised him freedom for a favor. Now it was time to deliver. Little did he anticipate an RGB agent had also boarded, whose sole assignment was to bring Do Yin Cho back and make an example of him to other defectors.

Five

The Hand Over

April 2019

The air smelled of burnished steel, laden with angry layers of smoke that strangled the city of Dandong, China. It rested directly across from Sinuiju, North Korea. The Yalu River had no allegiance as it obeyed the banks of both countries. The Sino-Korean Friendship Bridge was the main thoroughfare joining the cities for trade.

Ava Ryan arranged to meet Park Ho Jin, a high-ranking North Korean Reconnaissance General Bureau agent who worked for Bureau 39. He was to leave Pyongyang early in the morning and fly into Langtou International Airport, the hub in Dandong. It was also the main entry point where passengers could catch a fast train to Shenyang or Beijing.

Ava flew from Seoul to meet him in China, leaving the safety of South Korea. Australia had established a common arrangement with North Korea allowing diplomatic cross-accreditation and she used that excuse for a legitimate meeting, even though it was clandestine in nature. It was as down and dirty as the vernacular would suggest.

Ava lied to the Chinese customs officials, but she knew they tagged her, and a tail was imminent.

She made reservations at the Zhonglian International Hotel. Her room overlooked the river, and she could see a lot of North Korea's landscape.

Her instructions were to wait for her contact. She sat in the lobby, folded into a bright yellow bucket chair.

Ava wore a white-sleeved blouse and a quilted brown vest, along with green, loose-fitting slacks. A white leather shoulder purse contained a set of keys, lethal in the right hands. She didn't know what to expect but was wary, and her instincts were on full alert.

An unremarkable looking man with a dark complexion and greasy hair cleared the doorway. His drooping lids caused his eyes to look unfriendly and dull. His walk was brisk as he approached her. The multi-colored tracksuit and gold chain spoke volumes of an undercover agent trying too hard to fit in.

He held a motorcycle helmet. "Put this on," he said, as he thrust it toward her.

"Where is Park Ho Jin?"

"I take you to him," he said.

"Is it far?" she said as she followed him out to the street.

"Other side of town," he said. "Somewhere safe."

They mounted the Ducati and donned their helmets. The man checked traffic and slipped into the flow, racing across the grid. Bicycles, mopeds, and milling people vied for precious space.

They arrived at an apartment building in a neglected area of the city.

"Ho Jin in apartment eight," he said.

Ava knocked. Ho Jin slid the chain and eased open the door. She glimpsed the Beretta in his hand.

"Were you followed?" said Ho Jin.

"I think we're good. Your friend drives like a demon," said Ava.

"Come in. Would you like something?" said Ho Jin. He stuffed the gun back in his belt.

Ava sniffed and flared her nostrils. "Cooking something?"

"No. Just reeks of the previous occupant," he said. He opened a window.

The squalid surroundings increased Ava's discomfort. The small two-bedroom setup included a mattress on the floor and a stained, beat-up sofa. The kitchen area had dirty mugs scattered around the sink. There were packets of instant coffee and an ashtray full of Craven 'A' butts. Some had lipstick.

"Did you deliver the passport?" said Ho Jin.

Ava clasped her purse. "You, first."

Park slipped the flash drive from his pocket. "There's a computer if you don't trust me."

"Thanks." She took the flash drive and verified it. The information flashed across the screen. "It's a significant infraction of NATO sanctions," said Ava.

Ho Jin closed the computer and asked again, "Was the passport delivered to Do Yun Cho?"

Ava fumbled with her purse flap, retrieved her phone, and played the video Brian Pendergast had sent her of the handing over of the passport to Do Yu Cho at the airport.

Ho Jin said, "Thanks."

"No problem. Why are you risking your life for Do Yun Cho?"

He clenched his jaw. "You wouldn't understand. There is history."

"Nothing would surprise me," said Ava.

"You're taking a risk, too." Ho Jin tilted his head in consternation.

"It's my job."

"You need a reason?" he asked.

"Knowing makes it easier to live with," said Ava.

"My mother wants to escape North Korea. My father has held her against her will." Ho Jin paced the room and then stopped. "Using Do Yun Cho, she intends to reach out to her brother in Canada."

"I understand. But what about Do Yun Cho?" said Ava.

"He served us well and the passport is his out. One more message is his final task," said Ho Jin.

Ava bit her lower lip. "He was compromised?"

Ho Jin stopped and sat on the soiled sofa. He lit a cigarette and expelled it in a quick burst. Then suppressed a cough. "Through his former undercover work, he has been exposed. I'm saving his life."

"Does the RGB know about my involvement in helping him escape?" said Ava.

"This border city is crawling with North Korean agents," he said. "They are probably onto you."

"I won't be able to fly back with this flash drive."

"Agreed. Chinese airport security will never let you leave with it."

"But a phone won't raise an eyebrow," she said.

Ava looked at the flash drive. It was compatible with her iPhone. She inserted the drive and uploaded the information.

"The data is on my phone," she said. "As a diplomat, the security personnel would never check my phone,"

"You're safe to think that. But be careful anyway," said Ho Jin.

"I'll delete the flash drive, too," she said.

Ho Jin extended his hand toward her. Ava's lower lip dropped in confusion, then she passed the drive to him.

"Not for an expert data retriever," he said.

He dropped the flash drive on the floor, stomped hard with a heavy boot, and retrieved the pieces. Walked to the washroom and flushed them away.

He walked back breathing through his nostrils creating a wheezing sound.

"Time to move. My friend will drive you, back," said Ho Jin.

"I wish you the best," said Ava. She walked out of the apartment, aware of her surroundings.

The Ducati driver was waiting for her at the curb. Her attention focused on a brown sedan across the street. She walked past the bike and strolled toward the nearest alley. She rushed by, bumping into locals, threading her way to the next avenue.

On the next street over, she hailed a roving cab. The cab made a quick stop. A short bulky man stepped between her and the cab. Ava glanced behind her. Another man appeared, and he pointed a Makarov pistol at her.

Ava's lithe, agile body struck first. Her purse straps enveloped the short man's neck in seconds. The key to her flat was jammed tight against a thick artery.

"Don't move," she said. The man was on his toes, thrashing and gagging. Ava put her knee into his back and pulled harder. The serrated edge drew blood.

"Let him go," said the gunman. His diction was poor and his accent biting.

"Get the fuck out of here, before I kill him," she shouted.

The gunman stepped to the side angling for a better shot. Ava moved backward toward the street.

She heard the exotic exhaust notes of a racing bike behind her and shifted the struggling man to her right side. The biker lifted his right arm and pointed his pistol. Two thuds echoed off the walls. The gunman staggered back, and he toppled over into a pile of trash.

Ava twisted the leather strap until the man slumped. She let him drop where he was. People in the streets ran away in alarm. She reached the motorcycle as the biker buried the automatic pistol in the saddle bag. Jumping on, she embraced him in gratitude and they raced off.

"Thanks, you're not a wanker after all," she said. "Let's get out of here."

"Get bags. Go to the airport," said the driver.

***

At Langtou Airport, Ava's diplomatic status did not raise concern to Chinese security. The RGB agents trailing her turned around, foiled.

Sinking into the window seat of economy class, Ava mulled over her near capture by North Korean Intelligence. *I've got to pass the info on to Brian.*

"What can I get you?" said the attendant.

Ava returned to the present with a jolt.

"A glass of ... white wine please."

Shandong Airlines laid over in Qingdao for two hours. *Too much time for exposure and uncomfortable waiting,* she thought.

Ava exhaled a breath she didnt realize she had been holding when the flight landed in Seoul in the afternoon. She was safe.

The Boeing 737 rolled along the tarmac toward the gate when Ava called Brian. "I got out okay."

Brian smiled at the sound of her voice. He stuffed his phone inside his sports coat pocket, buttoned it and headed for street level and a waiting cab. He was relieved that she had slipped out of China.

Six

The Assignment

April 2019

The Central Committee Bureau of the Workers Party of Korea is often referred to as Bureau 39, the classified and covert North Korean slush fund and was directed by General Park Joon.

He arrived at his office in time for the briefing with his staff. His assistant and wife Kim Mi Cha placed his morning green tea and documents on his desk.

Joon oversaw the North Korea's Finance Department and protected Supreme Leader Ma's family's secret funds from the scrutiny of NATO sanctions.

The important building was home to the Central Committee of the Workers Party of Korea. Located in downtown Pyongyang, the third floor was restricted. It comprised Bureau 35 for intelligence, Bureau 38 for legal financial activities, and the most influential was Bureau 39 for maintaining the illegal slush fund.

Its main structure consisted of multiple stories with separate utilities. Its electrical power, water, and sanitation were separate from the tower block. It was also equipped with electronic devices to jam the radar at the airport and throughout the building.

Mi Cha smiled at the man who, deep within her soul, she despised. It seemed like eons ago when he dragged her over the Demilitarized Zone (DMZ) to escape her family. Mi Cha became an unwed mother, at the hands of Park Joon, the imprudent teenager. Her father Han was incensed and felt betrayed.

The years they struggled in the North were a testament to their survival. They were now in a position of power that few would reach, their position precarious in a totalitarian regime such as the Democratic People's Republic of Korea.

Mi Cha was forty-six and younger than her husband. She had grown into an attractive creature, had a tapered face, alert eyes, and an uncommonly small perky nose. The smuggled fragrance on her neckline left traces of citrus and floral.

Joon looked up at Mi Cha. He had paid handsomely for the perfume and was enthralled that she wore it to work.

"Thanks," he said. Picking up the teacup and giving her an appreciative wink, he took a sip of tea.

***

Park Joon replaced the cup in the saucer to cool and began to reminisce. After they crossed the border, they were arrested. After months of interrogation, they found Park Joon's uncle who was forced to take them in. He initiated them into the daily life of the North Korean regime. Mi Cha and Joon survived the tough conditions, the mental abuse, the extreme food shortages, the killing of smugglers, and the starving people.

They were astounded at their survival and their perseverance to succeed in an oppressive regime. His uncle forced them to work under the threat of concentration camps. Park Joon was required to join the army. He was noticed for his cleverness, and brutal personality. When Park Joon left the army with a high rank, he was recruited by the RGB and was trained in many covert arts including assassination techniques. Ma had personally appointed him Director of Bureau 39 with full responsibilities.

Park Joon sipped the warm tea, holding the teacup between his thumb and middle finger. His missing forefinger was a constant reminder of a reckless prank. Yet, no one ever mentioned it for fear of retribution. He extracted a Rothmans and lit up, blowing a veil upward. He tucked away the gold Pierre Cardin lighter, a gift from the Supreme Leader.

He waved over the group of agents and staff. They assembled around his desk.

His eyes glanced across the faces of his experts. The persons engaged in subterfuge and sanction-skirting efforts. But to him, this was his family. Their programs made money by any means. They excelled in the prolific manufacturing of armaments, illegal drugs, and currency, and selling retail goods abroad; besides retail slavery, which NATO banned.

Joon relaxed and lifted his teacup. All eyes focused on the director. His cigarette smoldered in an ashtray. The infamous organization only answered to the Supreme Leader, Ma, and his sister, Namu.

"*Donji*, comrade," rang across the room. Joon pivoted and faced the man.

"The Americans are flooding us with cyber attacks," said the associate, half turning from the bank of screens in front of him.

"Keep them out at all costs," replied Joon, withdrawing a final puff and expelling it, then extinguishing the butt.

"Now that we have first-strike capability, the allies are terrified," said Mi Cha.

"Our job is to keep them off balance and press forward," said Joon.

Joon's authoritative voice and physical presence empowered his minions. His need for control and his lack of remorse and guilt made him well-suited.

He was approaching fifty-one. He wore a light blue tie and dark suit which revealed a solid frame. His small eyes flitted around the room and his thin mouth stretched further as he stifled his annoyance. His nattering staff often offended him.

"Our leader Comrade Ma's mandate is simple: continue the nuclear war exercises and keep our enemies anxious," said Joon.

The office door opened and Joon's son stepped in. Park Ho Jin had been recruited into the organization when he turned twenty-one. A graduate of Kim Il Soon University he was good-looking, charming, intelligent, and open. Being of good stock, he was fast-tracked to be the successor to the office director, a maneuver that was accepted in this republic. Nepotism and family bloodlines entitled the few to high positions.

The personnel in the room turned and watched him swagger by. He was wearing a North Korean "Mao" suit, inspired by Mao Zedong's famous garment. His chest bore the traditional medals and badges. His full physique was intimidating. Black shaved hair and heavy plastic glasses gave him an eccentric appearance. But he was far from flaky and had trained in the military.

The country was under heavy sanctions, making acquisitions of restricted goods difficult, but not impossible. Park Ho Jin was instructed to use the Korean International Friendship Association as a venue to approach international factions or people who might be interested in weapons.

Joon called his son aside and escorted him into his private office. Ho Jin sat opposite his father in an easy chair.

"My morning meeting with the Supreme Leader was tense," said Joon. "He has new demands."

"How can I help?" said Ho Jin.

"Supreme Leader Ma made it clear that he expects us to sell more weapons," said Joon. He scratched an eyebrow while he contemplated. "Our intelligence agents uncovered a hotel, L'hôtel Expatrié, where arms dealers are known to congregate."

"Where is it?"

"It's in Seoul," said Joon. "Find the right dealer and get a signed contract."

"Is the hotel being watched?" said Ho Jin. He stared, expecting a reaction from his father.

"Undoubtedly." Joon rattled his teacup on the saucer. "I'll have a team escort you in."

"Entry should be smooth. The Korean Intelligence Agency (NIS) thinks I am a Chinese businessman," said Ho Jin.

"Your contact is the concierge, Andreas Huber. He works for us."

"Entrapment?" said Ho Jin. He had a curious look plastered on his face.

"There is always one way or another to get what you want."

Joon removed photographs from a folder and spread them along the desk.

"Memorize these men, one of them could be our future partner."

"Does the NIS know about them?"

"Likely, but get whoever is interested to Dandong right away. We can do the rest from our side."

"Yes, Director, I'll start immediately," said Ho Jin.

"Don't disappoint the Supreme Leader. Your mother and I have confidence in you." His eyes glimmered with respect for his son.

"I will not fail," he said, standing as stiff as a plank, then bowed his head in respect. His *Kibun*, his mood, intact for another day.

Joon picked up his phone and said, "Pull a team and follow my son."

Seven

The Memory

April 2019

While her husband and son were in the next room, Mi Cha inspected the bruises on her ribs. She splashed cool water on her face, washing away smeared mascara. Patting dry, she reflected upon her miserable existence and recollected better times. Her fond memories of the hamlet where she had grown up and the good days she held close to her heart. Her brother Min Su was seventeen and his name meant *gentle*.

They had sat around the kitchen table with bamboo bowls of kimchi fried rice before them. Her father Han had scratched their names underneath each bowl. They didn't fight, as there was only good harmony between them. Ownership of their bowls kept a sense of order in the kitchen and the dining room table.

Father Han was fortunate to have been given a Jingo pup as payment for a crop he'd helped bring in. He had to become an "alpha" to train and socialize the pup. Once Haru was integrated into community life she would hunt and guard them. Whenever Han appeared Haru's ears pricked up, her fawn tail wagged, and she howled in joy.

Mi Cha's name meant *beautiful daughter*. She swallowed a mouthful of kimchi rice, too hurriedly, and hiccuped twice before catching her breath. Her father complained she had reached fourteen much too soon.

Outside after lunch, she playfully rolled her eyes around in circles. Haru jumped up, snapping mid-air and landing on all fours. She barked, extended her paws and lowered her head. Mi Cha reached out to scratch behind Haru's ears.

The dog always snarled at Joon, the neighborhood toughie, as soon as he was around. He was nineteen and his name meant *handsome*. Mi Cha thought he was rather good-looking, but he was mean-spirited and put off by the dog, enough that he slapped Haru on her backside. The intelligent breed recognized a bully and growled back in frustration. Startled and incensed, Joon swore to kill *that four-legged bitch*.

The Jingo Korean breed was normally loyal and trustworthy until provoked, and the dog was well-loved by the villagers. Joon poked sticks at the dog, threw rocks at it and occasionally kicked it. Every time the dog was near him it would slink away and growl. The villagers were becoming confused about Joon's aggressive behavior. Whenever he drew close to pet the dog, Haru would grumble and growl under its breath. The kids were quite frightened.

Mi Cha was not frightened as she knew that the dog was noble. It had a good heart and allowed her to pet it. Haru got the scraps that she saved from dinner, so at least the dog had something decent to eat.

Mi Cha's job was washing the family clothing by the river. Joon arrived and threw stones and mud at the dog. "Stop it!" she cried out.

To avoid the assault, the dog ran around the children, got up on her hind legs, and snarled. Joon crouched on hands and knees pretending he was a dog too. Haru moved over and started nuzzling him. Joon jumped up, grabbed the dog by the neck and started to choke her. The dog was shrieking and yowling and whipping her legs back and forth and finally broke free. Joon extended his hand out to soothe the dog. The tormented Haru's pent up anger erupted into a powder keg of violence. She jumped up, bit down and wrestled with Joon's index finger, separating it at the second knuckle.

"Fucking dog!" Joon yelled in agony. He grabbed the stump as blood erupted like a geyser. He hopped and screamed and cursed the dog again.

Mi Cha was standing over Joon and trying to comfort him. She yelled at Min Su to chase the dog.

"Haru ran away with his finger. Go and get it," said Mi Cha. "Maybe we can fix it." She was young and naive and didn't know it was probably already too late.

She took a dish rag from the pile of laundry she was cleaning. She wrapped it around Joon's damaged finger to try and stop the bleeding. He moaned while Min Su ran after the dog. The dog kept running and left the village. No one knew what happened to that finger. Maybe Haru ate it because she had had enough of Joon's torture, or maybe she was hungry for some meat.

Eventually, all the family members and many villagers ran to see what all the commotion was about. Mi Cha's mother, Binna, escorted Joon to their home and into their shabby kitchen, doing the best she could. Joon's father, Park Gil Bak, took Joon a few kilometers away to a doctor in the next town. He'd need antibiotics and proper stitching, the type of medicine that couldn't be found in their small village.

After a few days of searching, Han found the hungry dog in the foothills behind the hamlet.

With great remorse, he found a new home for Haru in a village a few kilometers away.

***

Mi Cha rubbed an ointment into her bruised ribs and returned to her adolescent memories. Her legs shook. Her hands trembled. Her forehead was hot, and feverish, just like then.

She remembered how the heavy pounding on the side of the shack had rattled its walls, unnerving her.

Her checkered skirt hung from her thin body. A store-bought short-sleeve white blouse gave her a girlish charm. Her mother had embroidered a plain floral pattern along the neckline and front.

Mi Cha slammed her shoulder against the swollen door, freeing it from the warped frame.

"Come on," Joon said. Grabbing her hand and pulling her along.

She panted, the pace making her dizzy, then she heaved, a sour taste in her mouth. Her little swollen breasts pressed against the cotton of the blouse, sensitive and sore. Her bunny smile was subdued, her eyes narrowed in fear, by an uncertain future. Joon held her by the wrist and dragged her over the obsolete concrete bridge. "Hurry," he said. "They're catching up!"

"Let go of me!"

"Never! You're mine, now," said Joon. "You're going to be the mother of my child."

Joon wrapped an arm around his future wife. In a frenzy, they were swept along in fear. They ran along the edge of the old bridge. Pieces of fragmented concrete ground into their bare feet. They made it to the other side and headed up the rutted path toward the DMZ.

She stopped for a second. "You are going too fast. I can't keep up," she said.

Mi Cha rubbed a trembling hand across her brow. She swiped away the cold sweat as her legs began to shake. Her bones felt numb.

Joon and Mi Cha heard the yelling and the pounding of feet on the ground behind them. They were getting closer.

"I can't go any further. I feel sick," said Mi Cha.

"Your parents hate me, and your brother wants to kill me. I'm not leaving you," said Joon.

Mi Cha's straight-cut bangs were matted to her forehead. Her blouse was damp and stuck to her back. She was on the verge of tears.

"I want my mother. I don't wanna go with you anymore!"

"You're gonna have my baby! Who's going to be the father?" said Joon. The slap against the side of her face and ear stunned her. That was the beginning.

Mi Cha wailed; her bruised face was mottled from her ear to her chin. Her injured ear rang with a sound like mad crickets and tears rolled from puffy eyes. She wiped them away into the knotted mess of her hair.

The pounding of feet was getting closer. Mi Cha twisted her wrist, trying to break away. Joon gripped her wrist even tighter, until she cried out in pain. He yanked her forward. Mi Cha felt her heavy legs give way and she collapsed. He dragged her anyway, her bare heels scraping along the rutted path. The crunch of gravel and stabs of pain woke her from her stupor. He stopped, placed his arms under hers and pulled her up. Throwing her over his shoulder, he began to ascend the mountain path. An arduous trek of switch back trails up the mountains to North Korea.

Soon the pursuit by the Kim family would cease. Joon knew they wouldn't enter the DMZ for fear of getting shot or captured and tortured as spies, their death a certainty by the North Koreans' hands.

Mi Cha's phone rang, breaking her reverie. She picked up.

"Bring a writing pad and come to my office," said Joon.

"I'm coming." Mi Cha ran a finger at the corner of her eye. It was damp. She longed for her family, even now. She picked up a pad and pen, adjusted her dress, straightened her posture and walked out the door.

Eight

A Disciple of Terror

April 2019

In a sparsely filled parking lot, two men sat in a Hyundai Tucson. The recent cloud burst over Seoul left the asphalt with a sheen of dissolved oil and gas. A muted reflection from the lamp post light above was mirrored in the slicks, creating ghostlike images.

The two men in the front seats were ASIS. These Australian Intelligence agents were waiting to give Brian the damaging North Korean information smuggled out by Ava Ryan. Tonight, they were waiting to share it with the Canadians.

The window of the SUV was open, and a comfortable and cool breeze drifted in. A man approached, his appearance bathed in blazing red hues from the surrounding neon lights. The agents recognized him.

"Ava said you'd be here at eight pm," said the agent in a snarky tone.

"Look at the weather. Keep it professional, okay?" said Brian Pendergast.

"Alrighty, lad. We'll cut ya some slack," said the agent.

"Were you followed?" said the driver. He flicked the wipers and cleaned the mist from the window.

"I took precautions," said Brian, rather perturbed at the attitude.

"Info must be important to get a diplomat out on a rainy night," said the driver.

Brian had hoped to see Ava Ryan tonight, but she told him she'd arrange for her agents to pass on the information to him. "I would have loved to see you, but I'm busy with another case," she'd said. He patted his suit pocket reassured that his cell phone was there. His lifeline if the situation became unhinged.

The sound of a two-stroke engine along the adjoining road caused Brian to turn around and hesitate. He scanned the narrow alleys. He scrutinized all the buildings that were bedecked in cantilevered neon signs. One read *Fish Market*, the others, *Stamps, Kiss Bar*, and further on, *Nail Services*. His head swiveled again in the other direction. He saw hanging red lanterns. They were bright enough to distract him momentarily.

"Getting jumpy?" asked one of the agents, handing him the thumb drive.

Brian was distracted by the question. "Something's not right—"

A figure emerged from the gloom and moved with the grace of a jōnin, an elite ninja. The RGB had sent their best assassin. Within seconds, he was closing in. The North Korean agent glided toward the SUV as fast as Zeus's messenger.

Brian, rattled, slipped the thumb drive into his pocket and ran into the street past restaurants with colorful umbrellas and red plastic chairs, his leather shoes slapping against the wet pavement. Milling, dodging, and shoving through the crowds, Brian hoped he was safe.

The two agents reacted too late. The jōnin's left hand reached in and seized the driver's forearm. Then with his right, he drove a finger strike into the driver's larynx. Its effective force triggered a spasm. The driver struggled and gasped for air. Then the attacker darted on light feet to the opposite side of the SUV. The agent on the far side was exiting with a firearm. He slammed the door on his arm and his sidearm dropped with a clatter. He delivered a knife hand blow just below the agent's ear, cracking the mastoid bone. The agent tottered and grabbed the open door for support. The jōnin picked up the automatic pistol and shot him twice in the chest. The driver, still groggy, reached inside his coat for his Beretta, but was too slow. A well directed shot to the forehead flattened the driver.

The RGB agent ran back down the street, mounted his motorcycle and drove through a construction site, forcing aside crews who were working on another government project. Typical men with helmets and vests who were engaged in the endless job of fixing deteriorating infrastructure.

Then he maneuvered down the street searching for his quarry. Eventually, he saw Brian Pendergast weaving through the crowd in the market street.

He steered his bike, rammed people aside, braked hard, and engaged the kickstand. He reached the meandering diplomat, crept up, put his hand on Brian's shoulder and plunged the needle into Brian's neck. In an instant, Brian collapsed dead in the walkway.

Joon swept Brian's jacket and removed his phone and the thumb drive. He began walking through the market street, took the SIM card from the cell, placed it in a protective plastic sleeve and discarded the phone into a trashcan fire.

The SIM card would contain valuable information and contacts that would be useful to the North Korean government. The thumb drive, containing crucial information his own son had smuggled out, he would examine on his own.

Joon hadn't participated in wet work for many years, but he was still one of the best assassins ever trained by the North Koreans. The head director of Bureau 39 was his official title. But on a mission like this? He was in his element. A ruthless killer without remorse or feeling.

He never considered himself a bad man. He loved his son and wanted to cover up his son's betrayal. Besides, the whole mess could lead back to him. Supreme Leader Ma could have him and his family imprisoned, if not shot. Joon had no choice but to clean up Ho Jin's mess. *Who knew that having his son followed to Dandong, to protect him, would have revealed his betrayal?* That kind of information would jeopardize many long hours of skirting sanctions and bring serious consequences.

Pedestrians stumbled around Brian until a good Samaritan stopped, checking his wrist for a pulse. He shook his head, "He's gone," he said to inquisitive onlookers.

Joon didn't look back and pushed his way through the crowd. He pitched his poison pen down a rain sewer, started his motorcycle and headed in the opposite direction, away from the milling crowds.

***

Ava checked her Movado watch, concerned that her team was overdue. Her phone calls were being routed to Brian's voicemail. Sweat began forming around her underarms and a tightness was gripping her chest. She placed her fingers on her left breast. Her heart was pounding like a discordant piper's band.

She touched her forehead and bent her head in desperation. She began texting her team of agents. Nothing.

"Oh my God." Her desperate dirge echoed in the hollow, empty room.

She had the most horrible thoughts. *Did three men die this night in the service of their countries? Could a disciple of terror have slipped into Seoul and put to waste her agents and her lover?*

Tears of anguish stung her eyes. *What if her imagined scenario was true?* Ava wiped the tears away, smearing her makeup. She pulled her compact from her purse and stared at the mirror. She gasped at the wraithlike face and fumbled with her phone. *Time to call her supervisor.*

Nine

Be Watchful

May 2019

Special FBI Agent Patrick Reilly arrived in New York from his last overseas posting. He rubbed his dry eyes, battling jetlag. He did his best to shake off the weariness, as he mentally prepared for the appointment with Director Simmons of the Eastern District of the FBI.

Conditions in the Big Apple were partly cloudy, with a pronounced humidity which felt close. The weather forecast promised thunderstorms to end the day.

A cab dropped Patrick off in front of the FBI building at the Federal Plaza. After exiting the elevator, he pushed open the glass doors. Entering the open office space, he said hello to agents he recognized and proceeded past desks and meeting tables to the director's office.

"Come on in," rang the familiar voice.

"Sir, how are you today?" said Patrick.

"As you can see, nothing has changed but the color of my hair," said Director Simmons.

Patrick unbuttoned his blazer, sank into the tufted barrel chair, crossed his leg over, then grasped his ankle. Simmons slipped his hands onto the arms of the wheelchair. A sniper shot had crippled him physically but not mentally. The sitting president had made overtures to remove him. That is, until Simmons reminded him of President Franklin D. Roosevelt, and how well he ran the country from a wheelchair. Besides, Simmons had years of field experience behind him.

"Being recalled," said Patrick "Must be important?"

"We had a special meeting with the Five Eyes," exclaimed Simmons.

Patrick adjusted his tie and uncrossed his legs.

"The threat to our nation from the Chinese government couldn't be greater."

"That's been true everywhere I've been based," replied Patrick.

"The Chinese Communist Party has a successful history of hacking US technology, and stealing it," said Simmons.

Patrick opened his mouth to speak.

Simmons lifted a finger. "Hold that thought."

Patrick refolded his legs, sat back and waited patiently for Simmons to gather his thoughts.

"All our field offices are fighting the tide of China's hacking operations," said Simmons.

Patrick shifted in the seat, thumping his fingers on his thigh in anticipation of what Simmons was about to say. He knew from experience that his new assignment would be significant.

"Our goal is to stop the Chinese government's attempts to steal our innovations, intelligence, and technology," said Simmons.

Patrick ran his hand through his red hair, now scattered with a few gray strands. That year in Hong Kong had aged him. His handsome face had developed fine wrinkles at the corners of his eyes. As he approached his mid-thirties, his experiences had etched his features dramatically.

"I'm ready for the next assignment," he said.

"I am sending you as our legal attaché to our embassy in Seoul," said Simmons. "I need someone like you: grounded and with insight to handle a sensitive situation.

"You will join the Deputy Chief of Mission and coordinate with the Regional Security Officer (RSO). They have regularly scheduled meetings with the CIA and other agencies."

"Daniel Levi still the RSO?" said Patrick.

"Yes, he is."

"He's a decent man. We have shared a drink or two in the past."

"Then you'll get along just fine. I know you're ready for this," said Simmons, smiling. "Besides you're familiar with the Asian culture."

"Yes, spent plenty of time there." Patrick scratched his eyebrow and said, "Inspector William Fox and I had a hell of a time in Hong Kong."

"You two still friends?"

"He's been at Quantico for training."

"How did he do?"

"He finished the Yellow Brick Road fitness challenge with flying colors." Patrick grinned at the memory. "Took his yellow brick home with him. Sits on his mantlepiece."

"Now, about you. Are you over the phobia?"

"Yes, I saw our shrink. She suggested swimming lessons," replied Patrick nonchalantly.

"So, no more thalassophobia?"

Patrick said, "My fear of open water has been conquered."

"Excellent." Simmons shifted direction. "The Chinese Communist Party and the US have a good relationship diplomatically, but they have abused our trust."

"Anything I should be looking for?" said Patrick.

"There are CEOs of major technology companies who are concerned about trade secrets being hacked."

"But we are already on the alert for hackers and cyber criminals," said Patrick, perplexed.

"Yes, but southern Asia is a hotbed. There is a power struggle in the region. Intelligence agencies from China, North Korea and Russia are interfering everywhere."

"Their alliance makes their reach more intrusive than ever."

"Exactly. What makes it increasingly dangerous is the underground black teams engaged in secret missions throughout the region."

"Plenty of classified intelligence to intercept," said Patrick, he furrowed his forehead.

"We are especially concerned about North Korean agents infiltrating the area," said Simmons. "Our department is concerned because the RGB has kidnapped specialists from Japan to start a new program."

"If you don't have the talent, then steal it," said Patrick.

"That's what we are most concerned about. Especially with the Artificial Intelligence microchips."

"HUMINT. Our present situation needs on-the-ground human intelligence gathering," said Simmons. "That's where you come in."

"Give me a month and I'll give you my take," said Patrick as he shifted his shoulders back straight, confidence emanating from his blue eyes.

"We may not have a month," said Simmons. "Dandong, China, is key as it's across from Sinuiju, North Korea. Heavy trade is done between these two cities."

"Understood. Does Daniel have an established network I can tap into?"

"Yes, he will brief you," said Simmons.

"Sir, I'd like to spend a couple of days at the Academy to brush up," said Patrick.

Director Simmons shoved the file across his desk.

"This is your assignment. You have two days. Your tickets and accommodations are in the file." Simmons looked at his young protégé. "Be watchful."

The director picked up the desk phone. Patrick scooped up the file, stood smartly, and said, "I won't let you down, sir."

Patrick smiled at the gray-haired man he admired, and hoped that would be the case, considering how devious the Chinese had been the previous year.

Ten

Something is Off

May 2019

Montréal was amid a wet and cool spring. The buds were appearing on trees sparsely located in the downtown corridor of steel and concrete.

Monday morning was beginning to look like a typical day for René Bouchard, the former superintendent of the criminal investigation section at C Division. Recently he had been promoted to supervise the RCMP's National Security Enforcement Section. René and William were responsible for national security and terrorism activities.

William's boss, René, was perceptive and astute. One of his proclivities was his penchant for assigning his best investigator to international police forces to assist and provide support.

René wore a blue pinstripe suit, a light blue shirt, and a dark navy striped tie, his personal trademark fashion statement.

Most of the staff were wondering if there was moonlighting involved. Did he have a smart financial consultant advising him? Where did he buy the bespoke suits he always wore?

William knew the inside track, as his stock market acumen was his contribution to the stylish impresario's bottom line. William had helped his boss set up a Tax-Free Saving Account. The stock portfolio was a blend of dividend and growth stocks, averaging 20% annually. He wasn't telling anyone René's secret.

William had dropped Tracy off at Pierre Elliott Trudeau Airport earlier and arrived back at his office. He poked his head into René's domain.

"Bonjour," said William.

"Bonjour. Come," said René, waving him in and offering a chair.

William sat back, fixing his gaze on his dapper boss.

"I heard you are helping the police in Longueuil. A Detective Allard to be precise," said René.

William explained the encounter with Allard on Sunday.

"It's just my curiosity. The deceased has all the earmarks of a defector," said William.

"I expect you have a hunch?" René was pensive.

"Yes, it's this temporary Canadian passport they found on the body. Something is off. He doesn't show up in our data system. I've sent his photograph to Interpol, CSIS, and Five Eyes, too," said William. He held back the importance of the note with the dojang's address. He wanted more facts before bringing his friend, Mr. Kim, deeper into his investigation.

"Okay. Let's wait for the intel before decisions are made," said René.

"Sure thing," said William.

René tilted his head toward the door. The meeting was over.

William gave him a thumbs-up before leaving the office. He was relieved that René was not annoyed that he was meddling in Detective Guy Allard's investigation. He went to his desk and phoned Guy to get an update.

Guy answered on the first ring. "Inspector Fox, not on your boat?"

William let the sarcasm slide. He sensed the jurisdictional wall was rising fast. *Time to be diplomatic.*

"Anything you'd like to share?" William leaned back in his chair.

"I do. But, it's perplexing—"

"Yes?"

"I have a theory, though."

"Pushed off a cargo ship?" William interrupted.

"Oui. Tabarnak! No other explanation. His temporary passport was recently issued by our embassy in Seoul."

"That explains some of the mystery. The pathology report—when will you have it?" asked William.

"Tomorrow. I have a rush on it," said Guy.

"Good," said William.

"In the meantime, send me what you have," said Guy.

"Sure, I'll let you know when I have something."

Rather than pull his trump card early, William signed off. He was resigned that his department could end up with the case. He paused, trying not to get ahead of himself. The incident hinted that a breach of national security could have occurred. He felt the killing was a professional assassination of a North Korean. Mr. Kim refused to talk, and the note was pointing directly at him. William knew he had to get involved and help his friend despite the risk of fallout to his career. He got that familiar uncomfortable sensation whenever too many coincidences lined up.

***

William was awakened by blaring car horns. Through half open eyes, he peeked at the clock resting on the nightstand. *Six thirty!* He got up and opened the window blinds, squinting at the early morning sun creeping through sparse cloud cover. The blue-collar neighborhood was coming to life with people on their way to work. No sign of what caused the commotion. He shaved, showered, had a robust breakfast, and sipped on Sumatra dark roast as he mulled over the case.

The blast of city air buffeted him as he clung to the Triumph motorcycle. Beating the major morning traffic to his office, he arrived before the rest of his colleagues drifted in. William scanned his long list of emails, focusing on a sensitive transmission from Canada's Communications Security Establishment (CSE), the eminent cryptologic agency. The abbreviated report established the dead man as a North Korean smuggler.

His position in undercover operations had widened, and he was cleared for more sensitive materials. Should William want a more detailed report, he could request it, but this information would be adequate for now.

William phoned Guy and waited for the officer to pick up.

"Detective Guy Allard here."

"Hi Guy. It's William. I have some information on Do Yun Cho."

"Me, too," said Guy. "The pathology report came in."

"Great. And I just received foreign intelligence from CSE." William cleared his throat. "Do Yun Cho was a smuggler in and around Dandong China, across from Sinuiju, North Korea."

"Well, it makes sense. He was an inch shorter than average for most Korean males. A result of poor nutrition in his youth. It affects all North Koreans, except for the very privileged."

"What else have you got?" said William, waiting for Allard to dole out the rest of the report.

"There were rib fractures, lacerations of the liver and spleen, and the trachea and esophagus were completely severed." William heard a page shuffle and waited for Guy to continue. "The pathologist scanned for toxicology and found high concentrations of methamphetamine present."

A constable tapped on the office door. "Hang on a sec, Guy."

"Sure," said Guy.

The young officer handed William a thumb drive, and said, "Sir, we just received an intelligence report related to your case."

"Thanks." William inserted it into the computer and got it up on screen. "Guy, some new information just arrived."

"Okay, let's hear it," said Guy.

"Evidence points to Do Yun Cho as having been a North Korean escapee. Besides traveling across the border between China and North Korea selling contraband," said William, as he manipulated his mouse on the pad. "He was a low-level snitch wanted by South Korean intelligence."

"Our stiff has quite a story," said Guy.

"We both agree he was tossed from a moving ship. Our Coast Guard has radar, sensors, and CCTV along the seaway. They identified the container ship on my request. The *Sun Carrier* has docked and is unloading," said William, as he glided the cursor to shut down his computer.

"I would like to question the captain and crew," said Guy.

"Meet me at Terminal Fifty-Two." William was already pushing his chair away from the desk.

William stopped and entered René's office.

"I have some news for you on the Do Yun Cho homicide case. He was North Korean."

"So, we have a break?" said René.

"Yes. The ship we believed Do Yun Cho was on has docked," said William. He leaned against the door jam.

"Detective Allard has been informed?" said René.

"Yes, he has. The ship's name is the *Sun Carrier*, and it's flying the Philippine flag," said William.

"What's the reasoning for our department to get involved?" said René. Placing his finger over his lip in consternation.

William handed the thumb drive to René, who inserted it into the slot of his computer.

"It's all there," said William, as he waited for René's screen to fill with text.

René's eyes darted back and forth. "You're right. We need to investigate; this intel is quite disturbing. There's ample evidence of foreign influenced activities."

"This is why our intelligence forces should be on the ground in sensitive areas, all the time," said William.

"Conversation for another occasion. Let's have a look at your notebook," said René.

William passed over his police diary.

René looked over the jotted information. He closed the book and said, "Keep me up to date," he said.

"Absolutely. I'm heading to the docks now," said William, walking toward the elevators.

René picked up his encrypted desk phone, and said, "Connect me with the Assistant Commissioner of the NSCI Program." He was referring to the RCMP's National Security Information Network.

Eleven

Not as Bad as it Looks

William wasted no time as he stepped out of the elevator and into the underground parking. With long brisk steps, he arrived at the Triumph motorcycle, mounted it, then shot out of the police garage. He blasted southward along Notre Dame Street Est and switched onto Rue Port-de-Montréal before arriving at Terminal 52.

William propelled the bike past parked cars, bounced over train tracks, and stopped along the side of the *Sun Carrier*. The ship-to-shore container crane was offloading cargo. A forty-foot box swung across the wharf and precariously passed over William. He flinched, thinking the worst.

He dismounted his bike and stood waiting for Guy to arrive. Noting that Guy was fifteen minutes late, he decided not to wait and started toward the gangway, just as Guy's Ford Explorer arrived. Running and huffing, he caught up to William partway up the gangway. "Wait up!" said Guy.

"Thought you weren't coming," said William.

"Sorry, got held up," said Guy. He took two deep breaths and held onto the railing. William glanced at the officer standing by the car. Who's that?"

"My partner. He's going to keep an eye on the wharf."

"Good."

"So, what's the plan?" asked Guy.

"We line up the crew. Then see who is missing," said William.

"Let me speak to the captain," said Guy.

Before William could reply, he had pushed William aside on the narrow stairs.

When Guy reached the bridge, he flashed his badge and said, "Where's the captain?"

"I'm Captain Manolo García. What's this about?"

"Sir, are you missing any crewmembers?" said Guy, closing the bridge door in William's face. William stuck out his booted foot to prevent the door from being closed and yanked it open. He was annoyed with the overzealous cop and muttered, "Bloody hell."

"Why should I be missing anybody?" said the captain, in reply to Guy's demand.

"Guy, I'll take it from here." William flipped his jacket open and showed his belt badge to the captain. "I'm RCMP Inspector William Fox."

"What is this about?" the captain asked again.

"An ongoing investigation. Captain García, please line up your crew on deck," said William. He was infuriated by the delay and unprofessional behavior Guy had exhibited and began tapping his foot. García called his crew. It took fifteen minutes to assemble them at hold number three.

García led William and Guy down the metal stairwell to the deck where all the crewmen were lined up. After Captain García completed the roll call, he said, "Inspector Fox, two are missing."

Guy started questioning the crew from one end of the line and his partner, who joined him from the wharf, started from the other. William had the captain cornered. He shoved his phone into García's face.

"Do you know this man?" said William, his tone, frosty and firm.

García shrugged his shoulders and pursed his lips. "He's ... one of my crew! Who killed him?"

"Probably the other missing crew member," said William.

García's hand blocked his eyes in disbelief.

"The dead man worked in the galley," said García.

"And the other man?" said Allard.

"The chef's assistant," said García. "He's a replacement for the original chef's assistant. who became sick in Marseilles."

"What's he look like?" said William.

García retrieved his phone. Then showed him a picture of the missing crew member.

"His name is Chun Kwan," said García.

"Airdrop it to me," said William.

"Me, too," said Guy.

"Got it, thanks." William texted the facial shot to René.

> I think he is the killer. Can we do a data search on him?

William turned around and looked straight into García's eyes. "Could this crewman still be onboard?"

García crossed his arms. "Maybe."

Guy called his station. "We need an immediate backup at Terminal Fifty-Two."

"We'll hold tight until your men arrive," said William.

"Agreed." He turned to his partner and said, "Cover the gangway entrance."

***

Guy's partner figured if the suspect was smart, he would make his move before the police reinforcements arrived and create a distraction in order to slip away. Keeping a vigilant eye, the officer noticed smoke coming from one of the containers and in his peripheral vision saw a vague shadow of someone running toward the bow. Seconds later, the suspect was rappelling along the bow mooring line to the dock bollard, then sprinting across the quayside.

He yelled out. "He's getting away!"

Heads turned toward the running figure. Sure-footed, his speed was astounding across the empty wharf. The *Sun Carrier's* crew disbanded and ran to the smoking container to investigate. In an instant, William reacted and was only seconds behind the officer. He then ran past him, his lanky legs making long strides. William was closing the distance, but before he could reach him, Chun Kwan had disappeared into the maze of containers.

Crew members were extinguishing the fire in the open container when three police cars, their emergency lights flashing, came to a stop behind the terminal building. Six officers stepped out behind their cars with their weapons pulled. William had arrived at the containers and stopped to catch his breath. He waved his badge at the officers. He was looking at a line of eighty-four containers, six across and two stacked on top. Long narrow corridors separated the forty by eight-foot metal boxes with plenty of places to evade and kill the unwary at each intersection.

"You three, follow me," William said to the officers. "The rest of you head around to the other side. We want him alive."

They moved off at a quick trot. Guy and his partner split up and moved in from other entrance points. William had a firm grip on his Smith and Wesson, his finger on the index point. There was a round in the chamber. He swept the first two containers and found nothing.

William heard a scuffle, then a voice cried out, "Over here!"

William braced his back against the container and slid forward toward the voice. Cautious, he arrived at the narrow passageway. Guy was lying on the ground.

"Son of a bitch. He got me!" Guy's hands clutched his left side.

William checked his surroundings and ran over to Guy, who was writhing in pain.

"Hold on," said William as he called for an ambulance.

"How bad is it?" said Guy.

He pulled Guy's hands away, lifted his shirt and examined the wound. His fingers came away wet.

"You should be all right with a few stitches," said William. He placed Guy's shirt back, and said, "Press hard."

"Did you see where he went?" said William. Guy pointed to the adjacent passageway.

Two officers arrived with a belt trauma kit and attended to Guy. Satisfied Guy was receiving aid, William searched for the suspect. After five turns down empty corridors William stopped. He thought he had heard something.

The suspect dropped behind William from the top of a container with a thud. William's elbow block diverted the knife, grazing his forehead instead of vital anatomy. The gush of ruby red clouded his left eye. His reaction was swift as he pointed and shot. Kwan had already shifted, and the round penetrated the steel wall with a clang. William had no time to clear the blood. He fought one-eyed.

Kwan swung and parried, lunging the blade at William's abdomen. William swung the muzzle of his gun across Kwan's wrist with a downward force. The knife dropped. Kwan's eyes widened as he gasped from the pain. William moved in, shoving the barrel into his solar plexus. Kwan's face contorted as he screamed for air and collapsed to his knees. He thrust Kwan into the asphalt, his face scraping the harsh surface. William holstered his gun, took out his handcuffs, and restrained him. The officers, responding to the gunshot arrived to assist.

"You got him," said a police officer.

"Yes. Take him to the station," said William. "How is Guy?"

"See for yourself," said one of the officers pointing to Guy resting on the gurney.

"Kwan has been arrested," said William.

Guy cracked a weak smile, and said, "Très bon."

"You're in no condition to lead the investigation," said William.

"I know. You better take over."

"I'll talk with your supervisor about what happened."

"What about you? said Guy. "You, okay?" He pointed to William's bloody forehead. William touched the wound; his fingers came away sticky.

"Not as bad as it looks."

"We are lucky to be alive," said Guy.

William placed his hand on Guy's arm. "Leave everything to me. You get better, okay?" He turned to let the paramedics load the gurney into the medevac when the Emergency Medical Services (EMS) technician said, "Sir, let me take a look at that wound of yours."

"Thanks."

The technician led William to another ambulance and said, "Have a seat."

William winced as the technician stapled the gash on his forehead.

"You are good to go. But take it easy," he said in sympathy, offering him Tylenol.

Guy waved from the other ambulance and its rear doors slammed shut. William knew that the National Security Enforcement Section would take over. It was his case now.

Twelve

Time to Give Back

May 2019

Tracy called her father and left a message. Upon her arrival at the airport in Sydney, Nova Scotia, in the afternoon, she took a cab to the Membertou Cultural Centre. Months ago, the RCMP and the Cape Breton Regional Police Department had an altercation with the Mi'kmaq there. Now the center was a base where artifacts from the Ming dynasty site were cataloged and displayed. After entering the building, she went directly to her father's office.

"Good morning, Dad," said Tracy.

Jeffrey closed the screen on his computer, stood up, rounded the desk and embraced his daughter. "It's good see you, honey. You look chipper. Did you have a good time in Montréal?"

"I did, but I'm anxious to get back to work," said Tracy, unwilling to share with him the disastrous weekend with William.

"In that case, let me show you what we've done." He grabbed his belt, pulled his loose pants up and said, "Follow me."

Tracy frowned in concern. "Dad, have you been eating properly?"

"Just working hard. I could stand to lose a few pounds."

Tracy followed him down the hallway and into a large area. "Oh my gosh. It's a topographical replica of the excavation site. There's also a diorama of the tomb." Animated, she sped up toward the miniatures. "The model makers were flawless in capturing the details!"

"The site will remain off limits to all but the archaeologists," said Jeffrey.

"I like the idea Admiral Zheng He's tomb will be recreated in the museum."

"It's the best way to keep the integrity of the site."

"So, we kept the exceptional pieces of porcelain?"

"Yes, Sotheby's has auctioned off the others in New York and Hong Kong," said Jeffrey.

"That money will firm up the foundation and preserve our vision," said Tracy.

Jeffrey paused in concentration as his lips pressed into a thin line. "Tracy, I've spoken to the Dean at Stanford University and have asked them to extend your time on this project."

Tracy clenched her teeth in a moment of tension and a deep breath flared her nostrils. "I wanted to wrap up and go back to teaching," said Tracy.

"Chief MacDonald and I have a proposal. We'd like you to train promising Mi'Kmaq students to eventually become archaeologists," said Jeffrey. With a flick, he tossed his white ponytail over his shoulder. His steel-blue eyes asked for validation.

She gasped and her eyes widened in surprise. Etched into her father's face was the wisdom of Zeus, his advice like thunderbolts, at the ready.

"All right, this is important. Chief MacDonald and you have given it some thought. So yes, I'll do it," said Tracy.

"I knew I raised you well," said Jeffrey. He smiled and stepped away from the site models. "It's time to give back. Teaching the preservation of artifacts to future generations is so important."

"The Mi'kmaq are stewards of their cultural heritage and captains of their destiny," said Tracy. "I'll be happy to help."

Tracy flinched involuntarily and rubbed her abdomen. A bead of sweat glistened on her brow.

"Are you okay?" asked Jeffrey.

"Just a mild cramp. It should pass," she replied. She used her inhaler, exhaled and slipped it back into her purse.

"On another note, we have been invited to James' chalet," said Jeffrey.

Tracy straightened up and regained her composure. "Well, this is a surprise. What's the occasion?"

"James has a new business, *Fox Microchips*. He plans to build a microchip company in Ottawa."

"Well, I'm excited to go. I never can get enough of my biker guy," said Tracy, forgetting her annoyance with William.

"That's a week away, yet," said Jeffrey. "Time to acquaint yourself with the students." He placed his palms on the table and a half-smile exposed furrows of character at the corners of his eyes. "How about we get an early dinner?" said Jeffrey.

"Not feeling hungry. I'd like to go back to my apartment to rest," said Tracy.

"Now you're starting to get me concerned. I'll call later. We can grab some food then."

Tracy was feeling miserable, dizzy, and nauseous. She went to the powder room and splashed water on her face, retrieved a compact to apply some lipstick and was shocked at how pale she was. She stepped outside of the center, hoping the cool evening air would help relieve her discomfort.

Thirteen

Nanochips

James Fox's semi-retirement was far from the norm. After fifteen years as an Ambassador with Global Affairs Canada, he had taken an early pension and whenever he was called upon, consulted on diplomatic issues.

His appointment in Seoul was both a blessing and a curse, since it resulted in his younger son becoming wheelchair-bound. That tragedy had led to his divorce. After the break-up, he moved back to his chateau north of Montréal to be near his oldest son, William, who had enrolled at McGill University. His ex-wife, Annabelle, took Jamey to live in Toronto, where she pursued her financial career on Bay Street.

A high-energy person and a complicated policymaker, he was lanky with a slight paunch but still fit. His brown eyes were framed in black-rimmed glasses, giving him a stern but friendly look. His gray hair was full and neatly trimmed.

James was fond of his chateau in Sainte-Agathe-des-Monts. He had designed and built it as a retreat, situated on the shores of Lac-des-Sables. The chalet was an A-frame structure flanked by natural cedar planks. Attractive and rustic, it was suitable for a *Home and Gardens* review. A peaked gazebo was attached alongside it and added a private, relaxing lake view. Before the divorce, his wife had spent time creating terraced flower gardens leading along the back deck facing the lake.

A spirited person, he pursued various hobbies and activities. He took to travel, and recreation, like fishing and canoeing on the lake. He read popular fiction and socialized by volunteering at the local food bank. He enrolled in a writing course and began his first political thriller.

As rewarding as being semi-retired was, he realized that being free engaged his intellectual curiosity, and combined with a thirst for travel, it opened opportunities to participate socially. New friendships and experiences often mingled with delightful possibilities. But now it was time to turn over a new leaf and move forward.

James was close to people in politics and had made many business contacts. He cultivated good relationships in South Korea. The technological explosion in next-generation microchips was underway. He recognized that the world was on the brink of a massive change. He wanted to be part of it by combining his past public life experiences with the acumen of the businessmen he knew in Seoul. This partnership could benefit Canadian and South Korean trade and provide a great job for himself. He registered as a lobbyist with "The Office of the Commissioner of Lobbying of Canada". He had also registered his consulting firm as Fox Microchips.

After many years enjoying the Rolls Royce Corniche, he was tired of its idiosyncrasies and mechanical problems. His free spirit called on him to change. On a whim, he'd gone to a Montréal dealership well-known for buying and selling luxury vehicles. He finally said goodbye to the 1987 Rolls Royce Corniche and its old aroma of fine English leather.

James decided on the new electric automobile: the Tesla Model S dual motor all-wheel drive. He knew this safe car would be a joy to drive. After all, why should his son have all the fun? William's Triumph Rocket III was just that—a rocket.

He realized, as a lobbyist and chief executive officer of his own microchip company, that he should set an example. An environmentally safe car certainly did that in spades. As ambassadors come and go, they're nothing more than an official envoy. They are entrusted to provide and encourage the growth of trade between the host nations and to protect its citizens, keep diplomatic channels open, and thwart criminal activity.

The Canadian economy is part of the global economic engine. In foreign countries, that meant increased opportunities to sell and trade. The ambassador and his staff connect as intermediaries between cooperative businesses. This was the way James Fox ran his embassy when he was stationed in Seoul. Now he had a new agenda.

He knew that the Chinese were accessing secrets by using their state-owned companies to spy and steal trade secrets. With his new consulting company, on an unofficial basis, he could move freely from South Korea to Canada and report back if he learned of nefarious dealings by the Chinese. This would allow him to take advantage of information he had picked up over many years in the Republic of South Korea.

James planned to build a high-tech manufacturing center for semiconductor production in Kanata outside Ottawa. There were already many of the world's high-tech companies in Silicon Valley North.

His funding plans integrated a semiprivate and government investment strategy. His idea was to grow the complex into one of the world's largest connections to the other existing systems worldwide. In his estimation, it would take three years to build the basic manufacturing infrastructure. The expansion would follow as future demand needed it.

James was also cognizant of protecting the intellectual property of the venture. He approached the Federal Innovation and Science and Economic Development Ministry.

On a wet spring day, James went into the meeting prepared with a burning desire to win over the officials. He knew Rebecca Fallis, Senior Manager of Communications and Minister Olivier Gauthier's mandate was for Canadian businesses to succeed in their efforts to capitalize on the microchip phenomenon.

"Welcome, Mr. Fox. I'm Rebecca and this is Olivier. Make yourself comfortable."

James sat down at the boardroom table and opened his briefcase. He shuffled papers on the tabletop and began to present his financial projections and business plan.

"Let me begin by reminding you that Taiwan produces ninety percent of all advanced microchips in the world," said James.

"China has threatened invasion on numerous occasions and has promised to bring the province into the fold," said Olivier.

"The US is cognizant of this, and in the future, all American-designed chips will not be distributed in China. That includes all software and equipment," said Rebecca.

"I'm quite aware of this situation," said James.

"What do you propose?" said Rebecca.

"I have access to contacts in the South Korean microchip industry. They are interested in a partnership. Their best engineers will be available to help with the genesis AI chips. Next-generation nanochips are currently made in Taiwan and South Korea. The concentration in only two places is of major concern," said James.

"Strategically, both countries are threatened by communist military neighbors like North Korea and China, respectively," said Olivier.

"Our allies and companies like Apple are asking for offshore manufacturers to localize their operations. Fox Microchips is willing to answer this call at a time of uncertainty," said James.

"We like your business project," said Olivier.

"When can you start?" said Rebecca.

"As soon as I have official approval from the Ministry."

"I will have the paperwork over to you within the next day."

"Good. I will book my flight accordingly."

Rebecca tilted her head back, her eyes sparkled from the overhead lights. "James, I'm excited about your plan." Turning to Olivier, she said, "There are final details to discuss with James."

"I am expected in Parliament," Olivier said. "Why don't you two continue the meeting?"

"Perhaps we can discuss it over lunch," said James.

Olivier's eyes darted back and forth. His prolonged eye contact with Rebecca was pointless. She was smitten.

"I'll expect your report, Rebecca," said Olivier.

"Absolutely," said Rebecca, her voice eager.

"I know just the restaurant," she said. Her voice was sensuous, filled with the promise of more.

***

James called but found his son was distracted.

"Dad, I've got an important case. A North Korean national was found murdered in Longueuil."

"Sounds serious," said James. "Just wanted to remind you about the party next weekend at the Chalet."

"This case—"

"I know, son, work comes first."

"I'll try to make it, Dad."

Fourteen

The Interpreter

William phoned the Longueuil Police Capitaine. "The RCMP National Security Criminal Investigations is taking over the inquiry. Mr. Chun Kwan is suspected to be an international terrorist," said William.

"I see. It's a federal matter," said the Capitaine.

"Oui, he must be transferred to C Division in Montréal," replied William.

"I will release him personally."

"Any news on how Detective Allard is doing?"

"The doctors say he will be fine in a few months."

"Great news," said William. "I'll keep you in the loop on any developments in the case."

"Merci."

***

The next day William escorted Chun Kwan into the interrogation room. He opened the door, and Kwan hesitated; William encouraged him with a tilt of his head. The interview room was twelve by nine feet and painted off-white. The overhead lamps were fluorescent and bright as the midday sun. A corner camera commanded the room and the other focused on the suspect. Basic uncomfortable chairs were placed on both sides of a plain desk. One chair was bolted to the floor and the other could be moved freely. A cuff bar was fixed to the table. A two-way window allowed the onlookers' faceless participation. Well-insulated walls kept the room isolated except for the adjacent viewing room. Additional acoustic dampening came by way of a flat gray low-pile carpet. The heartless somber setting was meant to isolate the detainees, making them feel hopeless, but it affected William as well.

"Take a seat," said William. He wasn't sure if Kwan understood. William sat him down and locked the cuffs around the bar.

Kwan slouched; his legs stretched under the desk. His eyes were icy and sharp, like the knife he carried for killing. He clenched his hands tight, defiant, pulling at the restraints.

"Do you want an interpreter?" said William.

Kwan stared past him, past the room, but not past the reason he was there. His distorted features were pale as limestone and resembled a twelfth-century demonic figurine.

Mr. Kim and René stood on the other side of the one-way mirror. René was not alone in overseeing the process and Kim was asked to interpret. He had been a police officer in Seoul. William knew that René would make note of the suspect's mannerisms and tells, although trying to understand body language often didn't work.

The years of using the nine steps of the Reid Technique had ended. John E. Reid's method using conjecture of guilt had been proven to be ineffective. It was an adversarial, psychologically calculating procedure whose purpose was to obtain a confession, not positively an honest confession. With too many false confessions, the police had moved on. René had reminded William of the new PEACE procedures. Investigators allowed an accused to voice their account without interruption, before presenting the defendant with any variations or ambiguities between their story and other evidence. But could it work with a foreigner with poor language skills?

William texted Mr. Kim. The door to the interview room opened, and Kim ambled in, dragging another chair with him. He set the chair down, greeted Kwan in Korean, and sat down beside William. Kim flashed his cell screen at William. *There's someone here from the US Embassy with René.*

William said, "Please repeat my questions to him."

Mr. Kim listened to William's first question and repeated it in Korean.

"Mr. Kwan, do you understand the seriousness of these charges?"

Kwan remained motionless.

"You are allowed a lawyer," continued Kim.

William opened the file and revealed a picture of the dead Korean shipmate.

"What about this, Mr. Kwan?" said Kim shoving the photo closer. "You're a person of interest in the murder of Do Yun Cho."

Kwan pressed his lips together and was silent.

"We have your DNA index, your fingerprints, and the crime scene evidence. These include clothing fibers and your knife, with blood samples that match the victim's."

Kwan was transfixed, his eyes silent like the gloom of black lithified rock.

"This is what else we have, to prosecute you. Attempted murder of a detective. Deadly assault of an RCMP inspector," said Kim.

Kwan remained silent.

Kim continued, "It's in your best interest to speak to me."

Kwan didn't blink or shift. He sat like a stone, unmoved.

"Who sent you to Canada?" said Kim. He slammed his hand on the table.

William's rising eyebrows conveyed his disbelief. *I didn't ask him to be aggressive.*

Chun Kwan spoke in a low defeated tone. Mr. Kim straightened in his chair in outright focus as the suspect launched into his story.

William looked on captivated, although, he couldn't understand it. He had to step in.

"He needs legal counsel," said William.

"No, he is going to cooperate," said Kim, swinging his gaze at William and giving, a subtle reassuring nod.

William slid his chair away from under the table, and leaned back puzzled.

René opened the door and said, "Let's get him a lawyer before we trample all over his rights." A man in a gray-tailored suit stood behind him, shuffling impatiently.

"Sure," said Mr. Kim, startled.

"I want this done right. Follow protocol, comprends?" said René.

"Legal Aid should be here before we resume," said William, crossing his arms with annoyance.

Kim rubbed his neck and clenched his jaw. His attempt to access any clues about the note had failed.

"We'll go with the evidence we have gathered so far," said William.

"What's next?" said Kim.

"Outside," said William. "We need to talk." He touched Kim's shoulder in reassurance.

William was concerned Mr. Kim had violated the rules of professional conduct. If a lawyer made a complaint, the case could be jeopardized. "I'm taking a new tact before this case implodes."

***

In the corridor, William stood opposite Kim and scrutinized him. William raised his eyebrows, and his lips were firm.

"What was that in there?" said William.

Kim looked up and to the right, gathering his thoughts.

"Look, there was a chance to find out about the note," said Kim.

"My boss thinks I'm too cavalier as it is," said William. "That was bad."

Kim braced himself against the brick wall. It was an impassable barricade, like his guilt, forcing him to share his secret.

"I must tell you the truth," said Kim. "It's been bottled up too long. My sister got pregnant when she was a girl and was abducted."

His eyes became wet, he blinked at the moisture. "She was taken to North Korea. I think she's reaching out for help."

"You plan on finding her, just like that," said William.

"I was hoping you could help. You know—"

"With our resources," said William dryly.

"Will you come with me?" said Kim pleading. "To Korea?"

"I can't drop everything," said William.

"Never mind, I have old friends back home," said Kim, storming out in a huff.

William stood there stunned, stroking the bandage covering his cut forehead. René stepped out of the interview room and waved him over.

"The US Embassy sent a CIA agent here to observe the interview," said René.

"Bloody Hell! What are they doing poking their heads in here?" said William.

"You forget we share all intel. North Korea is a sore spot for them."

"I hope he is satisfied."

"We have a breakthrough," René said. "Kwan is grappling with English, but coherent," he explained, as they walked toward the interrogation room.

"In that case, would you interview Kwan?" said William. "I hope you didn't forget I have to go to Ottawa for some unfinished business with the Prime Minister's Office."

"That's right," said René. "The special position they offered you. Taking it?"

"Still thinking about it."

Back behind his desk, William reached out to Alexa Farouk, the chief of staff at the Prime Minister's Office.

"Good morning, Alexa how are you?" asked William.

"Excellent. Is this about the PM's proposal?"

"Yes, I'd like to talk further," said William. "See you tomorrow."

Fifteen

Confucius

William left C Division in Westmount to seek out Mr. Kim. He mulled over the interview and pointed discussions with René and Kim. William was annoyed and intended to straighten out the matter with Kim. Mounting his Triumph Rocket, he drove past the Seoul Chaco Korean restaurant on rue Sainte Catherines. He parked at the dojang and walked a few blocks to the eatery.

***

Kim was seated at his usual booth near the kitchen. The chef was a good friend and often surprised him with his favorite homemade meals. The owner was eternally grateful after Kim threw out two punks demanding protection. He sipped on a glass of beer and allowed his beef stew to cool by shifting the vegetables around absent-mindedly. His thoughts were lingering on his sister.

Kim turned at the sudden draft from the kitchen door. William approached, the door closing behind him. The full brunt of pungent, fermented soybeans followed him into the seating area. William blinked twice and slid into the booth without formal pleasantries.

"Have you reconsidered?" said Kim, scooping up a spoon of stew.

William bridged his fingers and leaned forward. "You and I have an unwritten covenant," said William. Then he leaned back and passed a hand across his forehead, preparing for the unpleasant discussion. "Tracy and I are indebted for your rescue of us in Seoul years ago."

"Don't go there, you don't owe me," Kim said, his voice strained. Kim spooned stew into his mouth, catching a dribble with the back of his hand.

"Tell me about your sister," said William.

Kim ran his thumbnail over his eyebrow in dread, hesitated and placed his spoon down. "Her name is Mi Cha. She disappeared with her abductor, Park Joon."

"You believe she's still alive," said William.

"Yes, it was my responsibility to protect her, and I failed," said Kim.

***

Applying the art of *Nunchi*, the Korean ability to gauge the mood of others, William assessed his friend's mood. He saw Kim was tormented, and that he was suffering.

As a young man, William trained at the Kukkiwon Taekwondo World Academy. Kim had explained that Kibun is a sense of dignity or face. If you lose your dignity, you lose your face ... such is Kibun. Nunchi was a way to sense someone's feelings.

William had first grasped the concept during a sparring session with a seventh Dan black belt. William had swept the elder flat onto the mat. The instructor's nobility duly ruffled, he seized William by the collar of his *dobok*. Instead of resisting, William began to apologize. The older man said, "It is I who should have known better and retained my dignity." The lesson stuck with him.

The Korean waitress stood beside the booth and asked William, "Want something to eat?"

"Come back later," said William. She left with her order pad still in her hand.

"You can't blame yourself."

"My family's honor was at stake," said Kim.

"What happened?"

"In our hamlet, Joon tortured our dog Haru. The dog retaliated and severed his finger," said Kim, pursing his lips.

"Mi Cha helped him. Misjudging her compassion, he responded by forcing himself on her," said Kim. His eyes became watery, and his fist wiped it away. He composed himself, leaning back against the booth.

"When Mi Cha was showing, the villagers assumed the worst," said Kim.

"What arrangements did the families come to?" said William.

"I beat up Joon and he confessed," said Kim.

"I would have protected my sister too, if I had one," said William. He considered touching Kim's hand in sympathy and thought better of it.

"Go on," said William.

"He abducted her before our families could intervene." Kim's timbre was bitter. "Our family followed them to the border, but we were too late."

"So that's why they live in the North," said William. "Joon must have kin."

"Yes, an uncle," said Kim. "Mi Cha is clever, and she could have sent a messenger."

"All right, this changes everything. I'm certain Do Yun Cho is the key," said William.

"Will you help?"

"My case is likely linked to your sister's messenger."

The waitress passed by, and William got her attention. She handed him the menu. "What's good?" said William.

"The chef makes a great bulgogi," she said, smiling.

"I'll have that and a bowl of kimchi," said William. "Oh, and a Heineken zero."

"Non-alcoholic beer?" Mr. Kim raised an eyebrow.

"On duty," said William. "Where do you plan to start?"

"Old friends in the National Police Academy."

"Do you know anybody in the Korean Intelligence Agency?"

"Kang Dae Yun," said Kim. "We've crossed paths."

William's chopsticks slipped the kimchi onto his tongue. "Whew, love this stuff." He seized the cold bottle of beer and swallowed, easing the bite of the spicy dish.

"This case is going to take us deep into the North Korean regime," said William.

"May we find refuge in prayer," said Kim. His hands were placed together.

"Buddha?" said William.

"No, Kim Min Su," said Kim, as he lifted his beer glass in a toast. William grimaced at the joke.

"Considering yourself up there with Confucius?" teased William. Their friendship had endured another rough patch. *What if the ramifications of his case and Kim's rescue attempt collided?*

Sixteen

I Hear Seoul is Lovely in Spring

May 2019

The VIA Rail train arrived in Ottawa two hours after it left Montréal. William's gut was acting up. The case of Do Yun Cho was full of inconsistencies and predicaments. His intuition was telling him something was not right, but police procedures had to be followed by justifiable, clear facts. He was compelled to follow the evidence, but he had a conflict to resolve in the capital. René could handle the multiple charges against Chun Kwan as he tried to unravel the rest. An Uber got him to Parliament Hill and Wellington Street. He noticed a large group of people milling about taking pictures in front of the translucent flame.

He had arrived across from the Office of the Prime Minister and Privy Council building and diagonally from the Centennial Flame. This was the monument to the Canadian Confederation. The rotund monument was surrounded by hundreds of stuffed animals, sandals and runners, flowers, and condolence signs: a reminder of the indigenous children who died at the residential schools. The old Langevin Block construct was light beige limestone with carved details and archways that included the sepia door entrance. William stepped into the elevator and sent it to Alexa's floor. She greeted him after the secretary showed him into her office.

"Please come in." She waved to a burgundy armchair.

William slid his lanky frame into the padded leather.

"I noticed people at the Confederation Flame honoring the indigenous children," said William.

"Yes, it's a sad time in Canadian history," said Alexa.

"I recently read the *Seven Fallen Feathers*. It touched me deeply," said William.

Alexa looked pensive and avoided the sentiment.

"You've come a long way to discuss human rights violations," said Alexa. She tugged the collar of her white blouse. Her thick red lipstick against her complexion accentuated the perfect balance of white teeth. She was striking and in a powerful position. She had the ear of the Prime Minister of Canada.

"I'm embroiled in a case, and it's a matter of national security," said William.

"Hold your thoughts," she said. "I'm putting the Privy Council office on speaker. The national security and intelligence advisor should be listening in,"

There was a hollow echo over the intercom as the man spoke.

"Good morning, Alexa," said Ted Bell.

"Ted, I have RCMP Inspector William Fox here. Please hear him out and give your impressions," she said.

William was uneasy by the PM's offer of a special position. He was about to refuse it.

"The offer we made is off the table," said Ted. "The Prime Minister believes it's not in the country's interest."

"Okay. It wasn't my thing, anyway." William relaxed in relief. "To the point, I am now a National Security Criminal Investigator for the RCMP," said William.

"So why come here?" said Ted.

"First, about the PM's offer. Second, a homicide victim from North Korea named Do Yun Cho," said William. He shuffled his papers on Alexa's desk. "He had a Canadian passport."

"You should be asking Global Affairs," said Alexa.

"I will. He was murdered in Canada. What was he doing here?" said William.

"That's the first I've heard about it," said Ted.

Alexa murmured. "What on earth is going on?"

"The NSCI is investigating. I'm taking the lead," said William.

"Counter-terrorism action?" asked Ted.

"Yes, and I need your cooperation," said William, consternation in his voice.

"And you want what precisely?" said Ted.

"For Global Affairs and CSIS to play nice. I don't want intelligence chatter compromising our investigation."

"The Minister of Foreign Affairs has the final say," said Alexa.

"Maybe, but I don't trust the Global Security Reporting Program. It's a faulty attempt at a spy agency," said William.

"I'll have you know it works," said Ted. "These Global Security Reporting Program officers develop contacts and deliver vital info."

"We know they have contacts with Hezbollah. It is bloody dangerous … they are not trained effectively," said William.

"All right, I'll deny you are investigating," said Ted.

"You wouldn't have to, if we had a specialized intelligence agency," said William.

"For what it's worth, our government doesn't want an MI6 equivalent," said Alexa.

"The US would be pleased if we did. But we have a good system in place," she continued.

Ted's cough was hoarse. "Trouble is the CIA intel is spotty. Kabul was overrun in weeks instead of months," said Ted.

"The Department of National Defense arranged an off-book mission last year that succeeded," said William.

"Deputy Minister Abbott pushed beyond his authority," said Ted. "He was reprimanded."

"It may have been his strategy," said Alexa.

"Adopting policies in legislation may have worked, too. But we don't have the luxury of time," said Ted.

"Agreed. We've got national security concerns. Our current agencies are performing well for now," said Alexa.

"I understand the politics. Our NSCI Program has a directive to investigate fully," said William.

"Okay, then do what you must," said Ted. "I'm done." He shut off the intercom.

Satisfied with the outcome William's fingers tapped a rhythmic beat on the desk.

William said, "Thanks. I'll take the—"

"—train back tonight?" said Alexa. She glanced seductively as she wet her glossy lips.

William caught the subtle nuance of an invitation.

"I'm trying to focus on the job," he said and rustled his notes together.

William stuffed his document tote, and said, "There's something rotten in Seoul."

Alexa smiled again. "Stay for a drink?"

He pushed back his chair and stood up. "I'll take a rain check."

Alexa's smile faltered. "Send me a postcard," she said. "I hear Seoul is lovely in spring."

His boots squished the carpet, and he was gone.

Seventeen

So It Begins

The US Embassy in Seoul was Patrick Reilly's recent assignment. It had been years since he was here last. In Hong Kong, his Chinese had improved with time. But now, arriving in Korea and interacting with locals, he acknowledged his Korean needed to improve. He struggled to communicate with the cab driver and was relieved to discover he spoke very good English.

He stepped to the curb with a suitcase in tow and glanced up. For a moment, Patrick sighed in wonder, while drifting clouds formed long cotton spheres, as if rendered by an artist's sweeping brush stroke. Mother Nature had again stunned him with her beauty.

The weather was partly sunny and hot. Patrick's cab had dropped him off at the white stone building surrounded by bulletproof windows. The panes let in vast amounts of light while protecting personnel. Architecturally the balconies were sound, and the lower portion was surrounded by wire fencing.

He entered the embassy compound and met with the Deputy Chief of Mission and the ambassador. They were like most diplomats he had met over the years. The ambassador was charming, clean-shaven, blue-eyed all-American, and the Deputy of Mission was all business, attired in a blue suit and red tie. The ambassador greeted him and resumed his affairs while Jeff Bloom, the Deputy Chief, escorted him around the offices and introduced him.

"We have a desk over there for you," said Jeff Bloom. He turned around and pointed at a security-protected door. "And access to the communications center is through here." He swiped his color-coded lanyard across the security pad.

They stepped into the din of busy research analysts. Patrick looked at the operations center. Agents sat along a lengthy desk with multiple viewing screens, separate monitors, and easy access to desk phones. Astute specialists were entering a variety of encrypted data and communications, making decisions or sending them up the ladder.

"Daniel Levi, the RSO, is down the hall." Jeff retrieved a set of keys from his suit pocket and handed them to Patrick. "These are for your apartment. The address is on the tag."

Patrick stuffed the keys into his windbreaker pocket.

After the meeting, Patrick made it his priority to visit Daniel Levi for info and updates. The RSO introduced him to the diplomatic staff with whom he would be working directly. Daniel oversaw other law enforcement agencies deployed at the embassy.

"I chair a law enforcement working group that meets regularly. The group includes many of the people involved like US Immigration and Customs Enforcement, the US Secret Service, CIA, NCIS, and of course the FBI legal attaché," said Daniel smiling at the new appointee. "The FBI coordinates with the CIA on any counterintelligence activities. So, I'll be at the meetings and share what we have. Just a reminder: the ambassador is responsible for aligning any common interests. In the embassy, he has the final say."

"I'd like to get settled in, then start tomorrow," said Patrick. "It's been a while since we've seen each other. Free for drinks later?"

"Sorry, not tonight."

"Well, I better get going, then. See you tomorrow."

Patrick's plan was to settle into his new job at the embassy and to embed himself into the subculture of intelligence gathering around South Korea, including North Korea, China, Russia, and Japan.

Patrick wanted to refamiliarize himself with the city and borrowed an embassy car. His first visit was to Interpol, the liaison to global enforcement agencies. It was situated at the National Central Bureau (NCB), a part of the Korean National Police Agency, located on Tongil-ro in the Seodaemun-gu district.

Patrick would expect access to Interpol's vast databases, as it pinpointed wanted people, stolen passports, and vehicles. With its constant updates, the databanks determined security threats in real time.

He introduced himself to an Interpol agent and asked for the assistant inspector. Over coffee, the assistant inspector was forthcoming on several matters of primary concern to Patrick. He unofficially informed Patrick that the police agency was experiencing issues of corruption in its ranks and areas of concern the Metropolitan Force encountered on the streets.

The vibration could be felt in the room as a helicopter landed on top of the roof. The assistant inspector looked up, shook his head, and resumed. "And because of a few rotten apples, the public perceives all of us as corrupt."

Patrick said, "I hear you."

"If I'm called a loyal dog one more time, I'll lose my cool," he said.

Patrick had received an education on the local gangs and exchanged information cordially about criminality, cyber-crime, and the immoral elements plaguing the city.

After his meeting, he enjoyed a quick lunch of Kalguksu, which pleased him, since he appreciated hand-cut wheat noodles.

Leaving the restaurant, Patrick drove back to the embassy and left the car there to resume his networking. The driving had been horrendous, and traffic enforcement was nonexistent. It was a blessing the taxis were abundant and cheap. He reached the National Intelligence Agency (NIS) and met with Superintendent Kang Dae Yan, with whom Daniel Levi had dealings. Here they discussed the main criminal elements and organized crime, cybercrime, and industrial espionage.

But one last question stumped the superintendent.

"Korea hasn't suffered any known incidents of homegrown Islamic-inspired terrorism?" asked Patrick.

"So far, we have not. Our forces are always on alert, ever since Flight eight-five-eight was downed, killing one hundred and fifteen people."

"A tragedy. Many of the preconditions exist now and are genuine," replied Patrick.

"I'll pass on your concerns. I am aware that an influx of foreigners could harbor terrorists."

"Our take at the Bureau is that you should consider increasing your diligence and communication sweeps," said Patrick. He rose from his chair and shook Kang's hand. "We'll be in touch."

Having made two solid contacts, Patrick knew each city had a secret nightlife where the corrupt and amoral connected. A place where certain things were concealed. He decided to find a bar after work where he could enjoy an absinthe. For good measure, Patrick normally visited the red-light district.

But in Seoul, the neighborhood was redeveloped, and the sex workers and drug pushers were driven underground and onto the internet. The area had transitioned into LGBTQ-friendly neighborhoods. Pocket bars and clubs accommodated transgender people with their welcoming signs. The area had become an oasis from prejudice, discrimination, and social barriers. Patrick knew that certain bars and hangouts would still be hotbeds of organized crime.

Information provided by NIS was that L'hôtel Expatrié was a hangout for arms dealers. He made a mental note to visit there later. After his first day in the city, he was determined to find a bar that served absinthe. Speaking with a taxi driver about his favorite drink, he found out about the Grigo-Grigo Bar.

Patrick strolled in and sat on a bar stool. Artists and illustrators gathered and created a hipster vibe where mingling and drawing were encouraged. There was wine, whiskey, and signature cocktails. Patrick felt immersed with an artist's sensitivity in this inimitable, rewarding atmosphere. He decided to relax among the artists and creatives and enjoy the unique experience.

"You're here for the Art Party?" said the bartender.

"Yes, it's my first time. Looks wild," said Patrick.

"Yeah, usually is," said the bartender. "What will you start with?"

"I'd like a flaming absinthe cocktail," said Patrick.

"Okay. I'll be ready with the extinguisher," said the bartender, as she chuckled and gathered the ingredients. Patrick swiveled around and surveyed the room. People were sketching portraits of each other, laughing and sipping cocktails. It was charming as the party got into the spirit of the evening.

"Here's your drink. Now sit back," said the bartender. She flicked a lighter and a blue flame, barely visible, flickered on the cube of sugar. When the sweet granules bubbled up and melted the mixologist extinguished it with club soda, then took the spoon and turned it into the absinthe, creating the louche. She stirred the remaining sugar into the liquor.

"Thanks." Patrick took a sip and smiled. "Should I get a pencil and sketchbook?"

"Hey, you! Stop. Don't move." Patrick turned around and was gobsmacked by a Korean beauty wearing a black sweater, beige pants, a thin belt, and red running shoes. She was a stunner.

"What gives?" said Patrick.

"I gotta draw you," she said. "You are so cool."

"Yeah, sure. What's your name?" said Patrick.

"Stay still. Let me finish it," she responded. "I love your red hair. Irish, right?" she said sketching on her pad, trying his patience. Patrick half finished his drink.

She handed him the sheet with a portrait of himself. "Very nice. Your work is excellent," said Patrick as he received it with both hands.

"Thank you. I'm Nari, and you?"

"Patrick, your faithful admirer."

"You move fast, Mr. Patrick," said Nari.

"Where are you studying?" said Patrick as he finished the absinthe and set the glass down.

"Seoul National University."

"Perhaps we can discuss art over a drink another time?"

"How about now?"

"Not tonight. I can't stay. But I would like to call you."

"Give me your phone," she said.

Patrick offered his cell with both hands. She received the phone in the same manner. Nari airdropped her contact information and handed the phone back to him.

"I'm in art class all the time. But I'm free on the weekends."

"I'll call you. We can pick up where we left off."

"I'd like that." She picked up her notepad and blew him a kiss and walked away.

Patrick rolled up the sketch, and left the bar, elated by his first day in Seoul. All the intense conversations with intelligence agents and police and finally an interesting woman who could keep him diverted when not on duty. He took the few steps to the curb and wondered how his assignment would unfold.

Eighteen

Flight to Korea

May 2019

The evening VIA Rail train to Montréal pulled out of the Ottawa station with an imperceptible shudder. William nestled into the ergonomic chair and spread his notes on the plastic tray table. The large window conveyed the serenity of the countryside, unmatched by the clamor of the city. He shuffled through his reports and glanced at the shadows of the clouds edging over the fields.

Frustrated with his official visit, William knew he should have expected the outcome. Bureaucrats present opportunities freely and remove them without consequences. Not with a wave of a hand, but with an insincere smile and prosaic remark. Visiting Alexa Farouk, an immature political wannabe had not been entirely futile because he had ensured that his presence in Seoul would remain low-key.

When William met Alexa Farouk last year, she impressed him with her understanding of the political landscape. She had offered him a special position suitable for his talents. He wondered how to explain that his true path was as an inspector with the Mounties. Now, he didn't have to. The Prime Minister had overruled his initiative since there were more pressing matters such as imposing carbon taxes during high inflation.

"C'est la vie," he muttered under his breath, packing his notes away in his leather tote.

The steward and trolly arrived beside William. He turned toward the uniformed man and searched the menu.

"I'll take the turkey sandwich with tomato pesto and provolone on multi-grain bread." William ran his finger down the menu. "No Jameson Irish?"

"Non," the steward replied.

"In that case, the VQA barrel-aged Chardonnay will do."

"Coming up, sir," said the steward. He placed the sandwich and wine on the tray. The galley cart advanced leaving the fragrance of gourmet cuisine wafting behind. William took a bite of the sandwich and raised his plastic wine glass.

The thumping of little feet along the aisle interrupted his lunch. He swallowed hard. The boy and the girl were likely with parents somewhere on board. But like a couple of rugby players, they trampled past the steward and bumped the galley cart. It hadn't been locked in place and was now moving at a considerable clip toward the gangway connection. The steward reached for the handle and missed. The children were determined to reach the front of the train and eventually the engine. As the cart reached William, he stuck his foot out into the aisle and his heavy boot took the brunt of the impact. The wine he was savoring cascaded over his windbreaker and trickled onto his trousers. He placed the empty cup on the tray.

The steward arrived and took control of the galley cart. "Are you all right?" he asked.

"Nothing tragic. It was a young vintage," William replied with a glint in his eyes.

The steward passed over paper napkins. "My apologies, sir." He snapped open another bottle. "With compliments."

The steward disappeared, and the adjoining passengers went back to their phones and magazines. The coach returned to normal, as if the disturbance hadn't occurred. William blotted his trousers, and the windbreaker beaded off the wine. *Who wants unruly kids?*

By the time the train arrived at Central Station, William was frustrated. He had not been received well at the Prime Minister's Office and the Privy Council Ted Bell had been rather abrupt. William was wet and two ill-mannered children were to blame. Their behavior disturbed him sufficiently to arouse annoyance.

He caught up with the family on the train platform and addressed their mother.

"Hello, I'm Inspector William Fox," he said. William retrieved his identification and held his badge up in front of the surprised little faces.

"I'm so sorry for the mess," said the mother. She tilted her head, and her cheeks blushed, eyes lit up in concern.

William saw a single mother, probably divorced or a widow. The disorderly children were a sure sign of a missing father figure. Her oversized, round-framed glasses gave her a homely appearance. The drab loose-fitting clothes implied a budget-minded individual. He knew he'd be footing the dry-cleaning bill.

"May I speak to your children?" said William.

"Yes, go ahead." She placed her hand on both children's heads as they stood in front of her. "I'm not going to arrest you," he said. "But you both broke rules," He put the badge away, and in a calm authoritative voice, he said, "There are consequences for your bad behavior. Your mother will likely take away your privileges." William looked into the apologetic eyes of the woman.

"Let's see if you can be orderly for your mother," he said to the children.

The kids' heads moved up and down in agreement. "Yes, sir, they chimed in unison." William stood up.

"Thank you, inspector," she said. The woman marched the kids toward the shops in the city center's famous underground pedestrian network. The passageways led to hotels, restaurants fashion shops, and even French-only bookstores.

She wheeled around. "You will make a good father." She turned away, jostling her children forward. The children waved back mischievously. William placed his hands on his hips and shook his head smiling.

***

William found an escalator and arrived at street level. He pulled the zipper up to his neck. Night in the city took on a certain vitality.

His cell buzzed. It was René. "Can you swing by the station on your way home? Something came up," he said.

"Sure, but my bike is at the marina," said William. "I'll have to pick it up first. Then head your way."

"No time to double back," said René.

"Okay. Be there in twenty," said William. He speed-dialed a cab. On the way over he deliberated about what awaited him. The situation must be important, as the impeccably dressed man usually would be out on a Friday night.

He paid the driver and rode the elevator to the office of the NSCI superintendent. René's door was open, and William strode in, his hands in his windbreaker's pockets.

"Sit down and get comfortable," said René.

William removed his hands from his pockets and dropped himself into the chair.

"What's so important?" said William.

"Brian Pendergast has been murdered in Seoul," said René.

"Bloody hell, when did this come in?" said William.

"In the last couple of hours," said René.

"How was he compromised?" said William.

"We don't know for sure. But two Australian Intelligence agents were also dispatched," said René.

"Over what, exactly?" said William.

"Some intelligence that they were after," said René.

"Brian Pendergast was my next lead for the Do Yun Cho investigation," said William. "Brian was the one who issued the passport to him."

"I need you on a flight to Seoul right away," said René. "Your flight for Toronto leaves first thing in the morning with a connecting flight to Seoul at five after one in the afternoon." He handed William the flight confirmation.

"When you arrive, the Korean National Intelligence Service will meet you at the airport. They expect your cooperation and, in turn, have offered you their help," said René.

"Thanks," said William. "I look forward to collaborating with them."

"We have received video footage of the hit."

"Any sign of the attacker?" said William.

"No, he leaped on the back of a motorcycle and bolted in seconds."

"So, no leads and no sign of him."

"Too soon to have a report from the locals. But FBI Special Agent Patrick Reilly is at the US Embassy," said René.

William leaned back in surprise. His eyes rode up in a bewildered expression and René explained. "He's helping our embassy with the Pendergast investigation."

"Excellent," said William. "If they haven't already, please ask the ambassador to seal Brian's office and to segregate his files and have them ready for me."

"I'll tell our embassy to expect you," said René.

"If we send the RCMP case file to Interpol—"

"They can get a head start," agreed René.

***

The streetlights lit up in the downtown core, illuminating the cool night air. William was glad he had his windbreaker as the river's airstream barreled through the high buildings. The cab shunted him through the night traffic over to the marina to get his Triumph. He retrieved his riding armor from the saddle bags, dressed, and placed his helmet on.

He headed out to Rue Notre Dame and homewards. His priority was arriving safely, facetiming with Tracy, and getting a good night's rest. It was going to be a long flight to South Korea. Before he left the marina, he texted his old partner, Patrick Reilly.

> Just found out we'll be working together again. Let's not get into the same trouble we did in Hong Kong. W.

> You're the one that's the cowboy. See you soon. P.

Nineteen

Okay, I Can Work With That

After an arduous trip, William landed in Seoul, South Korea, to investigate the murders of Brian Pendergast and Do Yun Cho. William reasoned the temporary passport that turned up at the homicide site in Longueuil was the connection. With that link, William concluded, Brian was complicit in arranging a visa for the confidential informant. *But why,* was the question.

Once he passed through security, he was escorted by National Intelligence agents to their offices in Naegok-dong District in the heart of the city. The high-tech facility resembled a semi-circle, not quite as elaborate as the US Pentagon across the Potomac from Washington, DC. Passing along the corridors to his meeting, CCTV monitored his every step. William glanced at a framed Korean flag hanging on the wall and it reminded him of his youthful days training at the Kukkiwon Taekwondo Academy.

Turning the corner, he saw security personnel patrolling the hallways dressed in khaki pants, military boots, and thigh holsters strapped to their legs. Security was never taken for granted with the North breathing down their backs.

William entered the office, remembered his manners and bowed to Superintendent Kang Dae Yun. He stood up and extended his hand in friendship.

"Pleased to meet you, Inspector Fox. This is my assistant Min-Ji," said Kang with a passing hand gesture.

On the plane, William had read Kang's file and learned he was a Korean Military Academy graduate, sixty-one, with salt and pepper hair. Today he wore a blue suit, white shirt, and a dotted navy tie. Min-Ji flaunted long midnight straight hair and wore a turtleneck sweater, a beige jacket and a pair of black-rim glasses. There were stacks of files as high as coffee cups dominating the desk.

"You have a beautiful facility here," said William. "Very impressive."

Superintendent Kang said, "Thank you. Please take a seat. May I offer you something?"

"Just some water if you have it."

Min-Ji pushed the intercom and said in Korean, "Please bring some water for our guest."

"Just a quick run-down, Inspector, of what we do here. Our chief purpose is to acquire intelligence on North Korea and suppress South Korean activists," he said. "For example, our service recently arrested a female union leader. She was a North Korean Intelligence agent. You see what we are up against." Kang shuffled a file and buried it at the bottom of the pile.

"The RCMP is well aware of the challenges you face." William took the bottle of water offered to him by one of the staff members. *"Gamsahamnida."* The attendant smiled at William's attempt to say thanks in Korean.

"Your case rang some bells here and we have taken over from the Seoul Metropolitan Police Agency," said Kang. "We'd like Brian's files from the embassy."

Min-Ji had crossed her legs and was transcribing notes for the superintendent.

"I am aware my participation is limited. But if you want Brian Pendergast's files then I need more latitude," said William sitting back stoically.

Kang produced a cigarette, lit it up, and deeply inhaled. He blew out a smooth rocket-like trail straight and true.

"Inspector, that is a big ask," Kang sighed and stubbed out the cigarette. "We believe North Korean agents are involved in the murder of your diplomat and two Australian Intelligence agents. You will get some freedom, but I expect you to follow my instructions to the letter and bring me every bit of information."

William was silent for a long moment and decided to trust Kang.

"Okay, I can work with that. I'm meeting with the Canadian Ambassador about Brian Pendergast's file later. Let me spend a day looking at them. We can talk about who will follow-up on the leads. Okay?" said William.

"You hold the cards. But don't get carried away," said Kang. Min-Ji smiled uncontrollably.

William shook hands cupping Kang's in the traditional Korean two-handed grip and gave a slight bow.

"I will be sure to follow the protocols."

"Now that we understand each other, I believe we are going to get along fine," said Kang.

***

William arrived at the Canadian Embassy. A couple of NIS agents in his shadow parked at the curb across the street. William met with the ambassador and had a private conversation with him. The message from

Ted Bell, the Privy Council, about keeping his presence confidential had preceded him and the ambassador was receptive.

As per Superintendent René Bouchard's request, the ambassador segregated Brian's laptop, diary, and other projects and left them in a locked office desk. During William's investigation, which was rather cursory, he found Brian had repeated conversations with Ava Ryan, a diplomat at the Australian Embassy. Because of the frequency and intimacy of the calls he determined they were more than close friends.

He asked the ambassador, "Do you know Ava Ryan?"

"Yes, I know her from diplomatic parties as she represents the Australian Embassy."

William noted her position as a consulate policy officer and location for follow-up and jotted it down. Then he checked for anything else and found Brian had spoken to his father, James. The conversation detailed the trade information from Fox Microchips who were interested in acquiring an engineer.

William introduced himself to the metro police and obtained copies of the investigative and autopsy report on the three bodies. An officer mentioned that he had met FBI Agent Patrick Reilly, and that he had already received copies of the reports. William was pleased Patrick was already on top of things.

He was beginning to make some investigative assumptions and had begun the grueling footwork to uncover the facts, when René called him.

"The Liberal government, on behalf of his family, has requested Brian's body be returned to Canada. Ottawa expects us to prepare an independent autopsy before releasing the body. They suspect we have better medical examiners. Therefore, you are to get the necessary paperwork from Global Affairs and get the body prepared for the flight back to Ottawa," said René.

He took a deep breath and continued, "You are to escort the remains and make sure that there is no interference by anyone during its journey."

William pressed his thumb against his pen and snapped it in two. "I'm not pleased. The investigation is starting to get some traction," he said. "Appeasing the officials back home is wasting my time."

"Do your job," replied René and he was gone with a click.

***

Kim was disheartened by the reception he received from the Korean Friendship Association. He had implored the representative for permission to visit North Korea.

The representative had said, "There is no proof your sister is in North Korea." His lips curved up in a sneer. "Sure, she didn't just run away from home?"

Kim was disappointed by the callous response and rather than admit defeat, decided to fly to Seoul to meet with his old police friends. There had to be another way.

Twenty

It's a Lot to Process

James had invited Tracy Jordan and her dad, Jeffrey, and his girlfriend, Brenda Tadler, to the chalet at Lac-des-Sables for the weekend. James had told them he had exciting news to share about his new endeavor. He had secured permission from the Canadian government to proceed with a high-tech microchip company in Kanata. William would also be joining them since his assignment had him returning to Canada sooner than expected.

In the kitchen, Tracy and Brenda were shaping hamburger patties and marinating chicken wings for the barbeque. The smell of raw meat, garlic, and spices were taking their toll on Tracy.

"Are you all, right?" said Brenda, alarmed.

Tracy seized her abdomen and curled over. "Cramps and nausea," she replied. She ran to the washroom and threw up. Staring in the mirror startled her, as a washed-out pallid person gazed back. Reaching out and touching her forehead, her elbow brushed against her breasts, which felt tender and swollen. An overwhelming sense of fatigue enveloped her like a dark blanket of despair. When Tracy did not return to the kitchen promptly, Brenda knocked on the door, then opened it, poking her head inside the washroom. Tracy sat on the toilet crying, her body leaning forward, hands covering her face.

"Dear Tracy, please sit up," said Brenda helping Tracy upright.

"You're peeing a lot? Maybe seeing spots of blood?" asked Brenda in a quizzical tone.

Tracy peered up in surprise. "Yes, and I'm not sleeping well, and I get heartburn, too."

***

Brenda, a mother of three grown children, recognized the symptoms of a pregnancy. She ran cold water over a washcloth and placed it on Tracy's forehead. "Hold it there and go lie down," she said. "I'll be back in half an hour."

Brenda went to the deck with drinks and explained to the men, "Dinner will be late. I have to go to town for an ingredient."

Brenda drove around the lake to the pharmacy in Saint-Agathe-des-Monts. Arriving back at the chalet, Brenda implored Tracy to take the pregnancy test. Tracy waited anxiously for the outcome of her future.

"Oh my gosh," said Tracy as she dropped the pregnancy tester. Brenda swooped down and recovered it from the floor.

"Tracy, you're positive," said Brenda, reaching out to touch her shoulder.

"Oh my God, this can't be happening. My career is over," said Tracy.

"How could this have happened?"

"I must have forgotten to take my contraceptive," she said. "It's the only explanation."

"Is William the father?"

"Yes." Her shoulders slumped.

"What are you going to do?"

"Not sure. It's a lot to process." Tracy sighed. "Please keep this to yourself until I have had a chance to talk with William."

"Of course," said Brenda.

***

Tracy strolled through the open sliding door and onto the deck. "William, will you help me please?"

"Be there in a second," replied William, shuffling into the large kitchen.

Tracy cornered him in the pantry while he was retrieving a fresh jar of relish.

She hugged him and whispered, "You're going to be a father." She rested her cheek against his chest. "I'm pregnant."

William stiffened like he had been embalmed in liquid nitrogen.

"Bloody hell," he shouted.

"What's going on in there?" said James. "Dinner's getting cold."

"Be quiet," said Tracy. "They'll hear us."

"You're sure?" he asked, his tone softer.

She squeezed him tighter. "Yes."

"They're waiting for us out there. Let's talk some more about this tonight before we tell everyone."

"Okay," said Tracy wiping a tear from her cheek.

"Besides, you should eat something," he said, guiding her to the deck.

James, Jeffrey, and Brenda sat at the picnic table while William and Tracy sat in Muskoka chairs. They enjoyed their burgers and wings, however, Tracy picked at her salad, her appetite was non-existent.

Michael Frank's *Popsicle Toes'* catchy beat had Tracy giggling momentarily over the mundane lyrics. Laughter and friendship helped her forget her worries for a moment.

"It's time for dessert," said Tracy, slipping away into the kitchen. Brenda joined her while Tracy retrieved the rhubarb crumble from the oven and dished out generous portions onto plates.

"How are you coping?" asked Brenda.

"Trying to overcome internal obstacles. Self-betrayal of my ambition, now at full stop because of motherhood," said Tracy.

"Don't be so hard on yourself. William is a good man. You two will work it out."

"I hope so."

***

William and Tracy met at the gazebo, while the elders admired the fading evening over the lake.

William had his qualms about becoming a father and its far-reaching ramifications.

"This is going to sound cruel, but should we keep the baby or not?" said William.

"I don't know if I'd be brave enough to give it up," said Tracy. "What if I become attached to the child?"

"It means a desk job for me," said William. "I don't want to take any chances."

"If we bring up this child my career will change, too," replied Tracy.

"Are we even equipped to bring up a child?" asked William.

Tracy's eyelashes were short and natural, allowing her blue eyes to shine. Her lower lids were darkened with pastels like an Egyptian queen. The mascara ran in rivulets along her chalky skin.

"Can we sleep on it?" she asked, her panic worn like the frayed edge of a torn cloth.

"Yes, let's do that," William replied, masking his disappointment. "But, we should tell the family at breakfast."

***

Assistant Commissioner McCauley of the National Security Enforcement Section and Supervisor René Bouchard reviewed Brian Pendergast's autopsy and toxicology reports.

"What do you make of this?" said McCauley.

"They missed the puncture wound above the hairline," said René.

"My take is the South Korean coroner thought the neck bruising was the cause of asphyxiation," said McCauley.

"After four days of waiting, we get astounding results. Tetrodotoxin caused the same symptoms," said René. "Paralysis of the muscles and diaphragm."

"This poison pen attack is an RGB assassination method. It's a lethal weapon imitating a Parker ballpoint pen. Virtually impossible to identify," said McCauley. "Are you sharing the information with the family?"

"No, we explained it was a heart attack. Too much stress," said René.

"That's our official finding released from the Prime Minister's Office," said McCauley.

"Yes, Brian Pendergast is interred at a Funeral Home in the city of Hull, Québec. His family has asked members of the Ministry of Global Affairs, including RCMP members, to attend. Of course, I'll be there," said René, a sadness in his voice.

"Send Inspector Fox back to Seoul. I want the case closed and whoever the son of a bitch is that's responsible," said Assistant Commissioner McCauley.

***

William's cell phone vibrated. It was Superintendent René Bouchard.

"Hello, sir."

"Bonjour, William. The pathologist report shows Brian Pendergast died from tetrodotoxin poisoning. Assistant Commissioner McCauley wants you back on the case," said René. "Swing by the office for a quick meet before you fly out."

"I'm at the chalet. Be there soon," replied William.

William's Triumph Rocket roared along Highway 15 South to Montréal. Tracy's look of disappointment had indelibly etched into the dark recesses of his mind. The security of the Canadian government must come first, he thought.

"I promise to call you from the airport and later from Seoul," he'd told her.

"Okay, that would be good." Tracy had paused, her eyes searching his. "Brenda's taking me for my first ultrasound later this week."

René was coordinating with the NIS, Korean Metropolitan Police and Interpol, a top priority now that the Australian Security Intelligence Organization had joined in. William's participation was an integral part of a multi-jurisdictional task force. Even with all the available resources, it still could be a difficult assignment to find the North Korean agent.

Twenty-One
The Job Takes Me Where It Takes Me

Time restraints did not allow William to attend Brian's funeral to pay his respects. This was his second flight to South Korea in a week. He turned on the overhead light of his aisle seat, aiming it directly at his notebook. In René's office, the personnel file of ASIS agent Ava Ryan had been sifted through like fine sand through a sieve. Salvaging the remnants of a dead end, Ava was William's primary lead since Brian's death. He found himself reviewing her profile for the second time. William's hands had trembled, oddly pleased at her features. What man wouldn't? Seeking a diversion from the long journey, William recognized Ava Ryan as a formidable equal as he laid bare her dossier.

Ava Ryan was a multi-raced indigenous native from New South Wales. Her mother originated from the Wiradjuri tribe, while her Irish father accounted for her dominant and recessive genes. She stood five foot eight inches, with a narrow nose, long neck, and greenish-blue eyes. Her long, curly blonde hair gleamed in the sunlight on her photograph. It gave her the manner of an angelic warrior.

William's inhalation was slow and controlled, spellbound by her exquisite qualities. Educated at the University of Sydney, the oldest and first school to admit students on academic merit as opposed to privilege, she had excelled in political science with a Bachelor of Arts and earned a master's degree in international studies. Recruited afterward, she sat the Foreign Office exam and was posted at the embassy in Seoul in the counter surveillance department. Adept at firearms, Krav Maga - the Israeli fighting technique, and jujitsu, she had aimed high, exceeding her classmates.

The portly man in a brown jacket, sitting beside him, puffed hard. "Excuse me, I need to use the washroom." William folded his notebook, stood up in the aisle and allowed the man to exit. The flight attendant arrived to collect the last remnants of food wrappers, snacks, and paper cups.

Upon arriving at Incheon International Airport, he was met by NIS agents who escorted him to the Four Seasons Hotel. Back to the busy thoroughfares and jostling crowds of the city, William was looking forward to resuming his investigation after the interruption to the case when he took Brian's body back to Canada.

***

After settling in for a couple of hours, William decided to call his friend, Patrick. He met Patrick in the lobby of the L'hôtel Expatrié. William reached out to shake Patrick's hand, but Patrick pulled William into a bear hug. "Missed you, brother," said Patrick.

"Me, too."

They retired to the Blue Velvet Bar, sitting on plush velvet-textured armchairs. There were couches laid out in intimate groupings opposite each other and facing low cocktail tables. The dark brown carpet had swirls of orange petroglyph patterns throughout. William thought it was mismatched and didn't work together.

"God, that's ugly carpeting," said William.

"No, on the contrary. It makes a bold and vivid statement," said Patrick.

"Is that the Bohemian in you talking again?" William teased.

Their drinks arrived, Jameson Irish for William and an absinthe cocktail for Patrick.

"How have you been?" said Patrick, taking a sip of his drink.

"Good," said William. "I have news. Tracy and I are going to be parents."

"Wow. That's sudden."

"Yeah, just learned about it two days ago," said William. "At first, I was surprised, but the idea of parenthood is growing on me."

"And you're here in Seoul, instead of with Tracy?"

"The job takes me where it takes me," he said. "This will be my last overseas job. Thinking of taking a desk job to stay close to home."

"Congratulations. Let's make a toast," said Patrick. "You're going to be a great dad."

"Thanks," said William, grinning.

They raised their glasses, took their sips and put them back on the table.

"What's it been? Six months since you graduated from the FBI Academy?" asked Patrick.

"It's been busy," replied William.

"Little scratch on your forehead?" said Patrick.

"Yeah, arrested the son of a bitch. Now I'm here on this case," said William as he leaned back. "What can you tell me?"

"Only that I've spoken to the local police. They've got video, a crime scene report, and Brian's autopsy," said Patrick.

"So, nothing new," said William. "I have something, though. Our pathologist did an independent analysis. He said Brian was injected with tetrodotoxin."

"A favorite of North Korean agents."

"It's why the local pathologist thought Brian died from asphyxiation."

"The Australians must be fuming over this."

"I've got Ava Ryan, one of their ASIS agents, as a lead," said William. "Before we meet her let's pay a visit to the National Intelligence Service for an update. I need to speak to Superintendent Kang."

"Sounds like a plan."

William yawned and checked his watch, "It's getting late, and I am still on Canadian time. Feel like catching some breakfast before we head over to see Kang tomorrow?"

"Sure. I'll meet you at the Four Seasons," said Patrick. "They've got an American style breakfast."

Twenty-Two

A Delicate Matter

Over breakfast, Patrick suggested that they be cautious about not being followed by North Korean agents.

"You go first. I'll make sure you're not tailed," said Patrick.

William finished his cheese omelet, took a quick sip of coffee and stood up. He buttoned his sports coat and headed to the lobby and out to the front.

Two minutes later, Patrick left sufficient money on the table for their meals, walked out and began tailing him.

William asked the cab driver, "Crisscross the streets to the National Intelligence Service building."

Patrick's driver, meanwhile, was not trained in covert operations and was speeding up. "Ease up," he said as he looked out the front window, scrutinizing the cars and mopeds. He noticed a black Kia was pacing William's cab ahead of him. He called William.

"You have a tail. Lose them and meet me in twenty minutes at the NIS," said Patrick.

"Okay," said William. "Stop here," The cabbie skidded to an almost instant stop. William paid the driver, stepped onto the curb and blended in with the crowd. He shuffled through and commanded another cab on the way to his meeting.

Patrick educated his driver on driving furtively. Minutes later the cabbie stopped the car and Patrick jumped out after paying. He walked briskly, occasionally looking at reflections in storefront windows. Confirming he had evaded the tail, he hailed another cab.

William arrived at the National Intelligence Service building before Patrick. Kang's security teams escorted him in at once.

"I've been expecting you. Good news, I suspect," said Kang. "But where is Special Agent Patrick Reilly?" His hand outstretched, Kang rose to greet William, his expression was resolute. He was tall but still shorter than William. He was dressed in a gray suit, his silver hair neatly combed, and eggplant-shaped pouches hung under his eyes showing the rigors of his position.

"He should be here any minute," said William, shaking Kang's hand firmly.

"Please, have a seat."

William unbuttoned his jacket and sat. Min-Ji's efforts at house keeping were evident as Kang's desk was free and clear of case files.

"I am pleased that the FBI is involved now," said Kang. "What do you know of Agent Reilly?"

"Patrick's a good man. We've worked together in the past."

A knock at the door interrupted the conversation.

"Sir, there is an FBI Agent Patrick Reilly who wishes to see you."

"Send him in and bring coffee for three," said Kang. "You will see that our agency has polite manners and is capable of attention to protocol."

Patrick arrived, and said, "Good to see you again Superintendent Kang," and sat down beside William.

"I believe your agencies have sent their best men," said Kang. "I expect both of you to comply with the laws of our country while you are here. Inspector Fox, our arrangement stands. We are deeply concerned about what has happened."

After the coffee arrived, Patrick and Kang filled their cups with sugar and cream. William sat back, enjoying his black. Kang brought the files up on his computer.

"I'm going to have these printed for you," said Kang.

Five minutes later, Kang's assistant Min-Ji came in with two copies, which she handed to William and Patrick.

"Thank you for these," said William.

"You have Brian Pendergast's documents?" said Kang.

William slid over a file. "Here are my observations so far. Brian Pendergast's movements, the independent pathologist report and my next lead, which is to interview Ava Ryan."

"Thank you," said Kang.

"Any other news to aid in our investigation?" asked William.

"The American government is concerned about the safety of foreign diplomats who represent G20 countries," interjected Patrick.

"Chatter has it the North Koreans are involved," said Kang.

"Agreed, and the answers lie there," said Patrick.

"Let's split up. The NIS follows the chatter. Patrick and I plan to interview Ava Ryan," said William.

"Gaining Ava Ryan's trust will not be easy," said Kang.

"I expect her full cooperation," said William.

"Besides, the Australians also want answers," said Patrick.

"Keep me informed of what you've learned," said Kang.

William and Patrick gave modest bows. Kang reciprocated, as was the custom. They left the national security building not completely prepared for what might come next.

A cab arrived to drive them to Patrick's apartment. William said, "That was a long meeting. It's time for lunch."

"Let's stop for takeout and talk about a plan over lunch," said Patrick.

"Approaching Ava will be a delicate matter."

Twenty-Three
Loyalty

The city of Seoul was well-known for its Korean BBQ restaurants and its alcohol-infused nightlife, along with its love for the cute and the weird. The capital was a massive, vast, towering megacity separated by the Han River and boasted fast internet throughout. The two main areas were Gangnam and Hongdae.

The area of Gangnam was luxurious like Beverly Hills, with beautiful designer shops and bright lights. Across the river was Hongdae, a university town. A bit more compact, and easier to walk from place to place. With its vibrancy, night markets, and amazing shopping at affordable prices it was the 'in' place to be. English speakers were more common making directions easier for visitors. This is where the US Embassy had purchased the apartment assigned to Patrick.

It was a modern minimalist style with a white modular sofa that rested on a wood floor. A round woven throw rug was placed in front of a contemporary coffee table. The room was dominated by wood materials and natural colors.

"Nice and comfortable." said William running his finger over the counter.

"I like it here," said Patrick, placing the takeout food on the kitchen counter. He removed plates from the cupboard and dispensed the food onto the dishware.

"Sit at the dinner table?" asked William.

"Sure, that'll be fine," said Patrick.

William placed their meals on the tabletop and took one of the file folders that Kang had given them and handed Patrick the other copy, who was sitting at the opposite end of the table.

"For our reading pleasure over lunch." William took a mouthful of beef and said, "This is delicious."

"Nothing beats Korean food," agreed Patrick.

William opened the NIS file and began skimming the report. "The National Security Service records are good at revealing what foreign intelligence officers were doing in Korea."

"The Brian Pendergast and the Australian agents' murder case is a complex one. The only thing we know for certain was Brian and the agents were killed over some intelligence," said Patrick.

"We should consider what Brian's intentions were by sending Do Yun Cho to Canada on a temporary passport," said William.

"Maybe he was motivated by some deep desire to help? But why and for whom?" said Patrick.

"Maybe Brian was killed for passing intelligence from Do Yun Cho to the Australian agents. Even CSIS and Interpol knew Do Yun Cho was a smuggler and informant," said William.

"Possibly for the Australians, this is where Ava Ryan is complicit."

"If the killer had been a North Korean agent, he may have decided to do the killing and retrieved the intel before it reached the Five Eyes. But who and why?"

Patrick opened his laptop and set up the video that the police had downloaded from a camera in the street.

"Wow, see that man on the motorcycle. The back of his head is all there is. No facial recognition or markings."

"There were no credible eyewitness reports from the shop owners or the passers-by?"

"Let's finish our lunch, go back to the scene and check out the street and the parking lot," said Patrick. He sipped his Dalgona, a hot beverage which was coffee, water, and sugar whipped up to a froth. He licked his upper lip. "Ready?"

"Not just yet," said William, shifting in his chair. "I have something more to share with you. It's about Mr. Kim."

"Mr Kim? How is he doing?"

"Not so great. The case is connected."

"How so?"

"Do Yun Cho had a note in his pocket with Mr. Kim's address."

"Holy shit!" Patrick exploded. "Why didn't you tell me this before?"

"Loyalty. He saved my life years ago. Jamey and Tracy's, too."

"So, what's the connection?"

"Kim's pregnant sister was kidnapped by Park Joon and taken to North Korea. She was only fourteen years old."

"That's terrible."

"Kim believes that Do Yun Cho had a message for him from his sister," William said.

"And now Kim wants your help?"

"Yes," he sighed, "But I don't know how."

"Is Mr. Kim coming to South Korea?" asked Patrick.

"Yes. He's determined to get his sister out of North Korea," said William.

"Don't get distracted," said Patrick. "He won't get far anyway."

"You're right. But I couldn't live with myself if the communists got him."

"I'll have our guys at the embassy watch him," said Patrick.

"They should be watching our backs, too," said William.

"Let's head out to the scene and continue our investigation."

"Hopefully, we'll find something the local police missed."

Twenty-Four
Do You Think She's Still Alive?

Kim managed to locate his old patrol partner Lim Kyu and called him at his dojang.

"How have you been? You old dog," said Lim.

"Better now that I know you are alive," said Kim.

"You well?" asked Lim.

"Yes, I'm coming to Korea," said Kim.

"Business or pleasure?" asked Lim.

"Old business," said Kim. "I'd like to catch up with the others. If they are still around."

"We're all retired from the police force now, but we've got jobs. But I'm sure we can arrange it."

"I'll be arriving at Incheon International within the next twenty-four hours," said Kim.

"You can stay with me," said Lim.

***

Kim endured the nearly fifteen-hour flight. Lim was waiting in front of the arrival gate and escorted Kim to his Kia SUV.

"Let's swing by my dojang. It's called Lim's Global Taekwondo."

"How's tomorrow? I'm beat," said Kim.

"All right, we'll all meet there in the morning and kick some butt," said Lim.

"I could use the practice," said Kim.

"We're almost home. I live at the Seoul Loft Apartments in Jongno District," said Lim. "Do you recognize the changes to the city?"

"Some things look familiar, but a lot has changed."

Lim drove along Yulgok-ro through the tunnel that passed under the palace grounds.

"We are passing under Changgyeonggung Palace," said Lim.

"I remember it well." Kim's eyes moistened, his patriotism strengthening with every memory. He decided to visit the royal palace when his business was finished.

"Why are you here, Kim?" said Lim, glancing at Kim before staring out the windscreen. "You said this wasn't a social visit."

"A dead North Korean washed up in Montréal."

"How strange, but what has that got to do with you?"

"He had a note in his pocket with my dojang address," said Kim. "I think my sister sent him."

"Do you think she's still alive?" said Lim.

"Yes, and I need help to bring her out," said Kim.

"Let's sleep on it. I will call the old gang," said Lim. "Let's see what we can do to help."

***

The next day they drove to Lim's Global Taekwondo dojang for a workout, where they met the other two men. Choi Wonho was a security manager at a financial institution and Sam Minho had become a cyber security analyst at an electrical vehicle (EV) auto manufacturing company. The four of them were dressed in dobok uniforms with black belts worn taunt around the waist.

"Look at us. Not much of a street gang patrol," said Kim bending over, holding his knees, and laughing.

"Did you forget who saved your ass when you busted the crazed drug dealer?" asked Choi.

"She jumped on your back and almost bit your ear off," said Sam Minho.

Kim straightened up, adjusting his dobok. "You are right. But let's get serious," he said.

He bowed at Lim as he ranked higher at 9th Dan. *"Sabomnim!"* yelled Kim, using the honorary title of master instructor. "Free sparring?" he challenged.

"Sijak!" yelled Lim. "Let's begin!"

After a few hours, the quartet of martial artists lay exhausted on the mat.

Lim had tested their strengths and their weaknesses. After the workout, Kim gathered them together. "I need to talk with you."

"Lim explained you need our help,'" said Choi.

"I'm back because a North Korean was murdered and found with a note. The message had my dojang address. I suspect that my sister wants to defect. I know it's a big ask but could you help me get her out of North Korea?"

"We all have jobs," said Choi. "It won't be easy getting time off."

"I would like your answers tomorrow," said Kim. "During lunch at the restaurant next to Lim's dojang. My treat."

***

The street gang unit went back a long way. Lives were saved including their own. Criminals were imprisoned. The old team had history. Kim cracked a smile when the three men arrived for lunch. As the men settled at the table, waiting for their orders, Kim asked, "My good friends, what have you decided?"

"We've talked if over, and we're going to help you," said Lim. "Thoughts on how we proceed?"

"We need to find a safe way to enter North Korea," said Kim. "That takes research and planning. That also takes guts." *Did they have the passion to carry this through to the end?*

"The question is how do we find Mi Cha and extract her from North Korea?" said Lim.

"No one in their right mind would try to cross the Demilitarized Zone," said Sam.

"How do we know she's even alive?" said Choi.

"Balloons have been used for years to send over medicines, toothpaste, money, radios, and even USB sticks with South Korean news," said Sam. "We could try and find out that way."

"What if we send leaflets that we are offering a reward for the location of Mi Cha?" said Choi.

Sam said, "The South Korean government hasn't banned balloons yet."

"But what if the military or RGB gets a hold of a leaflet?" said Lim. "They would hunt her down and punish her."

"I don't want to take that chance," said Kim. "Our plans must be covert in nature."

"That is why we must explore ways to find out exactly where she is and what she is doing," said Lim.

"We should find a smuggler who moves freely from one side of the border to the other," said Choi. "Someone, who for the right price, would be willing to escort Mi Cha safely to South Korea."

"She was taken by Joon years ago," said Kim. "He may have her compromised and in a difficult situation. We should be looking for him as well. They may still be together."

"Is there some way of penetrating the border?" said Sam. "Try doing this ourselves?"

"Don't think so. Our best option is to infiltrate a smuggling ring in or around Dandong," said Kim. "Maybe we can get a message into North Korea that way."

"Yeah, we could pretend to be tourists," said Sam. He took a mouthful of rice cake, finished his beer and burped.

The other three rolled their eyes and shook their heads.

"You haven't changed a bit," said Kim.

Twenty-Five

There's No Easy Way to Say This

Tracy parked her car in the Walmart parking lot to replenish supplies in the anthropology department. She needed a few boxes of latex gloves for her class.

She walked while checking messages on her iPhone, oblivious to her surroundings. A car backed out of its parking spot and the driver didn't notice Tracy. He realized his rear sensors were screaming and slammed the brakes too late. The momentum of the car sent Tracy reeling onto her back. She hit her head on the asphalt and was splayed out. Several concerned people checked her vital signs: she was alive, but unconscious.

A kind woman called 9-1-1 and the paramedics arrived. They stabilized Tracy, placed her on a gurney, and drove her to the emergency room at the nearest hospital. On arrival, the doctors discovered that she was pregnant. Their aim was to stop the heavy bleeding and possible subsequent infection. X-rays showed cracked ribs and a severe concussion. Her father Jeffrey arrived at her bedside, anxiously waiting for her to awaken.

***

The next morning, Tracy awoke, groggy and weak, took in the unfamiliar surrounding and asked, "What happened?"

"You were in an accident," said Jeffrey.

Tracy tried to sit up and felt the IV tug at her arm. Her eyes widened in alarm. With dread, she knew the tenuous connection between her and the tiny life growing within her had been severed. "I lost the baby, didn't I?"

Jeffrey's sallow skin and damp eyes were enough verification.

Tracy rolled her face into the pillow and wept. She didn't understand if it was anguish or relief. Her life was upended again, the sadness overwhelming. That thought fostered deep sobs, the patient monitor beeping in unison. Her erratic heartbeat registered on the machine, alerting the medical staff.

"She needs to remain calm," the nurse said to Tracy's dad. Turning to Tracy, she said, "We'll get something to calm you, honey."

After the injection, Tracy fell into a deep slumber. Relieved his daughter was resting, Jeffrey took a walk to the cafeteria and phoned William.

"Jeffrey, how are you?" said William.

"I've sad news," said Jeffrey.

"What's wrong?" said William.

"There's no easy way to say this."

"Go on."

"Tracy's been in an accident and has lost the baby."

The silence unnerved Jeffrey.

"Are you there, William?" he asked. "She lost the baby," he repeated.

"Oh God. She texted me the ultrasound only this morning." William's voice cracked. "How badly is she hurt?"

Jeffrey could hear the pain in William's voice.

"Her x-ray shows cracked ribs. She has a concussion too."

"Can I speak to her?"

"She's sleeping right now."

"Call me the minute she wakes up."

"Will do. For now, she needs to rest."

"Tell her I love her," he said. He left his coffee unfinished and called Patrick. "I need to talk with you."

***

Patrick met William at Holly's Coffee Shop near the hotel. He detected a deep sorrow in his friend.

"Tracy's in hospital," said William, grief shrouding his dull features. "We lost our baby,"

"I'm so sorry. Is she all right?" asked Patrick.

"Yes, but she needs me," he said. "I have to get home to her."

"That would be for the best," said Patrick. "If you are distracted, mistakes in the field can be fatal."

"My supervisor René is a reasonable man. I'll call and see about some downtime," said William.

"Give him a call. I'm heading to the washroom," said Patrick, giving William privacy to talk with René.

***

"Oui, bonjour, great to hear from you. Give me some good news," said René.

"Bad news, I'm afraid. Tracy's been hurt and lost the baby," said William.

"Oh my God, is she all right?" said René. "How are you holding up?"

"Okay, I guess," said William. "I'm requesting time off to support her."

"This is not the time. It will stall the case. The Prime Minister's Office has been pressuring us to close this investigation. Understand this is not personal, but a government priority of the highest order," said René.

"I'll do my best. Give me a couple of days to get something tangible," said William. "Then I need to get home to Tracy."

"Au revoir," said René.

William disconnected the call and threw his cell down on the table in disgust. "Inconsiderate asshole."

Patrick returned and sat across from him in the booth and said, "I got the last part of that conversation. That didn't sound good."

"No, it wasn't," said William. "Tracy is never going to forgive me."

"She loves you. Give her some credit."

"We should get started. The sooner we wrap up the investigation the sooner I can get back home," said William. "Let's head back to my suite at the Four Seasons. I want to check my notes."

"You're onto something?" said Patrick.

A determined gleam seeped into William's eyes. "Time to get the show on the road."

Twenty-Six

The Turk

Park Ho Jin slipped into South Korea using a Chinese passport. He traveled to hotspots searching for arms dealers or partners for the accumulation of wealth for the Ma dynasty.

He made the trip from the airport to Seoul and proceeded to the L'hôtel Expatrié, a five-star hotel. The owner, Jean Lapointe, a Canadian expat, had spent an enormous amount of money transforming the hotel. The chef, barista, and management style made the hotel famous for its ambiance and motif of western culture.

Well-dressed foreigners were seen mingling in the posh lobby and bar. In their bespoke suits, sports coats, and sharply creased trousers, they bought expensive scotch and champagnes, behaving like successful businesspeople. They were there to sell the latest high-tech weapons or technology.

Ho Jin explored the elaborately decorated lobby and the beautiful arrangements of furniture, then arrived at the Blue Velvet Bar. He entered the room and hesitated until his eyes adjusted to the muted light. His contact, Andreas Huber, the concierge, was nowhere to be seen.

Ho Jin observed many of the guests. He sat near a group and ordered a vodka spritzer. He noticed one outstanding man blessed with gentle manners and endless witticisms. Others seated among the intimate personalities were fast-talking, with the cunning of feral cats. Some had a commanding way of ordering drinks with easygoing flair. Ho

Jin sat close to overhear their whispered conversations. Remarks drifted across the short distance in an ambient conduit for arms sales. He caught catchphrases about funds being deposited in accounts in Belgium, Luxembourg, or the Cayman Islands. *He was in the right place.*

Ho Jin downed his drink and ambled over to the desk. Andreas was back at his station, fulfilling his duties providing information on local restaurants and attractions. If pressed, on occasion, he would arrange escort services. Andreas was an aging man with a long nose and close-knit eyes.

Ho Jin's father briefed him on the RGB Foreign Intelligence Service psychological evaluation file on Andreas's relationships. The exotic cars, drinking, prostitutes, and his gambling vulnerabilities. His lavish lifestyle exceeded the salary of a concierge and years ago, he had been compromised by the RGB, tempted by easy money to solve his problems. Andreas gathered information to subvert the South Korean intelligence service; the choice was easy, either help them or disappear permanently.

Ho Jin slid a folded bill across the desk. "I want information on your guests."

"You're not what I expected." Andreas's eyes widened in surprise. "Aren't you a bit young to be an agent?"

At thirty-one, Ho Jin looked young for his age, but nonetheless he was perturbed by the man's comment. "You are in no position to be impertinent."

"Excuse me, no offense was meant. This way please," said Andreas. "We better talk in here. More private." They slipped into a Porter's enclave. "So, what do you want to know?" he said, as he pocketed the bill.

Ho Jin pushed his forefinger against Andreas's chest and handed over pictures of the arms dealers. "Give me everything you know about these men."

"Most of them are here," said Andreas.

"Introduce me to the most promising." Ho Jin's brogues were tight and he wiggled his toes to release the tension. He was pleased with Andreas's agreeable mood.

"Come on," said Andreas. "Your best option is the Turk." He pointed to a large and distinctive man, who was tanned bronze. He was in his forties, hard, hair thinning on top, with a mustache and a scruffy beard. His mangled ears resembled misshapen morning glories. His long, slender fingers were ideal for piano, but more likely adept for triggers and grenades. The expression in his brown eyes pierced like an incoming sidewinder.

"Who is he?" said Ho Jin, taking in the gentleman in the pale blue suit and crimson tie.

"Amir Osman. He brokers multimillion dollar deals. A major player," said Andreas.

"Please introduce us," said Ho Jin, smiling at his host.

Ho Jin took in the large man whose belly spilled over his pants, despite the elegant tailoring of his suit. *He should take better care of himself.*

Andreas introduced them to each other and left them together. Over drinks, they discussed the possibility of each of them visiting Pyongyang and Amir's homeland.

"I am not Turkish. I am Armenian," Amir said with a slight wave of his hand.

"Oh, you're not Turkish?" Ho Jin grinned in confusion. "Why do they call you 'The Turk', then?"

"If we become friends, one day you will hear the story behind my nickname."

"Your expertise precedes you. Our government invites you to meet with us," said Ho Jin.

"Very good, I would be willing to discuss matters with the director of weapons production," said Amir wiping the sweat from his forehead.

"You realize that the director can't leave the country," said Ho Jin. "We will bring you across at Sinuiji. As a visitor to the Korean Friendship Association, there will be no complications. Then on to Pyongyang," said Ho Jin

"All right, but I am out of there in twenty-four hours or there is hell to pay," said Amir. His hand slapped the table.

"We shouldn't be seen together in Seoul. I shall leave first," said Ho Jin.

"South Korean intelligence is pervasive; be careful," said Amir.

"Meet me in Dandong next Friday. Come alone." Ho Jin stood, shook hands with Amir, and said "Here's to a successful collaboration."

"May our arrangement bring us much revenue," said Amir.

Ho Jin turned and weaved between the dinner tables, and on his way out, could hear the whispers and murmurs about the profit margins the next war would bring.

Twenty-Seven

A City of Secrets

The homicide scene was thirty minutes from the Four Seasons Hotel. Patrick and William chose the subway as the most direct route. Arriving at the closest metro station, it was a short walk to the Cheongnyangni Fish Market, located in the heart of the city. William and Patrick surveyed the crime scene, hoping to uncover a clue the first investigators might have missed.

They wandered through the narrow street to the parking lot.

"Anything interesting?" said William.

Patrick stood there pensively and looked around the entire area.

"The police must have missed something," said Patrick.

"Let's talk to a few shop owners."

"My Korean is fair. I'll interview."

After speaking with the owners of the Stamp Store, Patrick moved on to the Nail Services owner and finally, the bartender at the Kiss Bar. They came away no better off than before. William walked the route from the parking lot where the 9mm cartridges were found. He continued to the construction area where the assassin drove through.

"Get anything from your walk?" asked Patrick.

"Nada. A capable agent could have planned this out earlier."

"At least we can eliminate this portion."

Patrick took out his cell phone and looked at his email messages. "I have to get back. This is all the time I can spare."

"Thanks for your time. Ava Ryan is my next move," said William.

"Sorry I can't join you for the interview with Agent Ryan," said Patrick. "Call me when you have something."

"Will do," said William. He walked toward the street, past the shops, to hail a cab.

Patrick departed the other way to the Seoul Metropolitan Subway and headed back to his embassy.

***

The Four Seasons Hotel was close to the Embassy of Australia. William decided to see Ava Ryan and called from the cab. He asked the diplomatic staff to expect him as he was on official business for the Government of Canada. When he reached the Foreign Service Desk, he asked the officer on duty for Ava Ryan.

"She's busy, sir. May I take a message?" he said.

"It's urgent I meet with her," said William passing him his RCMP business card. "If she has time, please ask her to meet me at the Charles H Bar, at the Four Seasons Hotel, at seven this evening."

"Certainly, Inspector Fox."

Disappointed, William went back to the Four Seasons Hotel. He ordered in room service and cleaned up for the meeting with his prime witness.

It was a quarter after seven when William arrived. He was late on purpose because he wanted to throw Ava off balance. He intended to demonstrate his time was more valuable than hers, putting her at a psychological disadvantage. When he arrived, he found her sitting at the bar, tapping her red lacquered fingernails against the smooth surface of the bar. Her application of cherry lip gloss and short dress created a profoundly sultry vision. Ava was already sipping a cocktail and looking cross when William sat next to her.

"Hi, I'm Inspector William Fox."

"You're not fooling anyone Inspector," replied Ava. "With your silly mind games making me wait."

"Sorry about that," said William. He raised his finger to the bartender. "Jameson Irish."

Ava scrunched up her nose, and her eyes followed. She sipped her drink and shook her head. "You can bloody well be on time," she said, infuriated. "It's just professional courtesy."

"Can we start over?" said William. "I really am sorry."

Ava gave William a look that would have scared the devil.

"What can I do for you, Inspector?" she said.

"Tell me about Brian Pendergast. He was more than a friend, right?"

"I've already explained all this to the local authorities," said Ava. "Besides, you must know my government is also investigating."

"You know more than you're letting on," said William. He took a large sip of whiskey.

"This is a city of secrets. Why should I trust you?" said Ava. She finished her drink, turned around on the bar stool, ready to leave.

"Don't go. Let me buy you another one. We are on the same side," said William.

"All right." Ava pushed the glass toward the bartender.

"Another velvet martini coming up," said the mixologist.

"Tell me about Brian and why he was meeting with your agents," said William.

Ava looked over the frosty glass, sipped and made eye contact.

"We were lovers. He was a reporting officer with Global Affairs. We exchanged information," said Ava.

"Was that the case on the night of the—?" said William.

"Yes." Ava scanned the room, looking uncomfortable. "Can we talk privately?"

"Upstairs. I have a room," said William, draining his glass.

Ava finished her drink and followed William to the elevator. William's room was decorated in traditional Korean silks and ceramics, with modern traditional patterns in Kingfisher blue and warm earth tones. He offered Ava a seat on the square cushioned sofa.

"I am having a Jameson on ice," said William. "Would you like one?"

"Trying to loosen me up?" said Ava, adjusting her short skirt. "Sure, I'll have a small one."

"Brian's parents want to know what happened and why," said William, the lie coming easily.

Ava tasted the cool whiskey and explained how they met at the food market and became lovers and their covert exchange of information. Listening, William stood by the large window and viewed the city lights from several stories high.

"I need the loo," said Ava. William pointed to the bathroom beyond the King bed.

"Thanks heaps," she said. He heard the door click and the water began to run. William could sense he wasn't going to get very much out of her this time around. But if he could make her feel comfortable, perhaps she would open up and trust him. Maybe the next time he met her she would be more cooperative. He was certain there was much more to these homicides; the one in Canada and the murders of Brian Pendergast and secret service agents had a connection. They were linked, and he just had to unravel it. He knew that Ava was the key.

Ava returned and sat rigidly on the cushions like an uncomfortable feline.

"You, okay?" asked William.

"It's difficult talking about ... the whole situation," said Ava.

"If you feel you need to talk some more, we can get together another time," said William.

"I'm glad you understand. Coping is difficult," said Ava.

"I'll take you down and get you a cab," said William.

In the lobby, William got the concierge to order a cab. He waited until it arrived, then walked her out and opened to the back door of the taxi for her.

"I know we can figure this out together," said William. "Call me."

Ava tucked her legs into the cab and tugged down her dress. Just for a second, William realized how sexy those long legs were.

"Give me a few days," she said. William closed the door, and the cab disappeared into the city lights.

Twenty-Eight
Acute Micro Devices

James called William to tell him about his upcoming trip to Seoul. He'd already made the arrangements and packed his bags and was waiting for an Uber to take him to Montréal-Pierre Elliott Trudeau International Airport.

His son should be aware that he was heading back to the old haunting grounds. Maybe some old memories would be stirred up. James hoped he would be able to handle them.

He called William with the news. "Just wanted to let you know, I'm waiting for my ride. I'm headed to Seoul."

"Dad, your trip," said William. "It disturbs me."

"What are you troubled about?" said James.

"You have not been back for many years. I'm concerned you don't have an adequate security team."

"I've taken precautions and placed some calls to old friends. And the ambassador is expecting me. Don't worry. I'll be fine," said James.

"If you say so. Just in case, tell me where you're going to be," said William.

"Same hotel as you. The Four Seasons."

"Text me your flight details," said William. "I'll have a limo driver meet you at the airport. Need to ensure you stay safe."

"How many enemies do you think I have?" said James. "No, don't answer that."

***

James' flight from Toronto to Seoul was uneventful and lasted about fifteen hours. He inhaled the stale, recycled air of the air-conditioned terminal. It was no better than the airliner.

After securing his baggage and going through customs, he followed the driver to his limo. The fumes of the city were harsher than he remembered. The driver was a well-behaved man. He minded his business until James asked about the air quality. "Every day in our city is like smoking six cigarettes," said the driver in perfect English.

James was astonished at the city's transformation. "Thanks. It's been years since I've been here." *Had the Four Seasons Hotel changed, too?*

He remembered vividly the period of his diplomatic residency. His trusted staff collected delegates and envoys there. He had offsite meetings at the Charles H. Bar located in the hotel. It had a reputation as the best bar in Korea, making it a favorite hangout for dignitaries. This was the first time he had reserved a luxury suite at this hotel with his own credit card, having previously enjoyed a hefty expense account.

Checking in at the front desk, he glanced at himself in the lobby mirror. He looked dog-tired and his clothes were wrinkled from sitting too long.

After a fitful night, where he woke often, he was glad when morning arrived. In his studio, he had a quick shower and shave, then poured a cup of coffee and wolfed down a modest breakfast. He dressed in a brand-new sports jacket and casual slacks. He brushed his hair and adjusted his tie, made one last check in the mirror, and headed to the lobby. The limo would take him to the Canadian Embassy to begin a new endeavor.

The ride to the embassy took forever. Scooters were zipping in and out, even driving on sidewalks. Damaged cars were cutting in abruptly without regard or signaling. The city had morphed into a video game of smash and dent.

A bigger city with bigger problems.

When he arrived at the embassy, he heaved a sigh of relief: it was a pleasure to be away from the insane drivers. He was escorted to the Trade Commissioner's Office and met David McGuire.

"Welcome to your home away from home," said David.

"It's been a long time since I've set foot here," chuckled James.

"I understand you have a letter of intent and a business proposition."

"Yes, I am very excited to discuss it with you and the ambassador."

"Have a seat," said David. He waved his hand to a plush leather wingchair in front of his desk.

James, still wobbly from jetlag and lack of sleep, slid into the chair.

"Unfortunately, you've missed the ambassador," said David. "So, it'll just be me."

"All right, then," said James. "What's this I hear about my former protégé Brian Pendergast having been killed?"

"Yes. Unfortunately, he was slain. The Korean police are investigating," said David.

"That's terrible," said James. "Years ago, he used to work for me as an intern." James had an inkling that his son was here for the investigation but said nothing.

He opened his brief case and glided the document over the desk.

"This is my business proposal I presented to the Government of Canada. They've already signed off on it," said James. He massaged his temples to banish his weariness.

David picked up the document and verified the letter of intent. "The contacts and the market intelligence we provided have paid off."

"Yes, they have. We also have the approval of the South Korean Trade Office."

"Well, this is great news for Canada. When is your meeting with the company executives of Acute Micro Devices?"

"Tomorrow. I just wanted to introduce myself and advise you on the extent of the negotiations. It was a long flight, and I am still jetlagged," said James, rubbing his irritated eyes.

"That's understandable," said David, handing him back the paperwork.

"Keep it. That's your copy."

"Thanks," said David. "Seoul has changed a lot; would you like our driver to take you to the factory in Pyeongtaek?"

"Yes, if that's no trouble. My meeting is at nine in the morning."

"No problem at all. I'll have the driver pick you up at the Four Seasons."

"I appreciate that," said James, standing up to shake David's hand. "Thanks for your hospitality. I will let you know how the meeting with Acute Micro Devices goes."

"Great. Looking forward to hearing from you," said David.

James left the Trade Commissioner's Office, descended to the lobby and took a taxi back to the hotel. He planned a quiet day to refresh himself before meeting with his old friend, Steve Kumar, the CEO of Acute Micro Devices.

Twenty-Nine
The Chameleon

Patrick put on a Washington National baseball team jacket and slipped on a pair of Nike hands-free sneakers. It was a warm and comfortable June day. His steps were energetic as he threaded his way through the throng of morning commuters. He had spoken earlier to the RSO Daniel Levi for a list of safe houses in the city. He was on his way to a location, a secure apartment, away from the embassy. The Pendergast case and investigation needed a secure place far from the prying eyes of North Korean agents. The investigation into the deaths of Brian Pendergast and the Australian agents could put William and Patrick in a difficult situation. They would certainly obey the laws of the land, but they knew from previous experience this goal was not always attainable, especially when certain situations required immediate response.

After approving the safe house, Patrick returned to the embassy. Jeff Bloom, the Deputy Chief of Mission, escorted him to the communications room to show him interesting video footage one of the intelligence officers had uncovered.

"That man," said Jeff pointing to the screen, "has got us concerned."

Patrick reviewed a video of a man standing in front of the US Embassy giving a thumbs-up to the security camera. "Shit. Never thought I'd see him again."

"You know him?" asked Jeff.

"Sure do," said Patrick. "That's Ren Bo, a Chinese Ministry of State agent."

"What's he doing here?" said Daniel Levi, joining the two men at the screen.

"He snuck into the country for a reason," said Patrick. "But why is he in front of the American Embassy?"

"Good question. But how did he get into South Korea without us spotting him?" said Daniel.

"He didn't come in by conventional means," said Jeff.

"He's one of their best agents, capable and adaptive," said Patrick. "He wouldn't have taken a chance like this unless he has a message for us. What time was he here?"

"Video time-stamp shows oh-six-hundred hours," said Jeff. "He was only there for thirty seconds." The men watched as Ren Bo turned and disappeared into the crowd.

"He's a chameleon," said Daniel.

"Well, you better find him before the South Koreans do," said Jeff.

Patrick said, "They won't find him unless he wants to be found." He turned around to face the communications array and asked one of the agents. "Get a satellite fixed on him in front of the embassy and geo-fence him to his present location."

He turned to face Daniel. "I need a van and two diplomatic security agents. Send me the coordinates," he said, as he rushed out to the motor pool. *What could Ren Bo possibly want?*

Patrick and Ren Bo had met previously on a surveillance ship in the middle of the Atlantic Ocean. They had undertaken a delicate hostage exchange that could have gone south, had it been handled by less experienced men.

Ren Bo, with his military training and workout regimen, was a fit and cunning man, and a capable killer and strategist. Patrick recognized that Ren Bo was well versed in US tracking technology and would have left breadcrumbs for Patrick to find him.

The agent from the embassy texted Ren Bo's coordinates.

He's in the city, at a café.

Thanks, heading there now.

Ren Bo was drinking tea and pulled out a chair for Patrick when he saw him approach; the two US diplomatic security agents trailed behind him.

As the men stepped forward in a threatening manner, Ren Bo raised his index finger, and three Chinese agents stepped out of hiding.

"It's fine men. Stand down," said Patrick, turning toward his agents. The men stepped back for safety reasons. The café was crowded with tourists and locals. He had planned to escort Ren Bo to the safe house he opened earlier in the day, but now his plans had changed.

Ren Bo took off his sunglasses, turning his head away from the sun that had been blasting from the large store window. "It's been a while, Agent Patrick," his eyes bored into those of Patrick's.

"You're the last person I was expecting to see. What are you doing here?" said Patrick.

"My government wants to share vital information," said Ren Bo.

"Why should I trust you?"

"We intercepted communication indicating the North Koreans are after your smart bullet technology."

"Why would you conspire against your ally?"

"Yes, we have a good trade relationship with North Korea," said Ren Bo. "But we are worried about Ma's temperamental sister, Namu, who blew up the Inter-Korean Liaison Office. A symbolic building that was built to support dialogue between both countries."

"I'm familiar with the incident. She was pissed because citizens were sending hydrogen balloons carrying leaflets and food over the border."

"Because of her rash response and militant behavior, our government wants to keep certain high technology out of North Korea's arsenal," said Ren Bo.

"So, State Security sent you here to warn us," said Patrick.

"Yes, our agency wants me to investigate and find out how the North Koreans are interested in acquiring it."

"Thanks for the message. If I were you, I'd get out before the South Koreans find out you're here."

Patrick scraped the chair on the pavement getting up. Ren Bo stood up as well.

"Thanks. Starting to trust me now?" said Ren Bo.

"Maybe. But I want everything you've got," said Patrick.

"You probably know we have our smart thermal sensing ammunition for larger applications," said Ren Bo. "We are not going to share this with North Korea. We are concerned about the dire consequences should they acquire this technology and sell it on the open market. The regime's greed knows no boundaries."

"That's reasonable, as it could be used to assassinate world leaders," said Patrick.

"My job is to find the arms dealers who wouldn't hesitate to steal the technology," said Ren Bo.

"The Russians have experimented with the technology but stalled. They are more than capable of stealing the software, and the system needed to use it."

"You have everything. Now I've got to leave," said Ren Bo.

"That's it? You don't want anything in return?" asked Patrick.

"The whereabouts of all your agents in China," said Ren Bo.

"Are you developing a sense of humor?" asked Patrick.

Ren Bo stepped away from the chair. "It was good seeing you." His agents followed him out of the café to the waiting van.

Patrick sat back down on the chair and called over his own agents. He started thinking about what Ren Bo had told him and if it was true. What was his next move? He picked up his cell phone and dialed Director Simmons.

Thirty

Dark Overcast and Stormy

Director Peter Simmons arrived at the Federal Plaza as the morning sun broke the horizon in a blaze of orange red. He pushed himself through the front doors on his manual wheelchair. Powering his upper torso this way provided the physical exercise that gave him the satisfaction that he wasn't physically inept. In his office, he switched to the electronic wheelchair for his day at work, which made his efforts much less grueling and more focused. His electric wheelchair, although similar to Professor Stephen Hawkins', was more intuitive and allowed Director Simmons a direct interface with the onboard computer screen and dictating feature. The extension arm and the computer were hot spotted to the communications mainframe. He drove around his walnut leather top desk and parked himself. His secretary entered the office with his morning mug of steaming French roast.

"Morning, sir," she said. "Sleep well?"

"Yes. You're chipper today," said Director Simmons.

"Bought a lottery ticket. I feel lucky," she replied.

"Do me a favor."

His framed Ph.D. certificate from the University of Maryland had shifted and sat at an awkward angle. One of his agents had disagreed with his decision and slammed the door on his way out, causing the frame to sit askew. Two days later, he'd had enough of the incongruous position.

"Please straighten out the frame," he said.

"Sure." His secretary reached up and repositioned it. "Better?"

"Lovely, that will be all."

Director Simmons sipped his coffee, feeling quite pleased with himself. His desk phone rang, and he answered it. "Patrick, how's the weather in Seoul?" he asked.

"Dark, overcast and stormy," replied Patrick, using the code phrase to indicate the line was secure.

"All right, you can talk freely."

"Do you remember a Chinese state security agent called Ren Bo?" said Patrick.

"Go on."

"He's the one I negotiated with during the hostage exchange for Professor Jeffrey Jordan."

"The former CIA agent the Chinese want to prosecute," said Simmons. "They still after Jeffrey?"

"Not for now. He explained to me that the North Koreans are attempting to steal our smart ammunition technology."

"Can we trust him? And is that all you have to go on?"

"The Chinese government doesn't want the North Koreans to acquire this technology."

"It's worth billions of dollars to our US economy."

"Precisely. After looking into it, I was impressed with the sophistication of the system," said Patrick. "It does more than fly straight. It can dodge and dip and fly around obstacles and corners, providing enhanced sniper ability."

"I'm going to contact our defense contractors and ask all of them to run security checks on their people. Maybe someone has been approached by the North Koreans."

"I'll wait for further instructions from you."

"In the meantime, continue your efforts in the Pendergast investigation."

Patrick signed off. Since it was the end of the day for him, he decided he would call Nari. He left a message on her voicemail. *"Can we meet on Saturday?"*

***

Director Peter Simmons contacted the Attorney General Director of National Intelligence and explained his concerns, emphasizing that the information was obtained from a credible source. He then prepared a brief for the President and had it couriered over to the White House. It would be in the next morning's Presidential Daily Brief, a summary on all areas of national security.

Peter backed up his wheelchair and looked out the window. He turned to his computer to refresh his knowledge of the smart bullet technology. Its main features consisted of electronic commands, primed with satellite guidance systems, global positioning, and laser and radio software that delivered precision, exactitude and was remotely operated.

Peter Simmons took another sip of now cold coffee. This impressive technology had to be guarded at all costs. He was already formulating a plan in case any of the manufacturers found a security leak. The likelihood of a traitor willing to sell the software plans to their enemies was high.

Thirty-One
The Weapons Deal

Amir Osman had become an Armenian Lebanese refugee through no fault of his own. He grew up on stories of the fighting his grandparents endured to survive the Turkish massacres. His families' experiences made him a bitter man and those years of genocide drove him into international arms dealing so he could help the oppressed fight repressive regimes.

His interest in procuring armaments from a new source brought him to the North Koreans.

Park Ho Jin had heard about Amir and met him in Seoul and had organized a clandestine meeting in the northeast area of Pyongyang. Amir was staying at the Ryugyong Hotel. Ho Jin took him to see the *USS Pueblo*, the spy ship captured in 1968 by the North Korean Navy. Now a War Museum open to tourists, it was permanently docked on the Pothonggang Canal, separate from the Pothong River. Amir was impressed with the secret code room on board the ship, and said how visiting the ship was a wonderful experience.

***

"What are we doing here?" asked Amir, confused, his face scrunched up in disgust.

They entered the mushroom farm; the smell of raw sewage was drifting along the road from the block of crude shelters. A far cry from the plush hotel he was staying at in Pyongyang.

"This is not what our government would prefer visitors to see," said Ho Jin.

"But this is the real North Korea, isn't it?" said Amir, concerned about the location.

Ho Jin was not deterred. He threw back his shoulders defiantly, then pointed. "This way, this is it," he said.

The Pyongyang Vegetable Science Institute was a long building adjacent to the farm. The back door was barely on its hinges and scraped across the floor as it opened. They stepped down into the darkened basement. They were met with the click of a gun being cocked.

"Go to that door in front of you," said the soldier. He pushed Amir's shoulder with the gun and forced him toward the thick door. It was covered in black acoustic panels. Amir recoiled and glared at the soldier.

Ho Jin said, "Stand down. This man's our guest." He cleared his throat. "My apologies. It's this way."

They arrived in a formal meeting room that was well-lit with bright fixtures and in the center was a round table with several chairs.

"Look at that spread. There's hot food, beer, and wine," said Ho Jin.

"Is that a karaoke machine? I thought this was business," said Amir, flaring his nostrils.

"Relax. Let me introduce you to Jeong, president of our weapons production and this is Mr. Gok Cho, head of the medical industry."

"Gentlemen. I am pleased to meet you," said Amir. He pierced them with his eyes. Both directors had seen his type of hard character before, and although there was only a slim chance of this arrangement collapsing, they knew that trust had to be built between them all.

"Please sit, Mr. Osman, and enjoy our hospitality," said Jeong. Amir and Ho Jin sat across from both executives. They jabbed at the food with their chopsticks and helped themselves to drinks.

Young women brought in more food and refreshments and cleared away empty cups and dishes from the table.

During dinner, the *Kippumjo*, also known as the women of the pleasure, group sang, danced, and played musical instruments to entertain the guests. The Kippumjo were willing to offer more, should the men desire intimate attention.

Jeong clapped his hands. The women gathered their instruments and left the room. It became quiet and still as the four men and the two guards stared at each other.

"All right let's talk weapons," said Jeong.

"I'm interested in prices, quantities, and time to delivery," said Amir.

"You can have everything North Korea makes. Even our thermobaric missiles. You're familiar with those. The blast has a similar effect to a small tactical nuclear weapon. Or we can get a real nuclear weapon. It all depends on what you want to spend," said Jeong, his eyes rapidly blinking.

Amir's disposition was suspicious.

Ho Jin was equally dubious and said," I'm not sure about the nuclear weapons."

"Well, we will save that for later," replied Jeong.

"We should," said Amir shifting uncomfortably.

"I don't want to start a nuclear war," said Ho Jin.

Amir understood he was vulnerable, and this kind of talk was dangerous. He could be killed right there in the basement if there was any hint of deception. "Let's just stick to conventional weapons for now," said Amir, anxious to de-escalate the talk of nuclear weapons. "That would only bring unwanted interest from the USA."

"Let's not forget that methamphetamine is a good money maker," said medical director, Gok.

"I'm here for weapons only. I'm not interested in drugs," said Amir.

"We have interests in Africa with both drug and weapons manufacturing," said Gok.

"I suggest we find a place in Africa to build a weapons factory for you. We have blueprints and engineers. We also have North Korean workers who can build the factory," added Jeong.

"And I have connections in Qatar, Sudan, and Yemen," said Amir.

"We've been selling ammunition: AK47s, and RPGs directly to fragmented groups of freedom fighters," said Ho Jin. "We need someone like you to control the marketplace more efficiently. Like a broker."

"If I agree, can we build in Yemen?" said Amir twisting his onyx ring in a restless manner, impatient for the meeting to conclude.

"Yes, in Houthis-held territory, but we need guarantees and a large deposit," said Ho Jin.

"My connections are worldwide," smiled Amir. "And I have unlimited capital." He opened a soft pack and tapped out a Marlboro. He lit it up and exhaled, then sat back in his chair, satisfied.

Ho Jin twisted around in his chair to face Amir after the smoke cleared and said, "We should meet in a neutral country. Preferably in a hotel and sign the final agreement to place an order for the weapons," said Ho Jin.

"This is a possibility. Can we avoid the sanctions to transfer funds?" asked Amir.

"After the final contract is signed, the money will be used to buy oil in Yemen. It will be moved via ship-to-ship transfer. A Hong Kong oil trader will sell it and the proceeds will be sent to North Korea," said Jeong, running a finger along a document and added, "Ten million to start the first shipment."

"Ho Jin, how will you leave North Korea without alerting foreign intelligence agencies?" asked Amir.

"Who says I don't? But whenever I do, it's on a Chinese passport," said Ho Jin. Pressing his lips and checking his watch, "Nothing they can do about it, if I'm careful."

"I can work with this plan," said Amir, extending his hand.

Ho Jin fixed his eyes on Amir, grabbed hold of his hand and said, "This is a fantastic deal for you and North Korea. And a proud moment for Bureau 39."

The executives Jeong and Gok shook hands as well, sealing the deal.

The three North Koreans had secured a lucrative contract on behalf of their country and were pleased with themselves.

"Time for a toast. Do you enjoy *soju*, our national drink?" said Ho Jin.

A double clap brought the women of pleasure back with soju and cold Taedonggang beer.

"Tea will be fine," Amir said waving away the alcohol.

"Would you like some female company?" said Jeong.

Amir shook his head. "Get me back to the airport. I've got arrangements to make."

Ho Jin extinguished his Marlboro and threw back the shot of soju. He gasped, wiped his lips, then stifled a belch that triggered a sudden hiccup.

"Okay, can we go now?" said Amir leaving the tea.

The guards moved beside Amir and Ho Jin and escorted them up to street level. A state-owned sedan was waiting, and a guard held the rear door open.

Amir fastened his safety belt, sat back and stared at his host. "I might have somebody interested in your missile technology," he said. Park's lower lip quivered, and the car door slammed shut.

Thirty-Two
Now We Spring the Trap

Director Simmons had sent a classified warning to all the chief executives of the smart ammunition companies in the United States. He accepted the phone call that came in around twenty hours after the warning. Chief Executive Officer Paul Hobart of Trajectory Weapons Design was concerned when his security team found unauthorized messages from a foreign entity. He responded as soon as he was apprised.

"Director Simmons, my company has been compromised," said Paul Hobart.

"What have you found?" asked Simmons.

"One of our development engineers, named Johnny King, has received an innocuous message."

"Go ahead."

"A Chinese businessman has reached out to him and invited him to speak at a university in Thailand."

"What is his background?"

"He was a child prodigy. His family wanted more for him and got him of out North Korea. He earned an engineering degree from the University of California, Berkeley," said Paul. "Johnny believes his family to be dead."

"Interesting. I'm sending two of my agents to investigate the matter," said Simmons. "Oh, and make sure that Mr. King is in the dark."

"What do I tell my staff?"

"The government is exercising an audit for compliance matters."

"That should convince my staff."

Director Simmons replaced the phone in its cradle. He touched his forehead, questioning the validity of the information passed on by Ren Bo. How many holes were there in the US security networks around the world? Whatever it was, Simmons was determined to see that the technology would not be misappropriated on his watch. He called Patrick Reilly, who picked up right away.

"Yes, Director. How's the weather in New York?" said Patrick.

"Dark, overcast, and stormy."

"It's clear, here. You're free to speak."

"Trajectory Weapons Design has been approached. A foreign entity is trying to secure smart bullet technology by luring a top engineer to Thailand to speak at the Mahidol University."

"We need to find the source of the invitation."

"Precisely. Track down who really sent the email to Johnny King."

"Based on Ren Bo's intelligence, it's probably not China," said Patrick. "North Korea is likely using a phony businessman as their proxy. But I'll make sure."

***

Amir Osman and Park Ho Jin were sitting comfortably at the Blue Velvet Bar. Amir was dressed in a gray suit and blue tie, clipped with a gold bar. Park Ho Jin was thumbing text messages and had replaced his Mau suit with a traditional blue striped suit and burgundy tie. Both had sodas accompanying their *tteobokki*, a spicy rice cake, a specialty of the bar. Amir pulled the cocktail table closer, jarring a chopstick that rolled off onto the carpet. He plucked it up, wiped it superficially and began to eat. The spiciness of the rice cakes tickled his nostrils. Ho Jin took a bite and smiled.

"Not bad for restaurant food," Amir said between bites. "Delicious." Both were benefiting from the vast enterprise of North Korea's shadow war. Amir wiped his lips with the paper napkin.

"Johnny King has responded to our invitation," said Amir. "He was not interested at first. Until we sent him photos of his family. He was shocked. He thought they were dead."

"The RGB is pushing for specifics on the special materials and smart technology," said Ho Jin.

"If Johnny complies, the RGB may release his family from the camps," said Amir as he swallowed his soda slowly.

"He's confirmed his flight to Bangkok. He's bringing documents to make a presentation to a group of interested university professors and students," said Ho Jin.

***

Johnny King required a license to take sensitive materials out of the office and the country. Paul Hobart would not allow that, as per instructions from Director Simmons. The FBI team assigned to the case pretended to be auditors and got full cooperation. They reported back to the director.

"The recruitment was textbook. Applying open networking, they sized King up and coerced him for trade secrets," said Agent Paul Rand.

"When Mr. King tried to smuggle technical materials and blueprints out of the factory, we prevented his departure and detained him," said agent Ursula Davos. "I feel sorry for him. He only did this because he found out his family was still alive."

"It's a ploy used all the time to coerce," said Paul. "Nonetheless, it's treason."

"We intercepted another email which asked for Mr. King to secure the patent designs," said Paul Rand.

"We have taken over his email from his contact and they believe we are him. But do we know who Mr. King's contact is?" said Ursula Davos.

"No, I have an agent in Asia working on it from his end," said Simmons.

"We are controlling the outcome. Our classic double agent operation and the communications are positive. The contact thinks Mr. King has been recruited as a spy, for the RGB," said Ursula.

"Keep on it until we can find a source of the emails," said Simmons.

Director Simmons contacted the head of the Senate Intelligence Committee who empowered his Bureau to protect American business, technology, and intelligence collection. By now it was obvious that North Korea was desperate and was ready to buy, steal, or kidnap anyone to acquire the technology. After briefing the Senator, Director Simmons spoke with the head of the Defense Advanced Research Project Agency that developed the smart bullet. He asked for a brief outline to help him and his agents in deceiving the North Koreans.

Paul Rand and Ursula Davos were anticipating another email. When it arrived, the message requested Johnny King to pass on the design criteria, materials, and software programs.

Patrick called Director Simmons from the embassy communication center.

"Hello, Patrick. What have you got?"

"It's North Korean intelligence. The RGB, without a doubt."

"Let me check with my other team. I'll get back with my recommendations."

Director Simmons' smartphone beeped with a text. It was from Agent Paul Rand.

> King received an email explaining how to create a notepad document. R.

> My agent in Asia says it's the RGB.

> Should we comply? They sent steps to copy all documents and transfer them.

> Yes. Now we spring the trap. S.

Director Simmons' agents were in Arlington County, Virginia. He needed them back in New York with the information. The FBI agents stationed at Trajectory Weapons Design downloaded the directory of all the files to access proprietary information and the software to a laptop, as requested by Director Simmons. A Bureau jet flew them back to New York. Later both FBI agents were in the director's office, ready to proceed with the sting.

"Agents Ursula Davos and Paul Rand, meet special Agent Steve Yong. Agent Yong will impersonate Johnny King and deliver the laptop containing falsified data to the RGB agents in Bangkok," said Simmons.

"Interpol will arrest the foreign agents, and our overseas agents will assist," said Paul.

"We have the consent of the host country, and our Bureau has extraterritorial jurisdiction in this matter," said Director Simmons.

***

Special Agent Steve Yong flew from JFK International Airport at 9:00 pm and arrived in Bangkok at 6:10 am the next day. He was on time to meet his contact at the University of Mahidol at 11:30 am, before students broke for lunch. The twenty-four hours enabled Special Agent Patrick Reilly to arrive in Bangkok and prepare with Interpol. They were to meet the blackmailers in front of the Prince Mahidol Hall.

Patrick and the Interpol agents, including the Royal Thai Police, were present. They were spread out around the campus dressed as students. Placed strategically, they allowed their suspects to enter the area. When the North Koreans moved into the plaza around the hall, they would be surrounded by the grid.

Patrick searched the area and spotted two well-dressed men. Definitely not students, he thought. He adjusted the lens focus of the long-range camera on one man's face. Patrick thought he looked familiar. He had seen him before but couldn't recall his name. To identity the man, Patrick took a few photographs with his smartphone and sent the photos to the FBI communication center, hoping their facial recognition program would identify the man.

When two men approached Agent Steve Yong and began speaking with him, Patrick motioned for the teams to move. Interpol and the Royal Thai Police prepared to rush in. Ho Jin pulled out a gun from behind his back and aimed it at FBI Agent Steve Yong.

Thirty-Three
Move In Now!

"Hold back," said Patrick. All the team leaders of Interpol and the Royal Thai Police listened on their tactical earpieces for further instructions.

He assessed whether interrupting the dangerous situation of the man clutching the gun warranted action or patient consideration. Was he posturing or threatening? Agent Steve Yong showed no panic as he raised one arm in surrender and handed the doctored computer to Ho Jin, who then turned it over to his accomplice. Ho Jin proceeded to examine Agent Yong for weapons. When he finished, he zip-tied Agent Yong's hands behind his back and sat him on the ground. Clearly, Ho Jin had not intended to kill the FBI agent, and left the plaza with his accomplice and computer under his arm.

"Move in now," yelled Patrick. He watched the Integrated Police Services jog across the campus and overpower the North Koreans, who surrendered without resistance. Patrick ran a straight line over the plaza's precast concrete pavers and reached Agent Yong. He released Yong and they joined the other police while Ho Jin and his accomplice were led to an awaiting vehicle.

The initial questioning at the police station of the suspects fell to Patrick. The stolen technology case was uppermost on Director Simmons' agenda, which was why he wanted Patrick to oversee the interrogation before the case was presented to the Department of Justice.

Ho Jin had wanted Johnny King's computer, not realizing Agent Yong was posing as Johnny. Initially, they were to bring it back to Bureau 39, so the RGB agents could copy and download the specifications. While Ho Jin was in his cell waiting to be interviewed by Patrick, his impounded phone was examined. When physically searched, he was found to have been carrying cash and photos of Johnny King's family. The RGB had offered a few inducements: the threat of his family's death, their release from the prison camp, or the lucrative bribe.

Patrick and Steve were keen on organizing this new information. With Interpol's help, they found Ho Jin's cloud account and contact information about his employment, work and personal relationships. Even though he had a very good position, Ho Jin had written that his relationships with women and his finances were not going well for him. Beginning from his college to his university days and to the RGB, and finally, to Deputy Division Director of Bureau 39.

"His journal reads like a résumé," said Steve.

"We caught Ho Jin because he took unnecessary risks," said Patrick. "He was so confident he became reckless, although his professionalism in targeting recruits and development was top-notch spy craft."

With all the evidence that was collected, he was guilty of economic espionage and trade secret theft. The surprising piece of information that was found on Ho Jin's cloud account was the name, Do Yun Cho, the North Korean, washed up on Montréal's shoreline.

Patrick knew William Fox would find this of interest since he was currently investigating that murder, as well that of Brian Pendergast and the two Australian agents. This new information could be of vital importance.

***

Inspector William Fox smiled when he saw Patrick's name flash across his cell.

"Hi, Patrick," said William. "How're things going?"

"Great. I have some interesting news for you. We apprehended Park Ho Jin and his accomplice. After analyzing the data on Ho Jin's cloud account, we came across a name." Patrick paused. "Do Yun Cho."

"The dead North Korean. Interesting."

"This ties into your case directly."

"Could you postpone bringing Park Ho Jin and his accomplice to the United States for prosecution?" said William. "It's a big ask, but would you consider bringing the suspects to Seoul for me to question them?"

"I'll need to check with Director Simmons for permission to go ahead with your request."

"This could be a significant link between the murders of Brian and the two Australians."

"Can you leave it with me?" said Patrick. "I'm going to call Director Simmons right now."

Less than five minutes later, William's phone chirped again. It was Patrick. "We got the go ahead. Park Ho Jin will be arraigned in a military facility in Seoul. Once your interrogation of him is completed, he'll be flown directly to the New York FBI Eastern Division for further evaluation."

Thirty-Four
Family is Everything

During discussions with Kim Min Su, Lim Jun Seo, Choi Wonho, and Sam Minho about penetrating the border near the old hamlet, it became clear that the journey through the mountains would be precarious. The decision to fly to Dandong, the city across from Sinuiju, North Korea, would offer the best opportunity to seek help.

The flight from Incheon International was unsettling for Kim and his friends. They were worried about passing themselves off as tourists and decided that it would be better, once ensconced in the underworld of Dandong, to appear as low life hoodlums and criminals. When they landed in Dandong, it was a relief. The waiting was over; time for action.

At the Jinjiang Inn, the group took two clean modular suites with twin beds and writing tables. Their focus was to locate a contact in the black market. Everyone agreed it would be nerve-racking. The type of person involved in the shadowy world of smuggling would be cautious with strangers.

Kim tapped into his experience as a cop, providing him with unrivaled boldness and confidence. For a fee, the desk clerk directed them to Hongguan Karaoke Bar at the waterfront. "Wear this pin and someone will contact you," the clerk had said.

Sitting in the bar with local beers on the table, the group of former policemen hoped to blend in with smugglers, pimps and other nefarious characters. The four men surveyed the area, getting acclimatized to the seedy surroundings.

"The Sino-Korean Friendship Bridge is just five-hundred meters away," Lim said. "That's our way in."

Kim was wearing the North Korean flag pin that the clerk had given him on his jacket lapel.

The vibe in the bar was dark and Kim sensed someone was looking at them. It was a strange feeling he couldn't shake.

A man dressed like a trucker in a denim jacket and dark t-shirt made his way over. He sat down on the chair by Kim's left. Kim could barely make out his features in his periphery. Lim gestured at Choi and Sam, as their conversation was interrupted by the trucker's eyes settling on the group. He scrutinized each man as they continued to sip their beers. The trucker looked around the bar again, then leered at Kim. His eyes fastened firmly on the flag pin, then he averted his gaze, as if he was doing something he shouldn't.

Lim, Choi, and Sam were gripped by tension and were ready to react. Kim balled up a fist. The trucker's features were Korean, and the drinking and hard life mapped his face with loose jowls and dry wrinkles. On the table lay a few Chinese Yuan saved for the waiter. The bar was buzzing with idle chatter and the air conditioner blew cold air downwards on the table.

"Comrade," said the trucker extending his gnarled hand.

Kim met his greeting with both hands shaking back politely, invoking a half-smile from the other man.

Kim noted the unspoken deference as he explored the man's eyes. "I'm Kim Min Su and this is Lim, Choi, and Sam. What's your name?"

"Bae Hoon," said the trucker.

"You drive goods across the bridge every day?" said Kim.

"That's my job," said Bae. He swept his eyes around the table, taking in all four men.

"I have some interesting merchandise that needs to get across the border," said Kim.

"Why don't you use your usual channels, comrade?" said Bae.

"This is contraband cosmetics," said Lim. "A special order for a general high up in the military who wants to impress his mistress."

Bae rubbed his hands together, eyeing the money, "If the price is right, I should be able to slip this through for you."

Kim pushed the Chinese Yaun across the table toward the trucker.

"If you help us, there is much more for you," said Kim, waving over the waiter.

The waiter placed five beers on the table. Bae positioned his chair closer to reach his beer.

After four more rounds, the men had become comfortable with each other, barriers had been broken and a form of trust established.

"Where are you from?" asked Kim.

"My father's from South Korea, but I was born in Dandong. He came to work in the steel mills but lost his job." Bae took a sip of the beer and belched. "With the little money he had, he started a trucking company. I inherited it when he passed."

"Your father was clever," said Sam.

"Yes, he was," said Bae. "What about you men. What's your story?"

Kim decided to take a chance and confide in the trucker. "My sister was kidnapped when she was a teenager and is in North Korea," he said. "I am trying to find her."

"That's tough," said Bae. "So, this is not about cosmetics?"

"Yes and no," said Kim. "We do have cosmetics. But I'd like to get a message to my sister."

"What's your sister's name?"

"Kim Mi Cha."

The color drained from Bae's face. "You're joking."

"No, why would I?" asked Kim.

"She's married to Park Joon."

"Yes, he's the one who kidnapped her."

"You don't know," Bae's face was incredulous. "He's the General Director of Bureau Thirty-Nine!"

"Unbelievable. I can't believe it," said Kim. "Will you still help me?"

"Sure. That fat cat Park Joon needs to be put in his place," said Bae. "Besides, family is everything."

The five men clinked bottles together. "Here's to family," they said in unison.

The night ended with a lot of drinking and a friendship forged with Bae. By daybreak, a deal had been struck. Bae would help Kim get a message to his sister, Mi Cha, in North Korea.

Thirty-Five
I Wish You Were Here

William took a moment to settle into his room, got dressed in a sweatshirt, jeans, and runners. His concern about losing the baby with Tracy raced around in his mind. Deep sorrow and remorse were creeping into his thoughts, and his focus was drifting away from his duties. He wanted to share his state of mind with Tracy. This would be the first opportunity William had to explore the feelings they were experiencing. William texted Tracy.

> Feel like talking?

> Sure. Why not?

> I'll Facetime you.

Tracy was sitting up, snuggled in a hospital gown in an adjustable bed. She was brought to the Cape Breton Regional Hospital in Sydney, Nova Scotia, after the accident in the Walmart parking lot. Tracy tucked in close to the roller tray supporting her iPad Pro. She crumpled up the paper pill cup and dropped it into the waste basket.

Tracy's expression was somber, her cheeks puffy and her eyes bloodshot. They stared at each other for a moment before William asked the obvious question.

"How are you feeling?" said William.

"Shitty. I miss you."

"I'm trying to focus on this homicide case. But I can't," his voice choked, tears forming in his eyes. "My heart was set on being a father. And now there is no child to watch grow up, play ball with or go fishing."

"I was excited about our first ultrasound," she murmured. "I was looking forward to watching our baby grow."

"It's what could have *been* that made me so happy. Now I feel numb and angry," said William. His head was down and supported with his fingers, hiding his grief from Tracy.

She stifled a sob and reached for her third tissue. "When I found out about my pregnancy, I promised myself I would step up my health regimen: more yoga, staying hydrated, eating healthy, and getting a proper night's sleep." She wiped tears from her eyes. "What's the point now?"

"Oh, Tracy I wish I was there," said William.

"Me, too."

"I confided in Patrick," said William. "He really couldn't help much, but he listened."

"Since the miscarriage, there's been a slew of negative emotions. I feel a disconnect with my body even though it's started to recover. This is the worst time in my life. I am without purpose ... I feel so hollow."

"I can't begin to understand what you're going through," said William.

"The doctor says I am on the verge of post-traumatic stress disorder. Too much time to think is adding to my depression and anxiety."

The ball in William's stomach was getting tighter and heavier. He was close to throwing up. He sat quietly, staring somewhere off in the distance.

"You seem far away," she said. "And not just because you're in Seoul."

"Sorry, I think I'm in denial," he said. He rubbed his eyes with forefinger and thumb.

"My doctor told me that my feelings are common and can persist for up to twelve months. A therapist has been coming to see me here at the hospital. He says you should get help, too."

"As soon as my case is concluded," said William.

"My physician explained taking care of our health could benefit us. Our mental condition as well. He recommended I try post-natal massages, as it is very therapeutic."

"It's good advice," said William.

There was a long pause as Tracy looked up and to the right formulating her thoughts.

"Brenda Tadler realized before me that I was pregnant. I felt bad for us, especially *you*, because we never talked about a family," she said. Tracy started to pick her thumb with her fingernail. "Even though the pregnancy was an accident, I really wanted this baby."

"It was a shock. We were so careful," said William. "I was coming around to becoming a father, had come to grips with it ... and I was elated."

"It was amazing how quickly I developed an emotional attachment. During the nausea and vomiting, Brenda and I would mull over names for the baby. That first ultrasound ... wow. And now, there's no baby."

"This case is weighing on me and losing the child is making it worse," explained William.

"I feel so guilty," said Tracy. She reached for another tissue, and her tears flowed uncontrollably.

"It's not your fault." William felt the remorse in him intensify. "I should have been with you."

"I wish you were here."

"I'll be right back," he said. William crossed the room to the cabinet and poured a large Jameson. When he returned to his screen, he noticed Tracy had applied lip gloss to add color to her face. William took a sip of the whiskey. Its bite was sharp, scorching his insides.

Tracy acknowledged their different levels of attachment. When the loss occurred, they were in two different places emotionally. Tracy found solace in loved ones like her father and Brenda Tadler. William had not had time to come to grips with it since his boss, René had sent him on assignment.

Tracy didn't know how to broach the subject of another baby. Did they want to pursue another pregnancy and become a married couple? It was going to be a difficult discussion, but it would have to wait.

"When do you think you can go home?" asked William.

"Not for a few more days," she said. "It's isolating and lonely and this darkness envelops me ... *squeezing* the joy out of my soul."

"Did your doctor give you any more advice?" said William.

"He told me to have compassion for my healing process. So, I've logged out of social media and painful events that may trigger a panic attack or depression. My therapist helped me join a support group to come to terms with my emotional state," she said.

"I'm never going to forget my chance at fatherhood. There was a place in my heart for a child," said William. He let the statement linger because he wasn't sure about trying again.

Tracy now knew that under the proper circumstances, she *might* like to become a mother. It didn't have to be with William as the father, although he would have made a good one.

A patient services assistant brought a tray of food for Tracy, accidentally bumping the iPad as she set the tray down.

Tracy's frayed nerves finally unraveled.

"Can I have some privacy?" she shouted. Tracy felt her moorings snap and focused on coming back.

"I'm sorry."

"It's okay," said the assistant, as she ran from the room upset and bemoaning her patient.

"You should eat something, Tracy. You might feel better," said William.

"I suppose you're right." Tracy took a sip of her ice water.

"My therapist suggested a small family memorial for closure," she said, giving William a stern look. "I hope you can be here for that."

"Set it up and I'll be there," replied William. *I hope René will be reasonable and let me go.*

He worried that a bullet or knife could end him. His high-risk job was fraught with divorced colleagues or widows. He didn't want to put Tracy through that torment.

Thirty-Six

I Want a Lawyer

William sweated through his tracksuit after a vigorous workout in the hotel's fitness room. The hard pounding on the workout bag improved his spirit, but the lingering thought of Tracy's miscarriage was nagging him. No amount of punching would exhaust the grief he felt. But he had to focus on the present. The twenty-six weeks he spent at the RCMP Depot training academy had never prepared him for this type of tragedy.

He fingered the new scar on his forehead and was grateful he wasn't severely stabbed like Detective Allard. It was dangerous business being a cop.

The RCMP posted approximately thirty-five liaison officers around the globe in Canadian embassies. Their diplomatic duties consisted of international investigations and Canadian interests abroad. The officers interacted with other embassy staff, allies, and local police forces. But in Seoul, William was on his own, except for FBI Special Agent Patrick Reilly. The US Embassy had a safe room, also capable of hosting prisoners such as Park Ho Jin. The prisoner had been transferred from the military facility.

After a shower and a quick fruit bowl breakfast, William arrived at the US Embassy, ready to unravel the scattered puzzle pieces of Do Yun Cho's homicide.

Patrick Reilly allowed William the lead in the questioning of Park Ho Jin. The suspect had been cooling his heels for twenty-four hours. During that time, the FBI had sent his picture to all the intelligence agencies in the region. The Cabinet Intelligence and Research Office of Japan sent the FBI confirmation that their guest was a North Korean RGB agent.

William approached Ho Jin, who was still wearing his wrinkled blue suit.

"I'm RCMP Inspector William Fox. Mr. Park, we know all about your attempt to secure the smart bullet technology,"

Ho Jin sat stoically, calm and composed. William opened the dossier.

"Take a look at the charges. Are you prepared to spend twenty years in jail?" said William.

"I want a lawyer," said Ho Jin.

"Not yet," said William.

"In that case, I want to talk to Ava Ryan," said Ho Jin.

William's heart pounded in his ears like a hundred Taiko Japanese drums. "Bloody hell! How do you know her?"

"Just get her," said Ho Jin.

William gathered up the dossier and left the room, discouraged at the turn of events. Patrick was waiting for him anticipating his next move.

"That was short. He didn't cooperate?" said Patrick.

"He wants to speak to Ava Ryan," said William.

"This runs deep. We need a new approach."

"Keep him on ice. I'll speak to Ava and draw her out," said William. "Perhaps, she can shed some light on this."

William pulled out his Iridium phone then, placed a call to Superintendent René Bouchard.

"What's your status?" asked René.

"We are holding Park Ho Jin, a North Korean national, with ties to Bureau 39. He knows Ava Ryan, the agent responsible for Brian Pendergast's death, and has asked to speak with her," said William.

"This is a breakthrough," said René. "Tread lightly."

"Will do," William signed off. He called Ava Ryan. William's name flashed across her screen. She picked up on the third ring.

"I thought I'd never hear from you, when I didn't call," she said.

"Something's come up," said William. "We need to talk about Brian."

"The ambassador is having a gala tonight at seven. Get a tux. You'll be on the guest list," said Ava.

"Politics does have its perks," said William. "See you then."

Thirty-Seven
Crosshairs

Ava Ryan had been sufficiently rattled after her two agents and Brian Pendergast were murdered in the parking lot. She wanted to contact Park Ho Jin and find out what had been developing with his attempt to smuggle his mother out of North Korea. After the third day of reaching out, her phone went to Ho Jin's voicemail. She grew concerned and felt something must have happened to him. She wondered whether it was time to approach her supervisor about the North Korean agent who was her best informant.

Ava decided to wait until she had her conversation with Inspector William Fox later that evening. *Perhaps he knows what may have happened to Park Ho Jin. Should she try and mislead him or come clean?* She had noticed William's roving eye glancing at her slender and well-formed calves. The Russians were famous for their honey traps. Why not apply this tried-and-true method for the Australian cause?

Ava went shopping for an evening gown that would catch the inspector's eye. The Gangnam area had exclusive shops at the Galleria Department store where Chanel, Gucci, and Lois Vuitton were located. The store assistant helped her with an affordable sky-blue evening gown. When Ava looked at herself in the mirror she was delighted. The satin ruched, off-the-shoulder sleeveless gown and elegant split front design was edgy and sure to turn eyes.

William purchased his tuxedo from the Boss menswear shop in Gangnam. He passed on the suspenders and the cummerbund. He convinced the store assistant that a good leather belt and black buckle had a modern look not unlike Daniel Craig's Bond.

***

William told Patrick he was attending the gala at the Australian Embassy. He asked Patrick to be on standby, in case there was information coming from Ava. William arrived on time and was allowed to pass through the metal detector. He swaggered in and noticed the event announcement on the golden easel in the foyer. The occasion recognized the South Korean Business Chamber of Commerce. He entered the ballroom in the embassy, and it was full of dignitaries. Champagne and canapes were served on silver trays by bored servers. William was sure the guest list included bankers, artists, and executives of high-tech companies and businesspeople. The ambassador was dressed in his highland kilt and making the rounds with a glass of champagne in his hand.

William noticed Ava and other diplomats from the Australian Embassy socializing. She was ravaging in her pale blue gown and with every step the slit along the side would part, exposing her long slender legs. She waved toward him and moved on to another guest. Standing alone, he listened to intelligent banter, bad jokes, women gossiping, and the occasional mention of illicit sex.

As the evening progressed, a formulation of business deals came about, and the occasional roving eye caught a few women blushing. The well-dressed men and bare-backed gowns of fashionable ladies were flashing expensive diamond jewels and high-end watches.

William was getting tired and needed to find Ava in the crowded ballroom. These cunning cat and mouse maneuvers had gone on long enough.

William walked over to the grand staircase set in the far end of the ballroom. He mounted the steps halfway up, scanned the room and noticed Ava in her unmistakable satin blue gown. He hurried down the stairs and pressed through the crowd like a shark through a school of anchovies.

He tapped Ava on the shoulder. She turned and with those sea-green eyes, smiled. Ava grabbed his hand and said, "Follow me."

She took him past the kitchen, through the corridors and into the living quarters.

"There's a suite we keep for guests down the hall. We can talk there," she said.

"I've been waiting all night. What's the hold-up?"

"I had to make the rounds before I slipped away," she said. "Trying to keep my job, you know."

Ava opened the door, allowing William to enter and pointed to a comfortable leather tub chair adjacent to a cocktail table.

She said, "Would you like a drink?"

"Yeah. Jameson or Scotch, whatever."

She returned with two glasses and placed them on the cocktail table in front of William. She sat across from him and her gown slid apart, exposing silky soft skin tanned to perfection. William felt uncomfortable, imploring his eyes to obey and not falter. He focused on her unusual eye color.

"Let's talk about Brian Pendergast, Park Ho Jin, and Do Yun Cho."

"How did you find out about Park Ho Jin and Do Yun Cho?"

"Park Ho Jin is in custody and Do Yun Cho is dead. No doubt, you already know this."

"Ho Jin was my informant, and he was undermining the North Koreans," said Ava.

"What about Do Yun Cho?" asked William. He tasted the scotch and licked his lips.

"He ran messages between Ho Jin and me," she said. Ava crossed her legs, and the satin gown whispered as it fell to her ankle.

"So, Brian Pendergast helped you by getting a temporary passport for Do Yun Cho. He then delivers a message for Ho Jin intended for his uncle Kim Min Su. All to get Ho Jin's mother out of North Korea," said William.

"Yes. Then Ho Jin gave me the thumb drive with sensitive intel which I transferred to my cell. Once I got back to Seoul, I transferred the data back on a thumb drive meant to be given to Brian."

"Is that it?"

"Yes, that sums it up," said Ava. She picked up the glass and swirled the ice cubes around and sipped.

William looked at Ava, trying to appreciate what she was relating. He realized his conflict of interest. Ho Jin was Mr. Kim's nephew and that put his job and friendship in a precarious position. Ho Jin was complicit in corporate espionage and was going to be prosecuted by the US Department of Justice. If he was going to help Mr. Kim, he would have to make a deal with the FBI. He put that on the back burner with the full intention of following through later.

"Brian Pendergast and two of your agents died over that information. What was in that file?" asked William.

"Before the passport exchange for the thumb drive. I had to verify the information and transfer it onto my phone. It was shocking. An arms dealer named Amir Osman signed a deal with the North Koreans to build a weapons factory in Yemen. The Houthis, in turn, would be able to arm every terrorist group in the Middle East," she said.

"Isn't Iran supplying them arms? My understanding is the weapons are sailed over from Somalia and then transported to the city of Sana'a in Yemen," he said.

"Yes, NATO forces are patrolling the Red Sea and dismantling the network, but this changes the playing field."

Ava decided to drop the bombshell she was holding back.

"Bureau thirty-nine plans on kidnapping the chief electronics engineer from Acute Micro Devices. They intend to establish their microchip manufacturing facility somewhere in Pyongyang and develop Artificial Intelligence technology to disrupt the west. North Korean leader Ma and Director Park Joon are responsible for this covert assignment."

She finished her drink and walked the bottle back to the table. She poured William a double and the same for herself. Then dropped ice cubes into the drinks.

"Not pleasant news," she said.

William tossed back the drink.

"Besides this unsettling info, how are you coping with Brian's death?"

Ava knocked back her scotch and refilled the glasses.

"It hasn't been easy staying on the sidelines with the ongoing investigation. I'm in the agency's crosshairs over the deaths," she said.

Ava gave him a serious look, and said, "I heard you lost a child."

"It's been bloody hell."

"Brian and I were close. We both knew it wasn't going to lead to anything like marriage," she said. "But we still cared about each other."

"I'm sorry things are so tough right now."

Ava lowered her head into her open hands and wept. Her world was crashing down around her and the brave front she put on vanished.

William moved over and sat beside her. He put his arm around her shoulder, and she snuggled into his chest and cried.

"Hang in there, things are bound to get better," he said. William didn't know where that statement came from. He was feeling hollow and vulnerable himself.

Ava looked up into William's face and saw compassion.

"Will you stay with me? I don't want to be alone."

"You know I'm involved with Tracy."

"But she's not here and I am." Ava looked into his eyes, put her arms around his neck, and kissed him fiercely.

He kissed back, probing her mouth with his tongue. He couldn't hold Tracy, but he needed consoling. The passion was both familiar and exotic, and the moment consumed them both.

Thirty-Eight
Fish or Cut Bait?

William woke up, the pounding in his head was unbearable. He was paying for a night on the town. He was in his room at Four Seasons. His new tuxedo was haphazardly draped over a chair. He smiled as he remembered looking like Bond in Casino Royal. Skipping breakfast was sensible. He doubted he could keep it down anyway.

He reflected on his training at Mr. Kim's dojang. He had worked his students hard, and their reward being a night on the town with delicious Korean food and beer. Sometimes his students overindulged and would wake up with serious hangovers the next day. Mr. Kim was unsympathetic and insisted they show up at the dojang first thing in the morning to work out the toxins.

William seldom over indulged, but he remembered his sabomnim's advice. He was in his skivvies and decided a workout would get him engaged in the day. He started with a hundred push-ups, then completed fifty sit-ups. He drank water to help him rehydrate. Adjusting the shower water to a nice temperature, he tried to wash away the residual effects of the hangover. Toweling off, he slipped on a white shirt, pulled on designer blue jeans and donned a blue checkered pattern blazer and ombre oxford shoes.

William stepped lightly and floated down the stairwells to the ground floor. Every bit of exercise would help him get rid of the toxins. An embassy car waited for him in the pick-up and drop-off zone. A diplomatic service agent met him and whisked him back to the US Embassy. William had barely gotten into the building where he soon found himself in the RSO office. Patrick was pouring the coffee. The morning sun was filtering onto the well-waxed desk, creating hazy patterns.

"How did it go?" asked Patrick as he unbuttoned the black jacket of his suit and adjusted his blue tie before sitting down.

"The woman has some depth," replied William. His head continued to hammer, while he was trying to accustom his wits to the present moment.

"You dress up nice, but your face looks like shit," said Patrick. "Late night?"

"I should be in bed sleeping it off," said William rubbing his bloodshot eyes.

"What did Ava Ryan say?" asked Patrick.

"Park Ho Jin and Do Yun Cho were her covert operatives engaged in field intelligence," said William. He picked up a paper clip and proceeded to bend it into odd shapes.

"Interesting," said Patrick, raising his eyebrows.

"Do Yun Cho was compromised. Brian supplied him with a temporary passport to save his life. In exchange, Do Yun Cho was to deliver a message to my friend Mr. Kim. Then Ho Jin gave Ava Ryan the intelligence, which she asked her agents to deliver to Brian. Her agents and Brian were killed the night that information was to be exchanged. Ava is suspended from active duty and is under investigation over the failed operation," said William. "By the way, Ho Jin is trying to smuggle his mother, who is Mr. Kim's sister, out of North Korea."

"So, now we have the connection between the dead North Korean agent and Mr. Kim," said Patrick.

"Yes," said William wincing. "I could use a few Tylenols."

Patrick went to the bathroom, returned with two and handed them to William, who swallowed them with his coffee. "Hope that helps you focus," said Patrick.

"Thanks," said William.

"That's interesting. But what was the intel?" said Patrick.

"An arms dealer named Amir Osman signed a deal with that power tyrant, Ma. They plan to build a weapons factory in Yemen. The city of Sana'a to be exact. The Houthis welcomed them with open arms," said William. He tossed the twisted paperclip onto the desk.

"This is some serious shit," said Patrick.

"That's not the whole story," said William, finishing his coffee and setting the cup down. "The North Koreans plan on kidnapping the chief electronics engineer from Acute Micro Devices. They intend to develop AI technology," said William. "Applications of which will eventually be found in their military hardware and also used to undermine social media in the west."

"Wouldn't put it past them. North Korea kidnapped Japanese citizens in the nineteen-eighties," said Patrick.

"If you don't have the talent, you steal it," replied William.

"This is a massive shift. They have balls."

"Time to fish or cut bait," said William, using the old idiom. "Do we take action or wait?"

"I'll contact Director Simmons in New York," said Patrick.

"And I'll be speaking with René," said William.

William left the office and found a vacant meeting room to reach out to René.

***

Despite the hour, René Bouchard knew it couldn't be anyone other than Inspector Fox.

He picked up. "This better be good."

"It's better than good," replied William. He outlined the complete conversation with Ava Ryan. Then he made some points that were discussed with FBI Agent Patrick Reilly.

"You've made excellent progress," said René, pleased.

"Mr. Kim doesn't know the investigation includes his nephew, Ho Jin," he said. "He's one of the primary suspects in the smart ammunition espionage case."

"Encourage him to go home before the North Koreans kill him, or worse, put him in a concentration camp," said René.

"I have, but he flatly refuses. And he has old police friends helping him to search for his sister," said William. "It's just a matter of time before Mr. Kim finds out about his nephew's involvement."

"Under no circumstances are you to engage Mr. Kim in the investigation. Even if he insists on being involved," said René.

"He's a force to reckon with," said William.

"You and Mr. Kim go back a long time. Keep him out of the FBI's way," said René. "Get him on the next plane home."

"Agent Patrick Reilly has confirmed Park Ho Jin is being prosecuted," admitted William.

"All right. I'm also concerned about you. You are handling your grief well?"

"Yes, it's been hard, but I'm focused, and the FBI is helping with my case."

"Tracy is in good hands, so you keep an eye on the ball," said René "Comprends?"

William ran his hand over his face and sighed. He had fallen off the rails with Ava Ryan. *Now he could add betrayal to his list of failures.*

Thirty-Nine
They Know the Players

While William was talking with René, Patrick awakened Director Simmons from a deep sleep to pass on the disturbing news. He placed his cell on speaker and set it down on the desk. He slipped off his suit jacket and placed it over the back of the executive chair and got comfortable behind the heavy desk.

"Oh shit," said Simmons.

"Everything okay, sir?" asked Patrick.

"Do you know what time it is? I nearly knocked over my glass of water." Simmons sounded perturbed as Patrick relayed the seriousness of the latest intelligence.

"William was helpful in getting information from the Australian Intelligence Agent Ava Ryan," said Patrick. "The key issue we have is an arms dealer Amir Osman, who is building a weapons factory in Yemen to supply armaments to the Houthis."

"Let me get my laptop." A few minutes later, said Simmons. "I found a file on Amir Osman. A heavy player under investigation, but never charged. Downloading the files from the FBI database, now."

"He's like Teflon. But we have his partner Park Ho Jin in custody. They were both involved in the smart ammunition sting. Too bad he was not there for the takedown," said Patrick.

"Intel confirms that he is in Yemen building a weapons factory for the Houthis," said Simmons, clearing his throat.

"The Iranians are supplying weapons to the Houthis, aren't they?" said Patrick.

"Yes," said Simmons. "For now, our coalition Navy is dismantling their supply route in the Red Sea."

"Can we stop the factory before it changes the dynamics of the Middle East conflict?" said Patrick.

"We can damn well try," said Simmons. "I am sending a report to the National Security Agency. They can take care of it how they see fit. They know the players."

"I'll take care of our situation here," said Patrick. "We'll keep Ho Jin in custody here for the time being."

"Now bugger off. I need my sleep," said Simmons.

Patrick retrieved his jacket and started looking for William. There was much to do to wrap up the case. A buzzing and vibration stopped him. Nari had sent a text.

Feel like company? I'm thirsty. N.

Meet you at the Girgo-Girgo in ten minutes. P.

Patrick met William in the hallway just as his phone disappeared into a breast pocket.

"All done?" asked William.

"Yes, and now I've got to go," said Patrick.

"No time for a drink?" asked William.

"Some business to deal with," said Patrick. He turned his back and swiftly departed.

"If you change your mind, join me and my dad for dinner tonight."

"I'll let you know."

***

Patrick slid into the booth where Nari was waiting.

"Glad to see you," he said, as he reached over to kiss her on the cheek. She wore enormous drop earrings, and a light gray checked jacket. She had applied apple red lipstick and long wisps of black hair fell over her brow.

"Good to see you, too." Nari smiled. "I've already ordered."

The server arrived with their drinks.

"You remembered," said Patrick, as he sipped his absinthe cocktail.

"You are too cute to forget," said Nari, sipping her soju.

"Tell me about yourself ... again," said Patrick.

"Well, I was born here in Seoul. I am studying art at Seoul National University. I work evenings at a gallery, which helps make ends meet." She fiddled with a coaster and asked, "What's your thing?"

"It's not exciting. I am in the diplomatic service here at the US Embassy," he replied. He clinked her glass. *There is no reason for the complete truth.* "Cheers."

"*GeonBae,*" Nari answered.

They savored their drinks in silence.

"That's refreshing," said Nari.

"So, when did you get inspired to become an artist?" said Patrick.

"My mother encouraged me early in my youth, said Nari. "Against my father's wishes. He was in business and expected me to fill his shoes."

"Do you get along with him?"

"I dislike him complaining about the art scene," said Nari. "Starving artist's stuff, you know." She brushed her hair back over her ear.

"I'm going to frame the sketch you made of me," said Patrick.

No, you're not, let me paint a proper portrait."

"Okay, if you insist. How about I buy dinner, as a token of my appreciation?"

"All right. Let's finish our drinks and go," Nari said and grabbed his hand. Patrick stopped at the bar and gave the server Korean Won.

"Keep the change," he said.

***

They arrived at Nari's *yeollip jutaek,* a small sized apartment building.

"Come on, I'm on the fourth floor," said Nari. "Sorry, no elevators."

She opened the door to her home. Patrick stepped in, carrying two bags of takeout.

"Put the bags on the table," she said.

The small apartment had sliding windows and doors, with narrow stairs leading up to the loft, and a double bed. The functional kitchen was white. In the living room, there was a TV resting on a cabinet, plus plants and a loveseat. In the corner was her easel and paint table.

Patrick opened the bottle of Soonhari Soju and said, "So, why do you like this drink so much?"

"Because it tastes slightly sweet and crisp, and I like the peach flavor."

They piled their plates with Bibimbap, a dish of rice, vegetables, and pickled radish with fried eggs sunny side up, kimchi, the spicy fermented cabbage, and Bulgogi Beef barbeque.

After dinner, Nari washed the dinner plates while Patrick ambled over to a painting on the far wall.

"Watercolor on paper," said Patrick, appreciating the fine execution of her subject.

"Yes, my early work," she replied, looking over her shoulder.

Patrick stood, admiring it. A gaunt cherry blossom tree had an ax embedded into the trunk. Blossoms were floating earthward like snow. Standing nearby was a girl and an elderly man. They were both dressed in traditional clothing. He had his hand on her shoulder, a stern look on his face, as if accusing the girl of having heaved the ax into the tree.

"Very classical composition. The muted colors brilliantly combined," said Patrick. He was searching for meaning in the composition, hopeful it would reveal Nari's character. Something he could understand to appreciate her more.

"There is a whole philosophy behind the painting," said Nari. She was rinsing off the dinnerware and drying them.

"A diminutive exploration for the unwashed," said Patrick, tongue in cheek. "Just kidding, this is a significant work of art. It should be in a gallery."

Nari's cheeks flushed pink at the compliment. "Korean art is linked to the abstraction of naturalism and is defined by absolute balance of the artist's vision."

"I'm following," said Patrick.

"It should present a broad association with the environment. Naturalism is a concept exemplified by its earthiness, excluding the biases of the human mind," explained Nari, who was now standing by him. "You, see?"

"Yes, this is a brilliant concept," said Patrick. "Did you want me to pose now?"

"How about tomorrow morning?" she said, reaching around his neck and pulling him in for a kiss. She took his hand and led him up the narrow steps to the loft.

Forty

The Engineer

The limo driver from the Canadian Embassy had said to James Fox, "It will take about an hour to reach your destination."

The trip south to Pyeongtaek gave James ample time to reflect on his business venture and the changes and progress the city had accomplished. The area was Americanized with English street signs and fast-food shops offering French fries, chicken wings, and rice cakes in red pepper sauce, a heartburn ambush for the unwary.

James remembered the Acute Micro Devices semiconductor plant had been built on former pastures and farmland, previously scattered with livestock and manure. Pyeongtaek was home to a Korean naval base and US Camp Humphreys Military Base.

The driver pulled up in front of a massive glass edifice after entering the Godeok Industrial complex; the home of many Korean tech giants manufacturing state-of-the-art technology. The industries located here propelled it into one of the fastest growing cities in Asia.

James approached the venture with trepidation and excitement. A new era in microchip production was on the brink of exploding, and he was in the midst of it.

Upon entering the facility, he underwent the strictest of security protocols and was escorted to a reception area to meet his host.

"Good morning, Mr. Fox," said Jim Graham, the chief engineer. He reached to shake James' hand, and a friendly smile broke across the bearded face. The goatee gave him a professorial demeanor.

"Pleased to meet you," said James, grasping his hand firmly. "So, how long have you been in the microchip industry?"

"For about twenty years. Ever since I graduated from MIT," he said. "Let's get dressed for the tour."

Jim escorted James to the clean room filled with hooded white coveralls. Once dressed, they both put on booties and gloves.

"Follow me," said Jim as he strode out of the room.

They entered the pristine manufacturing facilities. Jim showed him the extreme ultraviolet (EUV) photography machines and how the process engendered the production of multilayer chips.

"Our process here produces three nanometer node chips, and we are gearing up to include four and five nanometer nodes," said Jim. "Your new company will need ultraviolet lithography machines."

"Yes, I am aware. They cost approximately two hundred million American each to start."

"And you'll need deep ultraviolet machines that Nikon makes," said Jim. "I suggest you pre-order the machines as it takes numerous years to construct them."

"Good advice," said James. "We have already taken that under consideration."

"Ultimately, the facility will have the capacity to generate one hundred and twenty-five wafers per hour."

"Just so you know, my partners and I have already acquired land in Kanata, near Ottawa, and we begin construction soon. We'll be building a power grid to ensure unlimited access to energy," said James. "Your recommendation to order the EUV units early will allow us to prepare for a timely transition."

The tour took forty minutes and when they completed walking the entire span James was curious about the facility.

"It's impressive. How large is it?" said James.

"Approximately twenty football fields," said Jim.

"And billions to build," said James.

"Yes, let's get you back to meet our CEO," said Jim.

"Steve Kumar. I met him years ago, when I was ambassador here," said James. "I'm looking forward to seeing him again."

Back in the clean room, James removed his coveralls, adjusted his tie, and ran his fingers through his hair. Satisfied with his appearance in the mirror, he retrieved his brief and followed Jim to the elevators. On the top floor, they slipped by the receptionist and Jim knocked on the door.

"Come in," was heard through the mahogany laminate door.

Entering Steve Kumar's office was a novel experience for James. He remembered Steve was born in Pakistan and immigrated to the US when he was ten years old. He skipped a year in high school and received an undergraduate degree in electrical engineering at Princeton University. He founded Acute Micro Devices when he was thirty-two and in 1991, took the company public. James was grateful for how his initial share position in the company had multiplied a hundredfold.

"How are you?" said Steve. "It's been a long time." He approached his old friend and hugged him. James winced from his powerful grip.

"Nice to see you as well," replied James straightening out the sleeves of the suit. "I see you are still hitting the gym."

"Never miss a day," laughed Steve. "Please, sit."

James' gaze swept the room. High ceilings and vertical windows overlooked the city. A glass cabinet with two flowering succulents rested on top. Awards were on the second shelf and books and manuals on the third. The low modular desk and a high-back executive chair faced away from the view.

Steve dropped into a leather buttoned armchair, inviting James to sit in the one opposite. James placed his leather brief on the coffee table between them and crossed his legs.

"I was an ambassador for Global Affairs Canada the last time we met," said James. "Now, I could use your expertise to improve Canada's development of microchip technology."

"My board of directors has approved your initial plan," said Steve. "However, the processor components need refinement to integrate AI with the gaming chip. Then we can firm up the architecture in a secure environment during development before sharing the technology under license."

"My venture group would like to borrow Jim Graham until we have our facilities up and running," said James. "After our initial public offering."

"Men of Jim's caliber are rare. Our engineers are in short supply, with a worsening problem of sector growth. And we're all looking for exceedingly talented individuals," said Steve. "In other words, we have a severe shortage of capable technical candidates."

"Nonetheless, you see why we need someone like him," said James.

"I know he loves challenges, and he might agree."

"Have a talk with him, and let us know," said James. "I'd appreciate this consideration."

Steve shook James' hand, "It was nice to see you again."

"If you've time, let's have lunch together," said James. "It would be nice to catch up."

"I'd like that."

"I'll only be here for a few more days."

"That could be tight," said Steve. "If we don't connect this time, have a pleasant trip."

The embassy driver held the door open for James and he slid into the limo. As they drove from the facility, James was relatively sure that Steve would convince Jim Graham to join his company.

"Take the scenic route back," said James, reclining in the backseat.

"Yes, sir." The driver merged into traffic heading toward Seoul.

Forty-One

You Are Out of Your Jurisdiction

The Four Seasons Hotel was in the Gwanghwamun district of Seoul. James Fox and Jim Graham retired to the corner suite for a private dinner and the signing of contracts. The luxurious suite had a corner window with a wraparound view. Over drinks, they admired the lights that flickered across the skyline like the ebb and flow of a distant galaxy.

While they were waiting for room service to bring their dinner, James said, "I was so pleased when Steve Kumar convinced you to join us." He tilted his head toward Jim indicating whether to top up his drink.

"Yes, please," said Jim. "A great offer is hard to ignore. Great scotch, by the way."

Robust banging on the hallway door interrupted their conversation.

"That's room service," said James, as he rose from the couch and strode to the door. He cocked his head to one side and peered through the door viewer. Acknowledging the hotel service staff was indeed here, James unlocked the door.

Three men rushed past the server and penetrated the room with military precision. Each held suppressed Type 68 semi-automatics, the standard service pistol of the North Korean Army, and they were aiming them at James and Jim. The threat froze them in place. The nervous server made a dash for freedom, and one of the intruders shot him. The server fell down spread-eagle in the hallway. Their attention diverted, James ran to the washroom with his phone. Against his better judgment, Jim pushed one gunman into another, allowing James time to shut the door. Bullets perforated the wooden door, missing James as he slid across the bathroom tiles. With shaking fingers, he texted his son who was staying on the next floor.

***

Men with guns broke into my room.

The soccer match William had been watching was interrupted by a chirp. He scanned the text. He pocketed his phone while dashing to the stairwell and ran up the steps two at a time. William found the server sprawled on the hallway carpet. He reached down and touched his neck. No pulse. Cautiously he entered the room. Empty. In cat-like strides, William checked the suite over. The bathroom door cracked open, and James exited the washroom.

"I'm okay. They took Jim Graham," said James. His eyes were glassy, and his breathing was labored."

William eased him onto the couch and said, "Call the police." He touched him on the shoulder. "And wait here."

William retreated to the stairwell, vanishing down four flights of steps into the underground garage. He caught sight of three men forcing a bearded man into a white van before the door slammed shut. He started to run forward as the van streaked out of the underground, up the exit ramp and bolted into traffic. William rushed out onto the street huffing.

He ran to the closest vehicle which was a Hyundai Porter, a commercial flatbed. The truck bed was stacked with cement bags. William opened the driver's door flashing his RCMP badge and pushed the driver over to the passenger side. He slipped in behind the steering wheel and pushed the lever into first gear.

The white van driven by the abductors began to move as the lights flashed to green. The Hyundai flatbed shuddered under its load as it merged into traffic. William ground his boot down until the accelerator was flat to the floor and picked up speed. It was a race if one could call an elephant chasing a gazelle a race. William prayed he could slow them down and expected the police were on their way.

He looked over at the stunned driver and asked, "Are you alright?"

"*Joh-eun,*" he stuttered, then repeated in English, "Good." The driver was dressed in navy coveralls with a name tag that said *Sampyo Cement.*

William retrieved this phone and speed-dialed Patrick.

"What's the soccer game score?" said Patrick.

"I'm on the road, chasing kidnappers. They took Jim Graham," said William.

"Who is Jim Graham?"

"My father's microchip engineer," said William, averting his eyes from the road to catch his phone drifting on the dash.

"Where are you?" asked Patrick. "And how can I help?"

"I'm driving on Saemunan-or. The kidnappers are driving a van, a white Kia Pregio. Registration plates fourteen-dash-eighty-nine-dash-fifty-six. We are seven cars back."

"We?"

"Yes, the driver is with me and he's 'joh-eun'," said William. "You know, 'good'."

"Keep cool, and we'll track him from here," said Patrick. He hurried along the hallway to the communication center and entered the busy room.

"Okay, people. Emergency, white Kia panel van registration plate fourteen-dash-eighty-nine-dash-fifty-six traveling south on route six. Get on it right now," shouted Patrick.

The embassy team swung into it, talking among themselves, and finding the van right where William stated it would be.

"Vehicle's on route six," said a communications expert.

"On screen, please," said Patrick. "William, the van is on route six southbound still ahead of you."

"Are the police blocking roads ahead?"

William swerved around a stopped vehicle, hit the curb and rode over it, dislodging three bags of cement. They careened onto the roadway, breaking open and spreading a fine gray dust over the area. Cars and vans screeched to a stop. William was too far ahead to hear the metal crunching and the drivers cursing.

He downshifted into third, weaving around a transit bus. The Hyundai hugged the broad turn and then finally came to an abrupt halt.

"Lost him at Tongil-ro," said William.

"They stopped at the NH Nonghyub Bank building," said Patrick.

"Headed there now."

"You better move fast. There's a helipad on the roof, and CCTV shows a helicopter about to land."

"Smart move," said William.

"Not good if they escape."

Pushing the Hyundai Porter into second gear triggered a lurch onto a curb. Several more bags of cement propelled onto the asphalt, causing another dust storm to halt traffic in front of the bank.

William left the Hyundai and ran through the revolving door and bolted toward the elevators. The confused cement truck driver stepped out, his arms and hands extended in apology, appealing for the crowd's sympathy.

William heard the metro police sirens before the elevator doors closed. On the top floor, he located the door to the roof and edged it open.

Thud. Thud.

"Shit!!" said William, ducking as two rounds pounded into the metal door above his head.

Men stamping up the stairwell finally arrived, and several armed SWAT team members pulled William aside and cuffed him. They were yelling at him in Korean.

"Hey, I'm with the RCMP!" said William. "Anyone speak English here?"

"Yes,' said the SWAT team captain. "You are out of your jurisdiction."

The kidnappers' helicopter rotated away when the pilot realized the mission was a failure. A metropolitan police helicopter circled the building once and took chase.

Trapped on the roof, the RGB agents were outflanked. The SWAT team captain said, "Seize them!" The door burst open, and the SWAT team took strategic positions, ready to fire.

The kidnappers that were hiding behind rooftop air-conditioning units dropped their weapons, raised their arms and surrendered. The Metropolitan Police SWAT team rushed out, retrieved the weapons and arrested the kidnappers.

As Jim was being escorted down to the main lobby of the building, he passed William, who asked, "Are you all right?"

Jim stopped and said, "Yes, thanks for coming after me."

Both men were taken to police headquarters, for debriefing, one in comfort, the other in cuffs.

Patrick's team had followed William's arrest on the CCTV, and he was concerned about William. He called the Metro Police Headquarters and demanded to speak with the superintendent.

"I am sorry, sir," said the receptionist. "The Superintendent is not available."

"Get him on the phone now! Tell him I'm with the FBI!"

***

The Metropolitan Police superintendent who oversaw the investigation was questioning William. "What the hell were you thinking? Tearing up the streets of Seoul."

"Trying to prevent a kidnapping. Possibly save someone's life," said William.

There was a light knock on the door and the receptionist entered. "Sir, there is a call from FBI Special Agent Patrick Reilly and he's very angry."

"Tell him I'll be right with him," he said. "Looks like you have friends in high places."

The superintendent picked up the phone, and his mouth narrowed in annoyance. Patrick's irate voice could be heard through the phone's handset.

"Agent Reilly, I am charging Inspector Fox with numerous traffic offenses, and I have confiscated his driver's license." The superintendent cleared his throat. "We don't normally offer bail to foreigners. Usually, we keep them in detention until our investigation is completed."

"Surely you know, William was a major contributor to the kidnappers' capture," said Patrick

"We have spoken with James Fox and Jim Graham and we do recognize William's role in foiling the kidnappers."

"As you are aware, William is in Korea as an investigating officer to help solve a murder in cooperation with the police, Interpol, and the National Security Agency," said Patrick. "His release is crucial to solving the case."

"Yes, I am aware why William is here. I will offer you this professional courtesy and I am releasing him in your custody," his voice was stern. "Tell the inspector to finalize his investigation and return home."

"Thanks," said Patrick. "I'll be over right away to pick him up."

***

Patrick and William arrived at the US Embassy and entered the meeting room to discuss Ava Ryan, Brian Pendergast, the two Australian agents who had been killed, and the capture of Park Ho Jin and his accomplice.

"Before we get started," said William. "Thanks for getting me released."

"What else are friends for?"

"I think I've waited long enough. Mr. Kim is headed for trouble if I don't intervene," said William. "I need to call him."

"Don't let me hold you," said Patrick, getting up to leave. "Getting coffee. Want some?"

"Yes, I could use a cup," William said and dialed Mr. Kim.

***

Kim and his friends were having breakfast at the hotel when his phone started vibrating in his pocket. He pulled it out and saw it was William. He excused himself, and walked to the lobby.

"Finally. I've been here for a while and now you call," said Kim.

"Sorry, old friend. I got caught up in a case. But now that I've got you, listen to this. We have your nephew Park Ho Jin on hold at the US Embassy," said William. "He is in a shitload of trouble."

"How is he?" said Kim.

"He's good. Where are you?"

"My friends and I are in Dandong. We have a cross-border trucker who will help us get a message across."

"Good. Don't do anything until you hear my plan. I can make this work favorably for everyone."

"I'm listening."

"Here's what I am proposing," said William."

Forty-Two

A Mishandled Mission

June 2019

During the Korean War, Pyongyang was destroyed. Rebuilt at a hectic pace, the high-rises and monumental buildings rose like phoenixes from the rubble. The regime had created the ultimate totalitarian metropolis, which included high-rises and a science and technology building that resembled a spaceship.

The financial arm of the Ma government was situated in a five-story building adjacent to Danmark Abellas Park. Divided by Changgwang Street, the contrast of rigid concrete and greenery created a divergence in a modern city.

General Park's office overlooked the early morning sun's illumination behind the manicured tall conifers that lined the street in front of the park.

Joon began his morning ritual. He was dressed in his tan military uniform, a *sangjang*, a Colonel General. His attire comprised three gold stars on his epaulets and embroidered leaves on his lapels. He placed his peaked cap on the desk. Along his chest were the most prestigious medals: the Hero of Labor and the Order of the National Flag First Class. The rest that adorned his chest were window-dressing, meant to impress his subordinates. He carried his mid-sized body through the office with a distinctive swagger. He had developed that swagger as a young man at the University of National Defense.

The reflection in the window mirrored a man with a round face, high cheekbones, and small eyes. He looked away from the Korean Fir lining the park and adjusted his recliner chair before slipping into the worn comfortable leather.

The mood in the office was sullen, and the harsh fluorescent tube lighting added to his agitation. Ho Jin had failed to report back to him on his mission. The assignment code name, Cobra Chip, was a joint effort between Financial Bureau 39 and Intelligence Bureau 35, intended to cross-train agents to be more adaptable in the field.

Joon picked up the desk phone and called the head of Bureau 35, the branch dealing in foreign intelligence.

"Good morning general. Is this about our mission?" asked Colonel Kwan.

"You were responsible for my son. Where is he?" demanded Joon.

"I was about to call you. He was arrested by the FBI in Thailand, along with my agent."

"Have you been to Chungsan?"

"The concentration camp. Never! Why would I need re-education?"

"I need straight answers or that's where I'll send you."

"The computer," said Kwan.

"What about it?"

"It was probably fake. A highly executed trap by the FBI."

"What a mess. I'll have your fucking head for the screwup."

"Get in line. I probably won't make it past the end of the week."

"Supreme Leader Ma knows about this failed mission?" asked Joon.

"Yes, the Director of Operations wants me at his office at eight this morning," said Kwan.

"Do something smart with the remaining time. Can we get Ho Jin back? Any ideas?"

"Our sources say he's at the US Embassy. It's impregnable. He will be extradited to the US and prosecuted for espionage," responded Kwan.

"Find a solution or I will be paying a visit to your daughter. She just had a baby, right?" said Joon, as he slammed the handset into the cradle.

He ran his hand over his forehead. He summoned Mi Cha. She tapped his door twice and stepped in. She wore a yellow one-button jacket and dress with black piping around the outside edges. She was smartly attired, attractive but not provocative. She sat without asking and waited.

"He's gone. The mission failed and the FBI has him," said Joon.

"You assured me, Ho Jin was ready. How did this happen?" said Mi Cha.

"A mishandled mission. The FBI set up a classic sting operation. Ho Jin was overly confident and was manipulated."

Mi Cha leaned forward into her hands and supported her face. The sobs were muffled. She cried for her son who she might never set eyes upon again. The agony sent her into a spasm, then a rage that even Joon had never seen before.

Joon stood up, stepped around the desk to comfort her. He placed his arms around his wife to settle her down. Mi Cha shrugged in his arms, twisting and stepping back. She pounded his chest with her fists.

"You failed us, you failed us," her voice trailed off. The sudden emotional exhaustion left her empty.

Joon called his assistant. "Please escort Mrs. Kim to our home."

"Yes, sir," said the assistant, eyebrows raised at this odd request.

"I will see you at home tonight," said Joon, turning to place a call to Senior Colonel Jun Seo at Bureau 121, the cyberwar agency.

"Good morning, Colonel," said Joon.

"How can I help you, General?"

"I'd like you to access the US Embassy communication center."

"What am I looking for?"

"Everything about Park Ho Jin," said Joon. "The FBI has my son in custody."

"You expect my department to drop everything?" said the colonel. "For a personal matter?"

"The department has thousands of cyber specialists. Find a couple of good ones for me," said Joon, "and don't force my hand."

"Yes, sir, right away."

Joon disengaged his phone. He focused on the operation to kidnap the microchip engineer Jim Graham, then turned his attention to the other part of his mission, Code Cobra Three, the Yemen arms factory. Yemen's political landscape needed intervention. The armaments factory would see its share of profits for all. Amir and his Houthis were well adapted to bring the project to completion. Time to talk with Amir Osman.

"Not a good time," said Amir.

"Is that machinery, I hear?"

"We are loading now."

"Call me back."

Joon didn't miss a beat and next contacted General Byung at the Ministry of State Security, who was in charge of counterintelligence services, overseas, prison camps, domestic espionage and capturing defectors.

"General Park, I was about to call you," said Byung. "I have bad news."

"Let's hear it," said Joon.

"Our operation to secure Jim Graham failed."

"What the hell happened?"

"The South Korean police captured our team," said the general.

"You chicken shits can't even tie your shoes without an adult in the room," said Joon. He slammed the phone down again, cracking the earpiece. *Could things get any worse?*

Forty-Three

Javelin

The ancient city of Sana'a was a masterpiece of architectural beauty. Multi-story tower houses and minarets made of basalt were decorated with intricate horizontal and vertical woven frieze. The window frames were painted white, making them jump off the pink façade.

Amir arrived in Sana'a with a cargo plane of materials and North Korean engineers. Accompanying them were architects with satchels packed with blueprints and structural designs. Once established, they had rented heavy equipment, and then razed the earth and laid truckloads of cement.

The local inhabitants had been told it was an extension of the existing clinic just north of the airport runway. The well-established clinic was under constant threat of closure from the vast number of patients who used the facility every day.

The Houthis welcomed the delegation from North Korea, who had traveled on fake Chinese passports. Bribes were paid and bribes were taken, and the official story was a modern hospital was being built to relieve the congestion. The Houthis spread the gossip, grateful that in nine months there would be a steady supply of assault rifles, light, machine guns, rocket-propelled, grenades, and ammunition.

Amir stood in the shade of a Bedouin tent. He was wearing a pale blue linen jacket, a Nero collared shirt, and sunglasses to reduce the glare of the sand. A dagger, called a *Jambuya*, was tucked into his belt. The handle was designed for a solid grip. The Damascus steel blade was curved, not so much for style as for effectiveness in various tasks. The leather sheath was decorated in silver motif, a symbol of Yemen's heritage and honor. He stepped into the tent and answered the phone. It was General Park.

"Hello, General," said Amir. "I meant to call you sooner."

"Hard at work?" said Joon.

"We've made progress these last three weeks."

"Sadly, Ho Jin is in FBI custody."

"An Armenian proverb says *birds are caught with seeds, men with money*," said Amir.

"My son is arrested, and you spout Proverbs."

"Calm down, no harm meant. Our project is on course, and I'll be leaving the country soon."

"Our government is concerned about Saudi Arabia and the coalition forces. Will they bomb the facility?"

"Not if they think it's a hospital and it's close to an established clinic," said Amir.

"Not likely on a humanitarian basis?"

"That's the understanding."

***

Director Simmons stared at the brief on his desk. The waiting was absolute boredom. He squirmed like a schoolboy in the dentist's chair. The analyst's summary wasn't about to open itself. He turned the page. He had contacted the National Security Agency hours ago about the armaments factory in Yemen. No response, so far.

Reading the document could prove useful. He began to appreciate the brevity and conciseness of the analyst's conclusions.

Yemen's Civil War started in 2014. Houthis took control of Sana'a, the capital city. They demanded lower fuel prices and a new government. In 2015, Saudi Arabia launched airstrikes and began economic sanctions. A United Nations transition council formed a government in the city of Aden.

Iran is supplying the Houthis in a proxy war. Coalition forces made an offensive push into the region to no avail. Iran's cleric-led government helped the Houthis to become one of the best military forces in the region.

Political analysts agree that the deep resentment driving the conflict is sectarianism. Iran, which is mainly Shia Muslim, and Saudi Arabia, which is Sunni, are using sectarianism as a tool, making the religious division between Sunni and Shia Muslims more upsetting and savage.

Simmons desk phone rang. He closed the folder and answered.

"Director Simmons speaking."

"Major General Mark Bruce from the NSA. Apologies for the delay. Director, your request is approved."

"The country is in turmoil. How soon can your team make it to Sana'a?"

"Javelin, our private contractor, is there in the region now," said Mark. "The Saudis requested them for special assignments."

"I am not familiar with this group."

"They are top-notch in intelligence analysis, security, and technical support. They are ex-CIA and know the drill."

"I'd like Amir Osman taken alive, if possible."

"Javelin's job is to destroy the facilities, and the North Koreans are casualties of war. There will be nothing left to rebuild," said Mark. "That's Javelin. They are thorough."

"So be it. Thanks, I didn't want my agents involved," said Simmons. "This operation needs to remain low key."

"That's what the NSA is for. Call anytime Director," said Mark and he hung up.

Simmons slipped the brief into the out file and breathed a deep sigh of relief.

***

Amir was satisfied with this new arrangement, now that he had his money. He decided to assign the building of the armament factory to the North Korean engineer and the general of the Houthis in the Sana'a region.

"Get my plane ready for departure," said Amir. He finished his meal of dates and *Qishr,* a sweet and spicy coffee alternative that he found refreshing. He would be glad to leave the oppressive heat.

"Yes, sir," said his assistant, as he sent for the Jeep and driver.

Amir was a survivor. Park Ho Jin was in FBI custody. Unfortunate, but a sure sign he was also in peril. He had worked with the CIA on multiple occasions and a major mistake with the US would burn that lucrative bridge.

Amir removed his Yemeni clothing and got dressed in a navy polo and Boglioli silk pants. He packed all his belongings, including the Jambuya dagger. He had a place for it in his London flat beside his other curios.

He knew how to set someone up for a fall. In a previous dealing, he had found out almost too late, eluding capture by mere minutes. This time, he sensed it would be close again.

An hour later, his personal jet, a Gulfstream G650ER, banked over the city with clearance from the General of the Houthis. Amir smiled, and knew he'd burned another bridge.

He had received intelligence that by nightfall, Javelin would be let loose.

Forty-Four

But Why the Lipstick?

Kim couldn't alter the past, but his sister's future lay in his hands. *But who was she? What was she like after all these years?* He didn't know. He couldn't fathom the enormous cost to both of them if he failed to get her out of North Korea.

Bae's truck convoy of goods had left early that day. By now the trucks had already passed Sinuiju and were approaching Pyongyang. Kim's first impression after meeting Bae in the karaoke bar was favorable. This was a lucky break, since neither of the ex-police officers dared enter North Korea with false papers. They were too savvy for that. All of them at one point or another had used a confidential informant for tricky assignments.

Kim and his friends were having lunch at Laghu Soup and Rice restaurant on the Yalu River. He sipped his sweet and sour soup.

"Do you think it'll work?" said Lim, sitting across the booth from Kim.

"We thought of every conceivable pitfall."

"Inspector Fox has a solid plan. I'm sure it will work," said Sam.

"We will know by tomorrow, so, hang tight," said Choi.

"Let's eat. I'm hungry," said Kim.

***

Mi Cha arrived at the beautifully landscaped apartments at 1180 Soehon Street. Disembarking from the elevator to the penthouse suite, she unlocked her front door. She replaced her shoes with her house slippers and placed her shoes into the *hyun-gwa*, the built in shoe cabinet. She reached the kitchen and placed the tea kettle on.

She had been in a daze since her son's apprehension by the FBI. On the ride over she forgot all about her plans to shop at the Sunrise Complex, where one could exercise at the gym, have dinner at expensive restaurants, and have access to 24-hour coffee service. She had planned a beef dinner for her husband Joon but missed the butcher as well.

She appreciated the privileges of the few, like shopping at Zara, Uniqlo, and H&M. What a divine experience. Her friends often mused about fixing their noses and chins.

There were times she was sad, but Joon would take her to the 47th floor of the Yunggakdo Hotel. They enjoyed excellent dining in the revolving restaurant, and it eased her heart. The panoramic view of the city was breathtaking. She could even see the replica of the Arc De Triumph that was thirty-five feet higher than the Paris original.

When the kettle erupted in a gritting pitch, she set aside the orange-striped throw cushion she'd been holding for comfort, rose from the white modular sofa and shuffled to the kitchen. Still wearing her yellow ensemble, she removed her jacket and placed it on the kitchen chair, then proceeded to make the White Mountain tea she loved so much. The tea reminded her of days past with her family in the hamlet.

Teacup in hand, Mi Cha returned to the sofa and noticed a piece of lint on the carpet. She picked it up, rolled it into a ball, and deposited it in the waste basket in the kitchen.

She returned to the living room and put her teacup on the round serving table, then snuggled into the sofa arm. She placed cushions around her and tucked herself in like a child seeking solace.

***

A courier on a motorbike pulled up in front of the building where Bureau 39 was situated on Changgwang Street. When he entered the security checkpoint at the front door the guards wouldn't allow him upstairs.

"I have a package for Kim Mi Cha," he said.

The security guard checked the sign-in log and looked up at the courier.

"She's not in this afternoon. Leave it with us and we will send it up to her office," said the guard.

"Sorry, no. She must sign or it goes back," said the courier.

"It's important, yes?" said the security guard. The courier pulled a carton of cigarettes out of his bag and passed them over to the guard, who scratched his ear as if making a hard decision. He looked over at the other guard for a confirmation of sorts. The other guard shrugged, passing the decision back.

"Okay," he said. "Here's her home address."

***

Their journey from immigrants to the penthouse was a long one. She had never heard of *Sonbun* before she arrived in North Korea. It was based on the system of accredited status. You were either core, wavering, or hostile. These tiers determined your suitability for opportunities within the regime. Mi Cha and Joon had achieved the coveted status of *core* and were bathed in luxury. Even the beatings from Joon were becoming less frequent.

But why was she sad about missing her whole family? Her parents would probably have passed on by now. At least her brother Min Su was alive. That gave her hope she might see him again one day.

She sipped her tea, and the teacup trembled back to the table. Her nerves were not under control. The red antique bar with pearl inlays was rarely used and contained a bottle of imported whiskey. Joon had gifted her with a glazed clay horse with a mounted traditional saddle, which she had placed on top of the butterfly bar's folding expandable doors. Less temptation that way.

The living room was well-adorned and comfortable, yet she felt hollow. The years passed yet something was missing. And now her son, the ultimate loss, to her already fragile psyche. Her eyes were wet again.

A solid knock on the penthouse door aroused her from her dark thoughts. She pulled off the pillows and walked to the door. She looked through the view glass, recognized the courier company and opened the door. She signed for the package and she returned to the sofa. Unsealing the flap, she removed a note and a red lipstick tube. She put the lipstick on the table and opened the note.

Baoguang Temple – Oppa

She smiled and almost cried again, but with happiness this time. She hadn't heard *oppa* for thirty-two years. That's what she used to call her older brother. An endearment from a younger sister.

She knew the temple was in Dandong. *But how will I get there?*

And why the lipstick? She took off the cap and twisted it. It was a soft, natural red color. She replaced the cap. Then it came to her. Her brother had provided an excuse in case her husband became suspicious of the package. The security guards might have told the general that a package had arrived for her.

If Joon asked, she would say my girlfriend from the museum sent me the lipstick to try. If she smiled and put on her best behavior, the deception could work. But then how would she find the opportunity to leave without causing too much concern from the administration?

It was also possible, Mi Cha thought, that the security guards at the Bureau had the package diverted to the apartment building against proper security procedures. She could only surmise that the guards were coerced or bribed. In that case, her husband might not know about the package. Nothing was certain, and she could make no assumptions.

Thinking the lipstick was something more than just cosmetics, Mi Cha retrieved her husband's Signal Detector and Bug-Sweeping unit capable of locating listening devices, hidden cameras, RF antennas, and GPS trackers. She isolated all her Wi-Fi devices and turned off the penthouse electrical power box.

She laid the instrument down near the courier package and picked up the lipstick. An audible high pitch emanated from the bug sweeper. Running the lipstick tube over the unit, it continued to beep and the graphic bar blazed red.

Her brother was able to track her GPS location. She had a way out. If only she was brave and took the initiative, her brother would be waiting at the temple in Dandong.

Forty-Five
Once a Cop, Always a Cop

After checking out of the Four Seasons, William stayed the night at Patrick's apartment. He spent the night tossing and turning, worrying about Tracy's condition and feeling guilty about having been unfaithful to her. He lay awake on and off for hours. In the early morning hours, he drifted into a fitful sleep, only to have the alarm on his cell phone jostle him completely awake. The hand on his analog watch swept past 7:00 am.

The short couch in the living room forced him to scrunch up. Probably another reason for the poor night. Getting up proved a challenge as he felt the stiffness in his muscles. His busy mind expressed his frustration in vivid dreams which meant despite the rough night, he must have had a partial REM sleep. He sat there, his eyes fixed on the ceiling. His thoughts lingered on his job and avoiding the harsh reality of the current circumstances. Tracy and he had lost their direction after their baby's loss: an ungrounding, leaving them shaky and sad.

William explored the fresh scar on his forehead. His fingertips caressed the healed tissue, confirming how close he had come to death. Another close call. Another reason he was reluctant to consider marriage. Not being able to turn off the cop in himself was impossible. Once a cop, always a cop.

William heard a key in the door and leaped up in anticipation. Patrick arrived holding a fast-food bag.

"Butterfinger pancakes and Café Americanos," said Patrick. As he handed a coffee to William.

"Smells good," said William, as he opened the bag with his other hand.

William sat back on the couch. Patrick sat in the accent chair across from him. The food was laid out on the coffee table. William sipped his coffee and lost his smile.

"Are you all right?" asked Patrick.

"Yeah, heavy caseload," said William.

"Bullshit, spit it out," said Patrick. He rolled up a pancake and dipped it into a takeout container of maple syrup.

"I've been going over when Tracy got pregnant. It concerns me," said William.

"If you're thinking about Kevin Steptoe, forget it," said Patrick. He licked his sticky fingers.

"Yeah," said William.

"You shouldn't have any doubts about her. She's gold," said Patrick as he picked up a serviette and wiped his fingers. "She only worked with him because, as a lawyer, he represented the tribe."

"Sorry I mentioned it. A little too suspicious for my own good," replied William. He forked a couple of pancakes and placed them on a plate, poured maple syrup on them and then mouthed a generous forkful.

"Kevin would make a better husband: safe job, steady work," continued William.

"What's that got to do with it?" said Patrick. "She loves you. Man, you can be obtuse."

"I could be killed or disabled at any time. The probabilities are high. It's not good," said William finishing off his last bite of pancake.

"You need to get out of that negative headspace," said Patrick, as he reached for his coffee and took a sip.

"Tracy wants a memorial service for our baby," said William. "Her therapist recommends the closure will help us all heal."

"Makes perfect sense. I'll come, if it would help," said Patrick, rolling up another pancake.

"I'm also trying to get past the fact I slept with Ava Ryan."

"Here's some brotherly advice. Get your head in the game. Do not dwell on the past or focus on the future. Be here right now. Be present," said Patrick. "Otherwise, your emotions will get you killed." He got up and took the remnants of breakfast to the trash bin and placed the cutlery in the sink.

Patrick had made perfect sense. William realized he had a job to do.

"Thanks for breakfast and the pep talk," he said.

"Anytime," replied Patrick.

"Can I use your shower?"

"Help yourself. I've got to go to the embassy."

"I have a few things to do before going to Dandong," William said. "I'll call you."

The apartment door shut with a click and the room was silent, except for the sound of traffic outside on the street. William showered and got dressed in a charcoal travel blazer, white polo, and tan Dockers. He slipped on fashion sneakers and a black New York Yankees ball cap. The cap was a present from Patrick and a few FBI agents who attended the ballgame after an intense training course in Quantico. William wore it more for blending in when working undercover, as he was still a Montréal Expos fan, through and through. He dropped his travel bag on the couch and began packing. After the frank talk with Patrick, he was ready and focused.

Forty-Six
You're a Sly Fox

William was on the verge of a breakthrough and decided to call Superintendent Kang on his direct line at the National Intelligence Service.

"Good morning, Inspector Fox. I see your recent ordeal hasn't put you off," said Kang.

"Not in the least. May I speak frankly, sir?"

"Make it brief."

"Your agency has been under fire on numerous occasions. No warning on the North's nuclear missile tests. No intelligence on the death of Ma's father," he said. "Then his sister, Namu, blows up the North-South Joint Liaison Office, effectively closing the door on any unification talks."

"Yes. We've seen how devious they are. Our accuracy rates on intelligence retrieval are low, I'll admit."

"Those incidents must have been embarrassing for the NIS."

"The poor outcome has caused our government to reduce our investigative powers."

"I have a proposal on how the agency can redeem itself and help Canada, the United States, and Australia."

"Inspector Fox, I always welcome any way to expand our influence with our partners. Please continue," he said.

"A lead for the Brian Pendergast case requires my travel to Dandong," said William. "Here's my plan." William went through the complexity of his proposal with the superintendent.

"That could work," said Kang.

"By the way, can we square up the damage with the Sampyo Cement Company?"

"Yes, that's a small price to pay for what you're about to do."

William disconnected and moved on to his next call, to bring René up to date. Noting the time, at least he wouldn't be rousing René from sleep.

"William, what have you got for me?"

"Yesterday, my father was nearly killed during a kidnapping attempt of his microchip engineer, Jim Graham."

"Fill me in," René's voice was grave.

"I took chase and was able to foil the kidnappers."

"And—?"

"Um, I caused a bit of damage in the streets of Seoul—"

"You were supposed to keep a low profile!" René exploded.

"I was arrested—"

"Tabarnak!"

"Temporarily. After they acknowledged I was here on official business, Patrick convinced the authorities to release me," said William. "I was instrumental in the capture of three North Korean agents."

"I don't know how you do it, but you seem to get yourself in and out of shit all the time," said René. "Stay focused on the case. And one more thing. Get your father and Jim Graham to Canada right away!"

"I will. I am working directly with South Korea's National Intelligence Service."

"Keep me posted," said René, ending the call.

William next sent a text to Ava Ryan.

> Can we meet?

> No can do. On my way to Canberra for an ASIS hearing.

> Talk later?

> Maybe.

William sat back disappointed. With Ava out of town, she'd be of little help now.

His close friend, Mr. Kim, required his presence in Dandong, China. For reasons not yet clear, there was a correlation that linked all the persons of interest into a common denominator.

William had been reluctant to share his full agenda with René. He fired off a secure message to René's email address at C Division that he'd be gone for a few days. Should he fail to report in, he asked René to contact Superintendent Kang at the NIS.

William retrieved his travel bag, opened the Uber app, and was soon driven to the Canadian Embassy. He had a busy morning and now there was only one more task for which he was responsible. It was imperative he get his father and Jim Graham to Canada safely.

He stepped into the meeting room where James and Jim were waiting for him.

"Time to leave, gentlemen," said William.

"What's all this rush-rush?" said James.

"Our government wants you home safe. Global Affairs has sent The Royal Canadian Air Force Challenger for your flight back."

"The VIP jet for the Monarchy and dignitaries?" asked James.

"The very same, with a few security agents on board for extra measure."

"Let's go then," said James.

"I'm beginning to like Canada more and more," said Jim.

"I'll be escorting you to Incheon International Airport," said William. "The driver's waiting."

They arrived at the carpool and entered the Toyota SUV armored vehicle. The driver wore a bulletproof vest and stored their bags while James and Jim settled themselves in the rear. William slipped into the front passenger seat.

When the airport security officers at the gate saw the embassy license plates, they opened the gate and allowed the vehicle entrance to the restricted airfield where the Challenger was waiting.

William hugged his father and shook Jim's hand. James started to walk the gangway to the passenger door, when William shouted, "From a silver fox to a silicon fox. It's quite a transition."

James turned around and smiled at his son, and said, "And you're a sly fox." He waved and entered the airplane.

William jumped back into the Toyota and said, "Mind dropping me off at the main terminal?"

"Sure, no problem."

"Thanks," said William. *Time to catch that flight to Dandong.*

Forty-Seven

Baoguang Temple

The constant flow of military personnel and RGB agents moving through security into the clandestine agency building slowed to a trickle. The lull encouraged the security guards with the opportunity to split the carton of cigarettes in half. They gave a few packs to the other guards around the lower lobby. Then the senior security guards flipped the five Won coin to see who would relay the news of the package to General Park. The fortunate guard deposited the coin in the hand of the other guard. He grinned, with satisfaction, then entered the elevators.

Ten minutes later he returned cheery and in good spirits.

"Get ready, he's coming down now," said the senior security guard.

All the guards stood at attention as the general paced away smartly toward his waiting armored limousine.

***

Joon stepped through the penthouse door and removed his tie, then threw his jacket onto the sofa. Mi Cha stepped out of the kitchen.

"You're home early," she said, her heart racing in panic. She hadn't disposed of her brother's note yet.

Trying to recover her composure, she said, "Dinner is not ready yet." She wiped her hand along her blue apron and reached for a hug.

"Where's that package that arrived today?" said Joon harshly enough to jar her senses. Mi Cha walked over to the coffee table and lifted the package and note.

Joon reached out and tugged the note from her hand. She deftly palmed the lipstick and sat down on the sofa, shoving the lipstick deep between the cushions. Her story about the lipstick being a gift from her girlfriend wasn't going to work now.

Joon read the note.

Baoguang Temple – Oppa

He wound up and slapped her across her cheek.

"Your fucking brother!" yelled Joon.

Mi Cha touched her flaming cheek and dabbed a tear. She stood up stoically and went to the kitchen.

"Have a drink, dinner will be ready soon," she said, displaying an act of courage she had developed over the years.

"I'm not hungry," he said, storming into the bedroom to change.

"Where are you going?" she said, knowing full well that Joon was going after Kim.

"Dandong," said Joon, as he slammed the front door in exasperation.

Mi Cha went to the cabinet and removed the ceramic horse statue. Opening the liquor cabinet, she poured a Johnnie Walker and sat on the sofa. Scotch in one hand and the lipstick cradled in the other. She could hear the guards shuffling outside her door.

How am I going to get out of here?

***

Joon sat in the back of the limousine cruising toward the airport. The answers he was receiving from his subordinates were in keeping with his mission. A four-member infiltration team, including a sniper arranged by Colonel Kwon, was assembled at the runway and ready to fly to Sinuiju. The infiltration team was dressed in street clothing typical of Chinese Nationals. One lone agent was carrying a custom-fabricated violin case. Inside repurposed foam supported the scope, rifle, and four magazines. Each member was armed and highly trained in Black Operations.

Joon escorted the team onboard the Soviet era Mi 17 helicopter. Built in the Cold War, it still functioned well, enough to fly forty-two minutes and land at the deserted airport on the outskirts of the border city of Sinuiju, North Korea. Reaching the highway and the Sino-Korean Friendship Bridge would be the best way to enter Dandong, China.

The driver stopped at the security gates on the north side.

"Identification," said the guard.

The passports were handed over, scrutinized, and returned. The guard raised his eyebrows, realizing with whom he was dealing and opened the gate.

"Have a nice day shopping," said the guard, carrying on the façade. The team relaxed in the van, relieved the border crossing had been mundane and uneventful.

The driver of the van said, "Baoguang Temple?"

"Yes, but stop a few blocks away," said Joon. "Then we set up our ambush."

The driver stopped the van on a side street near the entrance of the West Gate of the Botanical Gardens. The Baoguang Temple was inside the gates, accessible to tourists and citizens alike.

"Follow the plan. If we get compromised, get across the border and wait at the helicopter," said Joon.

The team exited the van and entered the park in pairs. The temple had a traditional Buddhist design, with an arched and tiled roof and large Foo Dog statues protecting the entrance. Its bold, garnet pillars and chalk-white balconies were striking. Joon expected the encounter to take place at the top of the wide staircase beneath the archway in the gray stucco wall, where visitors passed through into the temple.

Joon regarded his agent. She was an attractive older woman, a capable killer, who had been in the service for years.

"Stay under the arch," said Joon. He had selected his female agent for her age and approximate physique and similarity to Mi Cha. She moved up the steps and took a passive position, waiting.

"The rest of you take up your positions," said Joon. Three agents scattered to various secluded spots. Joon sat on a park bench beside an elderly man who was eating a sour candy. Joon kept vigil while pretending to read a newspaper. Waiting for Kim Min Su to arrive was risky for him and his team. The Chinese were tolerant, but only to a point. The good measure of trust he gave his team was now beginning to wear on him.

***

"Joon took the bait," said William, lowering his binoculars. He compared the image on his phone with the man sitting on the bench. "It's him," he confirmed. "He's missing part of his index finger. Remember, we only want him."

"They're all settled in," said Lim, talking into his mic.

William patted Kim on the shoulder, reassuring him the plan was on schedule.

"All right, Sam, go over and tell her she's pretty and ask her for a date," said Kim.

William, Kim and his friends stood way back, pretending to admire the Rose Garden. William had his ball cap down to obscure his face, while coordinating the deception.

"She may not be your sister," cautioned William. "Don't forget, he's come for you."

"We'll see in a minute," said Kim.

Choi and Bae covered two of Joon's operatives.

Sam walked up the stairs, stopped under the arch and approached the waiting woman.

"You're pretty. Did anyone ever tell you that?" he said, with all the sincerity he could exude. She smiled, revealing the stained and irregular arrangement of teeth.

"Yes, I'm waiting for my boyfriend. Now go away," she said realizing the man before her was too young to be Kim. Besides, there had been no signal from the park bench.

"That's not her. Mi Cha has two prominent front teeth, like a rabbit," said Kim.

William pulled off his ball cap, wiped his forehead and placed it back. That was everyone's signal to engage. Kim ran toward the park bench. Lim, the mature man who had been sitting beside Joon, reacted instantly and threw an arm around Joon's neck. Grabbing his other arm, he put Joon in a headlock. Joon's arms flailed about trying to fight off the attack. William and Kim arrived on either side of Lim and wrestled with Joon. Three men on one. Joon was pinned to the bench in a chokehold.

"Hold him down," shouted William.

"Trying to," said Kim.

"Got him," said Lim, as Joon passed out from lack of air.

The female RGB agent reacted with the speed of a peregrine falcon, attacking Sam. He buckled over, holding his groin, unable to pursue.

She flew into the wandering crowds and disappeared. Joon's other agents didn't fare as well as her. Choi and Bae disarmed them. Hand techniques only; there were to be no deaths on Chinese soil. They dragged the men behind some ornamental bushes.

The RGB agent with the sniper rifle could not get the shot. Curious garden lovers were beginning to film the disturbance in the archway which created a diversion for him to pack up. He folded up his gun and retreated before being seen, and merged into the busy crowds. Choi and Bae headed out of the west gate to join the rest of the team.

"Bae, can you get the van?" asked William. "We need to get Joon out of sight as soon as possible."

As discreetly as they could, Kim, Choi, Lim and William escorted Joon through the botanical garden entrance, meandering toward the parking area on the adjacent street. They encountered a pair of policemen in white hat protectors and green-striped vests patrolling the area. The police could be troublesome, as they normally conducted high-intensity searches and questioning to control public mischief. They also functioned as political enforcers suppressing negative comments about the communists.

Kim's eyes met those of the policemen and said, in perfect Chinese, "My brother, he's had a bit too much to drink. We're taking him home to sleep it off."

The officers nodded and continued their patrol.

Forty-Eight
The Broken Bridge

William and Kim watched over their shoulders as the policeman walked away. They turned Joon around and shuffled in the opposite direction. The police continued to patrol toward the gardens, observing the public, who were appreciating the fauna and blooms.

Joon awakened and pretended to remain unconscious by hanging limp while being shuffled along. Using the firm grip of the two men on each side of him as a pivot point, he raised both legs to waist level and thrust them forward like a long jump athlete. The sudden movement thrust William and Kim forward and off balance. Joon landed on his feet. Pulling away, he turned on a dime and sidekicked Kim who he fell on his back, dazed. William braced his feet, moved into a ready stance with a knife block and a right middle fist but before he could act, Joon ran into the street, dodging cars and people. William's plan was splintering before him. He began to pursue Joon, the man whose orders had killed four people and ruined another agent's reputation.

Joon dashed through four lanes of traffic, avoiding near misses, and stopped a BMW sport utility by waving his arms frantically, then forced the driver out onto the asphalt. William reached the passenger door handle and held on until it was too foolhardy to continue. While catching his breath, he took a snapshot of the license plate with his cell.

Bae pulled around the corner in their van and spotted Joon jumping into the sports utility. Joon launched the BMW and weaved through traffic. Bae's van tire kissed the curb and pulled alongside the men. William jumped into the front passenger seat, Kim staggered over, recovering from the sidekick. Sam, still recovering from the indignity of the well-aimed kick by the North Korean agent, limped behind him. Choi and Lim helped Sam and Kim into the vehicle, moments later the van accelerated in pursuit of Joon.

"I see the Bimmer," said Choi.

"He's headed for Xingan Road. Turn here," said Kim, pointing at the side street.

"Get ahead of them," said William. Bae cut off a slow Mercedes, then scooted over two lanes and floored the accelerator.

"Joon is going for the Friendship Bridge," said Lim.

"There is a faster way parallel to the railway line," said Bae.

"What are you waiting for?" said Kim, agitated. "Move it!"

Bae signaled and turned left onto Xingyi Road, heading south. William texted Patrick the license plate of the black BMW at the last location.

Patrick's response was quick. His team at the US embassy in South Korea hacked into the Chinese city's vast array of CCTV cameras.

He's on Xingan Road. Parallel to you now.

"Bae, drive to the broken bridge and hold your position," said William.

"That's cutting him off from the Friendship Bridge and back home," said Kim.

"We can take him at the broken bridge," said William.

Bae caught up to Joon. As the van was overtaking Joon's vehicle, William grabbed the steering wheel from Bae and swung left into the BMW. The broadside caught both drivers off guard. Effective, but dangerous, it forced the BMW into a concrete barrier.

Bae tried to open the driver's door, noticed it was stuck and shoved his shoulder to open it. William's door was undamaged. He opened it and headed for the wrecked BMW. Joon knifed the airbag and got out of the BMW, scanned the accident and ran up the stairs along the entrance to the broken bridge. William ran after him and stopped when Joon grabbed a young woman hostage, stood behind her, holding his knife against her abdomen.

Both men stared at each other, sizing the other up.

"Stand back," said William to the tourists. He treaded lightly on his feet.

Joon's eyes bored into William, "Don't move or I will kill her." Keeping the knife pointed at her stomach, he gave a voice command to his phone and put it back in his pocket. He released the heavy grip on the woman and shoved her toward William who nearly fell back trying to break her fall.

Joon sprinted, reaching the end of the broken bridge, which was halfway across the Yalu River to North Korea. The Allies had bombed it during the Korean War and now it was just a tourist site. William barged into a group of tourists, within reach of his quarry.

A speedboat raced toward the bridge from the far shore. Joon pushed aside a few lingering bystanders and jumped the rail. Although William's reaction was swift, he missed Joon's arm. Joon skipped down the stairwell under the girders to a wharf under the bridge, then jumped in the waiting boat. It took off and vanished before William reached the bottom steel beam supporting the wharf.

Looking up, there were tourists and four policemen yelling at him in Chinese. Two officers began tramping down the metal stairs, intent on arresting him.

William braced for the cold and dove into the river. Broad strokes brought him within reach of a fisherman's boat. He was hauled on board and given a blanket.

***

Kim, Lim and Choi joined Bae to examine the extent of the damage to the van.

"How bad is it?" asked Kim.

"We can still drive it," said Bae, pulling the front fender away from the tire.

"Where's Sam?" asked Lim.

"I'm here," said Sam, climbing out of the van.

They saw William and watched the motorboat with Joon on board speed across the border.

"He got away!" said Kim.

"I don't believe it! William just jumped in the water!" said Lim. Soon after, they saw William climb into a fishing boat.

Kim reassembled the group, and they slipped by the police. They drove along the river to the abandoned textile factory, where they agreed to meet should any of them have become separated.

***

William's scheme had collapsed and here he was in a North Korean smuggler's boat, up to his eyeballs in contraband cigarettes, alcohol, and ginseng. William and the smuggler used hand gestures to communicate. William offered money and then drew him a map of the river and where he needed to be let out. The fisherman kept on the North Korean side, piloting down the river toward the outskirts of Dandong.

William offered a second bundle of Korean Won for a bottle of North Korea's first whiskey, based on Johnnie Walker Black.

Night fell on the river and a slow cruise brought them to Binhai Highway overpass. The smuggler crossed the invisible border and entered an old canal under the Huanghai Avenue Bridge. He kept the boat true until they reached the abandoned textile factory.

After disembarking, William shook the old man's hand and shoved the boat toward the middle of the canal. The smuggler waved his floppy hat, sat down and took the tiller. The *tut-tut* of the motor grew fainter as the boat slipped away.

Forty-Nine
No Stopping for Anything

Every morning Pyongyang was awakened at six by the loudspeakers from the railway clock tower. The electronic resonance of the haunting music would play a ballad, *Where are you, dear General?* It was a reminder to its citizens of their second Supreme Leader of the northern regime. For Mi Cha, though, it was too far away, the lyrics often distorted and unrecognizable.

She got up, irritated at having had to listen to that melody for far too many years. The previous evening had provided a period of intense reflection. She decided this was the day to go all in—leave, or die trying. She dressed in her military uniform, then slipped the lipstick tube into her front pouch pocket.

Ma had promoted her to a Colonel, even though she had no previous military experience. Ma, in his latest political shift, had surrounded himself with leading women. Against the old guard's advice, he began creating a new generation of leadership. He thought the gesture would improve his image.

Mi Cha was going all the way starting with her unearned military authority. Her capability was never a question in her mind. With her rank and uniform, she intended to force her will until she reached the border.

After a quick breakfast of rice, grilled fish and steamed eggs, she called the office to send a car.

Mi Cha opened the penthouse door, dressed in her military uniform. The guard outside stepped back, surprised.

"Excuse me, Colonel? You have been confined to your home," said the guard.

"I have new orders to report to Bureau Thirty-Nine," she said, lifting her valise and stepping out into the hallway.

"Follow me," she said, parading and swinging her arms. The two privates glanced at each other, shrugged their shoulders, and fell in behind, following her to the elevator. On the front grounds, a domestic car stood parked at the curb. Mi Cha entered the Pronto GS, the state-owned company's flagship sport utility vehicle.

One soldier sat in the front and the other beside her in the back. They drove the short distance to the Bureau on Changgwang Street. The small group passed through security.

On the top floor, she greeted her staff members. A few of them waited to engage her about today's agenda, and where the General was. "He's out on assignment," she said.

"Do you have any special orders for us today?" asked a staffer.

"Just carry on with your normal duties." Mi Cha turned to the guards. "No need to wait for me. I plan to work here today. Come back at the end of the day."

Mi Cha entered her office, closed the door, relieved her ruse had got her this far. She sat at her desk and picked up the phone to make a call.

"Colonel Kwan speaking."

"Good morning, Colonel," said Mi Cha.

"How can I help Mrs. Kim today?"

"Where is General Park Joon?" asked Mi Cha.

"Classified."

"Our son, Park Ho Jin, is being moved from the US Embassy," she said, improvising. "My husband will want to know."

"How do you know that?"

"A message from the cyber agency," said Mi Cha, trusting the lie was convincing.

"I'd be pleased to pass it on."

"No, thank you. As this is a family matter, I would like to tell him myself," she said, as her voice edged up. "Where is he?"

"Sinijui Airport. That was his destination. After that, I don't know," said Colonel Kwan.

"Good day," she said, replacing the phone in the cradle.

Mi Cha eyed the stack of paperwork on her desk. She decided it was best to act as if this was a normal working day. She glanced at the wall clock periodically, the hands moving like molasses on a cold winter's day. At lunch, she pressed the intercom and said, "I will keep working at my desk. Please ask the cafeteria to bring my favorite."

"Certainly, Colonel."

A short while later, her assistant placed the savory dish of *pulgogi*, grilled meat and *myŏn*, noodles on her desk. Even though her appetite was not robust, she knew she should eat. *Who knows when I will have a good meal next?*

The business day was about to come to an end. Mi Cha swiveled her chair around and stood up. She entered her husband's office, approached the picture of the Supreme Leader and removed it from the wall, exposing a safe. Her husband had given her the code for emergency use. In her mind, this was a desperate emergency. She typed in the numerals and opened it, then removed a Type 68 automatic, a stack of currency, and fake passports for the Park family. She buried them in her valise and left the office.

Mi Cha said to her two guards, "General Park needs this valise for an important meeting." She detached herself and walked away. The guards stood dumbfounded, then hurried after her. "It's imperative I get this to him immediately," she said, over her shoulder.

She signed out at security, wondering which guard had sold her out about the package. Mi Cha seated herself and told the driver to take her to the airport in Sinuiju.

"Colonel, it's permanently closed," said the driver.

"Except when it's an emergency," she said, forcefully leaning over the front seats to make her point, her hand in the valise, gripping the automatic. "No stopping for anything."

"Yes, right away," said the driver as he slipped the Pronto GS into gear and pulled away.

One guard sat uncomfortably close to Mi Cha. The one in front used the rearview mirror to observe her. Gazing at the scenery streaming by she pondered her next steps.

The North Korean government was inflexible and monitored all work attendance. Traveling throughout the country was stringently regulated and administered.

Mi Cha had two strikes against her already. She had disobeyed orders to remain at home. Traveling on a false pretense only added fuel to the fire. She had three hours to get to a safe point. She was not planning on spending her retirement in a concentration camp. She trusted whoever was tracking her GPS signal would intervene to help her.

The tempo of the journey with the guards was boring, but the time passed. Arriving three hours later at the abandoned airfield without intervention was a blessing, but she had to be convincing about her special mission to any military personnel in charge.

"Driver, stop beside the helicopter," she said. "Let me out here."

The pilot walked over to Mi Cha and began to scrutinize her, his eyes traveled up and down her body, her uniform not concealing her curves sufficiently.

"Colonel, do I know you?" asked the pilot.

"No, I'm here on special assignment," she said, holding up the valise.

"What kind of mission?" he asked, lighting a cigarette and exhaling.

Mi Cha pushed her rank. "For General Park. I see he's not here. So, I will wait with my guards," she said, and walked away with all the authority she could muster.

Entering the main doors to the airport lounge, she made use of the facilities, grateful the water was not shut off, she washed her face. The wetness and coolness brought a refreshing relief.

Mi Cha stepped into the passenger area, intending to rest on the commuter benches. She turned to the guard who had been shadowing her, and said, "It's been a long day. I'd like some privacy."

"Colonel, the men are also tired. One of us will be outside patrolling," he said. He turned on his heel and strode outside.

Mi Cha was not an atheist. In her childhood, she had practiced Buddhism along with her parents. Wiping the dust from a bench in the deserted lounge, she sat and prayed.

All the indoctrination she had endured over the last thirty-two years was melting away. She prayed for something larger than an empty political belief. Her blind faith tugged at her soul, inciting a promise of deliverance.

Mi Cha took off her jacket, placed it over herself like a blanket, lay her head down on the valise, whimpered, and fell asleep. Her arm was tucked underneath her, and her right hand clutched the firearm.

Fifty

William Fox, at Your Service

The abandoned textile factory outside Dandong had endured years of neglect. It waited patiently for a renewed purpose and today it had one.

Kim sat up front, navigating the route from the GPS on his cell. The late model SRM T50 Cube van passed along the curve in the road.

"Not long now," said Bae, as he swung the steering wheel to exit the highway. The asphalt gave way to a long gravel laneway. The van pulled up in front of three old buildings. Kim went around to the back of the van and opened the double doors. The former police officers jumped down.

"God it was hot in there," said Lim.

Choi placed his hand on Lim's shoulder, braced, and jumped down.

"Stinks, too," said Choi.

"Think your cop friend is okay?" said Lim.

"Wish I knew," said Kim, kicking a stone across the ground in frustration.

"Hopefully he will make it to our rendezvous point here," said Sam.

"Bring the food," said Choi. "I'm starved."

"I'm hungry, too." Bae dropped down from the cab with two bags of take out.

"What the hell is this place?" said Choi, his eyes glancing around the debris.

The broken windows and busted doors had allowed the weather into the deteriorated structure. The dirt-covered floor was well-worn. Metal drums were stacked in corners and along walls. Wood skids were leaning on the walls and piled up haphazardly. Wooden barrels lay discarded along the outside fence line. Rusted bicycles were stacked on top of each other, propped along a wall. The second floor had collapsed and was exposing open doorways to a lengthy drop. From the upper floor, metal shelves had tumbled, and lay strewn about the rubble. Old hoppers, feeding tubes, and steam pipes stretched along the wall.

"Home, until we can figure things out," said Kim.

"Let's start a fire. I feel a chill," said Choi.

"Help yourself to the wood. I doubt the owners care," said Kim.

The fire started warming the men as they sat around on makeshift seats.

"Where did Bae go?" asked Sam, warming his hands in the heat.

"I had a snooze in the back of the van," replied Bae. He rejoined the group and sat on one of the old benches.

"I'm worried about William," said Kim.

"He swam to a fishing boat. He made it," said Sam.

"But to where?" said Bae, shaking his head.

"Do you hear that?" said Kim turning his head toward the sound of a two-stroke engine.

"By the canal," said Lim, standing up to look. "Can't see a damn thing."

***

William smelled the smoke and walked toward the light of the fire.

"Who goes there?" said Kim, forming a fist.

They all stood up to see a man, cloaked in a blanket, shuffling toward them.

"William Fox, at your service," he said, extending his arm and holding out a bottle of whiskey.

"Thank Buddha you're here," said Kim. "You got whiskey, too?"

"Joon got away," said William. "For that, I'm sorry."

"We ate before, but have food left," said Kim. He offered William a takeout container filled with fried rice. "Hungry?"

"You bet," said William. He took the container of food from Kim and wolfed down his meal.

"What now?" asked Choi, crossing his arms.

"Now, we drink and forget," said William. He cracked the seal on the whiskey, tilted his head and swallowed a mouthful. "Decent but needs aging," he said, passing the bottle to Bae.

"This knockoff shit?" said Bae, well acquainted with the brand. "Not the best quality." He took a small sip, grimaced and passed the bottle to Lim.

"Not that good," said Lim passing it to Sam who took a gulp and gave it to Kim.

"No thanks," said Kim, handing the bottle to Choi.

William placed his phone near the fire to dry out. The cover and battery removed; it sat on a handful of tissue. He took the bottle from Choi, had another swig, and handed it to the next friend.

After a while, no one complained about the quality of the liquor. They doled out the whiskey until the bottle was empty.

"I'm catching some sleep," said William, as he snuggled under his blanket.

"I'll take first watch," said Kim, sauntering over to the van. He stepped up and slid into the front seat.

Except for William, the rest of the men crawled into the back of the cube van, each finding a spot to sleep.

William huddled around the fire, covered in his blanket, holding his reassembled phone. René would be worried. His exhaustion prevented him from following up with his boss. Consumed with the burden of failure, he tried to sleep. He tossed and turned, regretting how events had unfolded. Overconfidence had humbled him, and he felt terrible. His plan had disintegrated before it made any traction. Embarrassed in front of Kim's friends, he held out hope for a break. The fire crackled and fizzled out as William drifted off to sleep at last.

Fifty-One

Gunshots!

William was awakened by the chirp of his phone. The GPS system alerted him that the subject was on the move. He checked his watch; it was 12:15 am. He tapped the screen on the phone and the location appeared on a map. It was time to move. Getting up to roust the other men, the smell of ash and polluted canal water was overwhelming. *He'd be glad to get out of here.*

"Wake up," William whispered, waking Lim, who had taken over watch from Kim.

"It's still dark," he said. He yawned and blinked a few times.

"We got a break," said William. "I'll wake the rest of the men."

William reached the back of the truck and pounded on the door.

"What the hell!" yelled Choi.

"Get up," he hammered again. "Kim, wake up. Your sister is on the move," said William.

William showed the map to Kim.

"We have a GPS hit. Sinuiju airport!" said Kim.

"Now we have a fighting chance," said William.

"This is why we're all here," said Lim. "Let's go get Kim's sister!"

"Men, we should go over the game plan," said Kim. They all clustered together, sharing the light from the truck's headlamps. "William, explain your strategy," said Kim.

"There are six hours before daybreak," said William.

William addressed the critical factors each ex-policeman would face. "We'll need to split up into two teams. Kim and I will organize our escape from China to South Korea. We'll be using the motorcycle."

Kim said, "Not looking forward to being on the back of that thing."

William cracked a brief smile at the older man's comment and said, "Bae, you will take the van and get over to the logistic depot to pick up your transport truck. Then drive over the border with Lim, Choi and Sam. Lim, you have the most experience, I'd like you to coordinate the strike," he continued.

"Taking out armed men is crazy," said Sam.

"Don't worry about that," said Bae. "I have a couple of guns you can use."

"Thanks, we're well trained," said Choi. "And we have the element of surprise, but guns will help."

"Get my sister out alive," said Kim. "That's all I want."

"Bae, do you accept this arrangement?" said William. "We understand the risk you're taking, using your truck."

Bae grinned and said, "You have paid me well. I can afford to retire after this."

"Even so, thank you," said William. "When you get to the logistics depot, text me."

The men scrambled into the cube van and lowered the motorcycle to the ground.

William mounted the motorcycle, handed the helmet to Kim and said, "Let's go!"

***

Sam drove at a snail's pace along the gravel lane before merging onto the highway. They traveled for about an hour before entering the depot. After a few minutes, Bae located his transport truck and said, "Its over the there." The truck was attached to a green shipping container with HANJIN painted on its sides.

Lim, Choi and Sam entered the empty container and settled in for the long drive. Before Bae closed the transport's rear doors he said, "You'll need these." He handed them the two guns.

It was 2:20 am. when he texted William.

> Good to go.

The eighteen-wheel rig passed through Dandong and rumbled across the Sino-Korean Friendship Bridge. The country was in total darkness with not a city light anywhere. At the North Korean security station, Bae waved his fake manifest.

"The city's shut down. There's no deliveries now," said the guard.

"Look at the manifest. It's emergency medical equipment for the hospital," said Bae, his voice rising.

"Let me check with my supervisor." He stepped back into the security guardhouse. Phone tucked between his cheek and shoulder; he stared through the window at Bae.

Bae drummed his fingers against the door with impatience.

The guard poked his head out the window. "He's not answering right now."

"I can't wait all night. This equipment must get through!"

The guard placed the phone down and came back outside.

Bae held his breath while the guard walked around the truck with a flashlight. He exhaled when the barrier lifted and the guard said, "All right. Just this time."

Twenty minutes later, Bae arrived outside the gates to the airport with his lights off. He opened the rear doors of the container and the three men jumped down together.

"She's in this building," said Lim, sharing the phone and the location. They hopped the fence and split up until they reached the arrivals area.

"Choi, take out the guard," said Lim. Choi blended into the night. Sam and Lim followed a few paces behind. Choi used a rear choke hold on the guard. The guard squirmed and flayed about, then passed out. Choi handed the guard's pistol to Lim and kept the Type 88, the new AK 47.

Sam checked the guard's pulse, gave a thumbs-up and said, "He'll be out for a while." The three men moved to the front of the airport lounge.

Crack, crack. "Gunshots!" said Lim.

The arrivals door to the terminal opened, and a wild-eyed woman stepped out holding a gun. She reacted at the sight of the men and aimed the automatic at them.

"Put your hands up!" said Mi Cha. The men placed their guns on the ground, and she walked closer.

"Who are you?" she said moving the barrel up and down.

"Kim Min Su sent us. You're Mi Cha," said Lim. She lowered the gun.

"Yes," she said adjusting her torn blouse to conceal her vulnerability. "I've been expecting you."

"What happened? Are you okay?" asked Lim.

"The pilot attacked me," she said. "My personal guards are coming so hide around back. I'll lure them to you."

"Men, get ready," said Lim. His group ran around to the back of the building.

One of the guards and the driver from Pyongyang stepped outside in their t-shirts with their assault rifles, "Colonel?" one of them said. "The pilot's dead!"

"He tried to rape me!" said Mi Cha, "I had no choice." She walked out empty-handed. The guards cautiously approached, rifles at the ready.

"Now what?" said Choi, in a low voice.

"We jump them," said Lim.

"Are you alone? We heard voices," said the guard.

"Right behind you," said Sam. They forced their gun barrels into the guards' backs.

"Drop your weapons," said Lim.

"Do as they say," said Mi Cha.

Lim and Choi searched both guards. They zip-tied their wrists together, then led the guards inside the lounge and tied them to pillars.

"We are done here. Time to go," said Lim.

"Let's use the SUV!" said Mi Cha. "He's got the keys," she said, pointing to the driver.

Choi, Sam and Mi Cha piled into the SUV while Lim drove to where Bae was waiting in the transport truck.

They reached the truck and drove up the ramp Bae had prepared to enter the container. Bae smiled, pleased there were no casualties. He started up the truck for the journey back and sent a text to William.

> Everyone is safe for now.

Fifty-Two

The Defection

The new Yalu bridge, built in 2011, joined China and North Korea. A bigger and better bridge, it would accommodate more volume of trade but in 2019, North Korea's highways did not yet exist to connect the bridge to the central population. The North Korean government, for whatever reason, never completed the roadway infrastructure.

This meant the old bridge was the only plausible way for Mi Cha and her rescuers to escape. The way they had come in.

Bae suggested to wait until daybreak. The truck traffic would be backed up. Impatient guards would be lax as countless container trucks would overwhelm the check point.

Six hours and fifteen minutes had passed since the team left the abandoned textile factory. The new day brought fresh guards who had not seen the truck before. Time was crucial. Bae arrived at the security check; the point of no return. As predicted, the overworked and harried guard waved the truck past with only a cursory glance. Bae sighed in relief and drove the big rig across the bridge where freedom waited for Mi Cha and the rest of them.

At the terminal, Bae backed the truck and trailer into the empty slot. He surveyed the yard before opening the rear doors, then gestured for the group to come out.

"Stay here," said Bae, "I'll pick you up."

Several minutes later, they piled into the cube van. Everyone remained calm, except Mi Cha.

"I'm worried about my husband, General Park. He will find the mess we left. He will send someone. Maybe he'll come himself," she said.

"Leave the worrying to us," said Bae. "We'll get you out of China."

"First, we have to wait for William and Kim to make arrangements for our escape," said Lim.

***

Joon was frustrated that it had taken so long to reassemble his infiltration team. It was well past midnight by the time the four-person team was reunited with Joon. They returned to Sinuiju and rather than head to the decommissioned airfield, Joon and his team stayed the night. They headed toward the airport the next morning and arrived at six-thirty.

Joon glanced at the open gate, then noticed no one was guarding the helicopter either. The pit of his stomach churned. The driver halted the Jeep outside the terminal.

"Out," said Joon. The infiltration team spread out and began searching the area.

"In here," one team member called out. Joon and his Black Ops team assembled in the lobby. The three guards from the Pyongyang garrison were playing cards.

"Attention!" shouted a soldier.

The guards jumped to attention. Joon's team watched the nervous guards as they fumbled into formation.

"Where is my pilot?" said Joon placing his hands on his hips.

"He's dead," said a guard and pointed to the body on the bench.

"Who's responsible?" Joon barked.

"Colonel Kim Mi Cha ordered us here on a special assignment," said a guard. "She claimed the pilot assaulted her,"

"She killed him?" said Joon, his voice was incredulous. "What else?"

"We were attacked by some men. They knew her and she left with them."

"At ease," said Joon. His infiltration team and the guards from Pyongyang stood about, waiting for direction.

Joon stood motionless, his mind blank. His son Park Ho Jin was held by the FBI. His foolish vendetta against his brother-in-law had failed. Now his wife had defected. The Park family had failed the Ma regime. He had to at least bring back his wife or lose everything.

"Dismissed," said Joon. He sat down and dialed the State Security Department. He gave Mi Cha's cell number to an agent to run through her provider, Koryolink.

"We lost the signal at the Sino-Korean Friendship Bridge at six-thirty this morning," the agent said.

"Hack into the Chinese CCTV network and get her location," said Joon.

Minutes later the agent replied, "She was in a transport truck when the signal was lost."

"Where is she now?" asked Joon, standing up. He was irritated. His restless feet began strolling the lobby. "The CCTV cameras show they switched vehicles at the logistics depot. To a cube van."

"And from there?"

"They traveled from Dandong to an abandoned factory," said the cyber intelligence agent.

"Black Ops team with me," said Joon.

"You three, stay here," said Joon to the Pyongyang guards. "I will deal with you later."

Fifty-Three

Eyes on the Border

It was the end of the day when the news broke. RGB Deputy Director Chang oversaw all espionage operations. He was alarmed when staff members of Bureau 39 reported that Joon and his assistant Mi Cha were missing. Also, a Soviet Cold War helicopter and special Black Ops team were unaccounted for.

The Deputy Director, Lieutenant General Chang, reported directly to Supreme Leader Ma.

"The Park family have disappeared, and I am deeply concerned," said Chang.

Ma summoned his sister, Namu, who was responsible for Bureau 39 staff and officials.

"The Park family is missing," said Ma. "Find out what's going on."

She assembled her entourage and began her investigation with a trip to the Bureau building. She entered the communications center like a warthog marking her territory. She had a way of tilting her head up that displayed a pointy chin. Her demeanor of entitlement and her flat smile emanated a ruthlessness not seen in many women. She removed her black Dior coat and opened her Lady Dior bag. She rummaged for her taser, pressed its button and smirked as the electrical discharge arched a blue light.

Her entourage of four RGB agents were identically dressed in blue ties, black coats, and sunglasses. They towered over the most dangerous woman in North Korea. A constant rumor voiced she would be the next leader of the country. Known for her savagery, she reportedly ordered officials executed for simply annoying her.

Everyone in the room stiffened at her arrival.

"Where is she? Where is Mi Cha? Where is Director Park Joon?" she demanded.

Staff members turned around from their computers at her command. None ventured forward, afraid the messenger would be the brunt of her fury. After a stillness and dead air, a young man stepped forward and admitted, "Assistant Director Mi Cha arrived for work as usual and then signed out at the end of the day."

"Search everywhere," said Namu.

The staff scattered throughout the building while others made calls to various departments. Namu burst into Park Joon's office. The open safe door indicated a hasty retreat.

"Check it," she said. One of her agents looked inside. He turned back and shook his head.

"It's empty," he said. "If there was any money or papers in there, they're gone."

She searched the desk for any hint of where the couple went. In a single, angry swoop, Namu scattered files and in-trays across the carpet. She lay down her taser.

"This will be my headquarters," she said.

Settling in behind General Park's desk, she called Chang.

"Lieutenant General Chang speaking,"

"General, it's Namu."

"Yes, Deputy Director. What can I do for you?"

"Close the borders. Get our helicopters up. Notify our field agents. These two cannot escape," she said.

"My best officers will be in charge," said Deputy Director Chang, disconnecting the call.

Within minutes, the borders were closed. The military and field agents were put on high alert. Next, shore patrol boats set up a search pattern along the coast. Helicopters intensified their regular routes along the DMZ. This was a substantial undertaking to locate two missing officers of the state.

Namu paced around the room, waiting for news from Chang. She reclaimed General Park's executive chair when the phone rang.

"Good news?" she asked.

"Not yet. Your instructions have been put in motion," said Chang. "I'll be in touch when we have them in custody."

Namu glanced at her Cartier diamond-encrusted watch. It was almost six-thirty. Ninety minutes to sunset. The search in the dark would make it harder, but not impossible. Even if the hunt were to go into the night, the visibility would be remarkable under a full moon.

Namu and her entourage of agents and secretaries went to work. The Bureau staff stayed fearful, anxious to supply all the support she required.

"I'd like eyes on the border," said Namu.

One of her personal bodyguards placed a laptop computer on the desk, plugged it into the system and smiled at her. "Border cameras on."

The country's connection to the international internet linked Pyongyang with Dandong, crossing the China-North Korean border at Sinuiju. The streaming arrived via fiber optic cable to many classified locations. The Bureau staff stationed in the various departments saw real time video images.

Elaborate attempts to prevent the missing officers from fleeing had been initiated too late. The damage was already done.

Fifty-Four

Tie Them Up

Bae pulled into the yard at the textile factory and parked the cube van. Lim stepped out from the passenger side, walked to the rear of the van and met Choi and Sam who had just disembarked from the rear of the van and were helping Mi Cha down.

"Choi, Sam, look around," said Lim. The men started a cursory inspection of the yard.

"Let's get you warmed up," Bae said to Mi Cha. He took off his jacket and wrapped it around Mi Cha's shoulders. "I'll start a fire and then we can eat," he added. He broke up pieces of old skids and piled them up and lit the fire.

"Just got a text," said Lim. "William and Kim should be back anytime."

***

The night unfolded in a pattern of events neither side could have anticipated. It was fear that drove Joon to be reckless. The last forty-eight hours had passed without any substantial results. His mission to capture his brother-in-law never materialized and now his wife had escaped to China. Soon, the top echelon of the North Korean military would be searching for him.

"Head to the patrol boat," said Joon, jumping into the front seat of the Jeep.

Arriving at the jetty, his ops team stepped into the bridge of the patrol boat. The gunmetal-gray motor craft tacked into the river, bringing its bow in line with the opposite shore. It swept alongside the river traffic mirroring the intangible border.

"Slow and steady," said Joon.

The pilot followed the course under Joon's direction. Thirty minutes later the GPS coordinates they had set for the abandoned factory indicated they were close to their destination.

"Helm, hard right," said Joon.

As the boat changed course a silvered white froth broke the murky surface. Joon said, "Quarter throttle, ease her in. Stop."

The team slipped into the rubber raiding craft and left the patrol boat mid-river. The inflatable boat entered the old canal under the Huanghi Avenue bridge. They were back in mainland China.

"We'll ease up the canal and surprise them," said Joon.

"Careful, no noise," said the lieutenant. The team checked their weapons and their headsets in preparation for the raid.

"Pull up here," said Joon. One of the men attached the bow line to the wharf while another man secured the aft. The team swept the area in unison, exactly as they had practiced in training exercises. The raw-boned lieutenant led the team while Joon marched toward the back, covering their flank. The area was empty as the team spread out, searching throughout the factory yard.

"Clear," said the lieutenant, speaking into his headset.

Reaching the abandoned factory from the canal rather than the road gave Joon and his team a distinct advantage. His earlier ineptitude melted away as the confident general barked out his orders.

"Lieutenant, post our men here, here and here." Joon pointed to strategic positions, laying out a perfect assault.

Joon watched the group through his binoculars. A fire was roaring, and the smell of fast-food wafted over to him and his men. Takeout bags of Panda Express were being passed around. The group, unaware of the danger they were in, indulged in a mélange of noodles, vegetables and spicy shrimp.

Joon said, "Now!"

Joon and his lieutenant stepped out of the recess hidden in the ruins. The machine guns covered the powerless group from several directions.

"Stay where you are," said Joon. Everyone froze. Mi Cha's brow furrowed, and her eyes bulged in shock. Joon called the other team members out. Mi Cha's arm was behind her back. She thumbed the safety off her pistol.

"Stop moving," said Joon. He stepped over and relieved her of the weapon.

"How did you find us?" asked Bae.

"None of your concern. The woman will come with us," said Joon.

"Shit," said Lim as he shifted his feet, helpless. He prayed this would play out without any mishaps.

"Tie them up," ordered Joon. Two ops team members zip-tied each of them with hard plastic wrist cuffs.

"Where are Kim and his friend?" said Joon. He scrutinized Mi Cha with a fiendish glare.

"How should I know?" she said. Joon swung fast and a hard slap spun Mi Cha's head sideways. She composed herself, straightened her back and said, "Why should I tell a bastard like you?"

Joon grabbed Choi and placed his 9mm at the base of his skull.

"Where is Kim?" he shouted.

Lim stood up, "Be patient. He'll be here soon."

"Sit down and shut up," said Joon. "Spread out," he motioned to his men. They took up positions along the periphery of the yard. The grounds were silent except for the crackle of the fire and the faint hum of the highway. Then a roar of a heavy motorcycle approaching caught everyone's attention. William entered the driveway, decelerated and extended his right leg, taking the corner leisurely. The bike stopped on the crushed rock. He nudged Kim behind him.

"No guard," said William. "Something's wrong." Kim dismounted. William extended the kickstand stood up and lifted his left leg over the saddle to step down beside Kim. William tilted his head, puzzled. "Where's Lim?"

"What the hell?" Kim mouthed "You left the motor on?"

"The engine noise will attract someone," said William. They rolled the bike to a pile of rusted girders nearby and stowed it away out of sight.

"Go see why they stopped," said Joon, sending one of his men ahead along the gravel driveway.

William and Kim heard the cautious crunching of stones as the man shifted toward them. Kim stepped out and the Black Ops member waved his muzzle at him. William elevated himself onto the top girder and launched for a sidekick. The heel of his right foot caught the soldier in the cervical vertebrae. The soldier's head snapped sideways, and the rest of his body followed. William landed beside him. Kim helped William drag the body and hide it behind the pile of rusted steel.

"You take his AK47," said William. "I'll take his sidearm."

"Joon's men?" said Kim.

"Yes. How many is the question," said William.

"They have Mi Cha," said Kim.

"Not for long," said William. "Take the flank." He pointed at the roofless building.

William crept diagonally toward the periphery of the courtyard and peered around the corner, facing the fire pit.

Fifty-Five

Stop or I'll Shoot

Joon grew more impatient with every second. The elite operative he sent was due back ten minutes ago. The motorcycle engine's rumble continued to echo in the distance. Agitated, Joon's right thumb rubbed the stub of his missing finger. He suspected Kim and William had arrived and were playing cat and mouse.

"Round everyone up," said Joon. His remaining two operatives forced the five captives to sit around the fire pit. Joon and his men continued to train their weapons on the captives.

"Kim, I know you're out there!" yelled Joon. "Step out or I'll kill your sister!"

Scanning the outside fence line, Kim wavered. This was not the play they'd planned. William would have to go it alone.

"Don't waste my time," shouted Joon.

"I'm here," said Kim, brushing past the stacked metal drums.

"Place the machine gun down," said Joon.

Kim placed his gun on the ground. When Joon's lieutenant stooped to retrieve the weapon, William caused a distraction by veering away from the wooden skids, shooting several rounds over Joon's head.

Kim took advantage of the diversion to kick the lieutenant under his jawline, catching him off guard before he could reach the gun. The lieutenant fell over unconscious.

Next Kim vaulted toward Joon and before Joon could react, swatted away his gun and thrust a knife hand strike to the trachea. Joon's eyes widened in shock. Kim grabbed his arm and threw him over his hip, judo style.

William stopped in astonishment as he watched Lim, hands bound behind his back, let loose a double sidekick at the operative. His boot broke the man's knee, and the next damaged his ribs. Before the operative could recover, Lim delivered a final front snap kick to his head.

Choi, also with his hands restrained, slid forward and delivered a roundhouse kick to the last operative's head. The man lurched backward, landing on the ground, senseless.

William cut Lim and Choi loose. Mi Cha and Bae were next.

"Nice work," said William. Lim and Choi smiled in relief.

"Mi Cha?" said Kim, spellbound by his sister's presence.

"Min Su?" She made eye contact with the short, heavy-set man and immediately realized it was her brother Kim. She stopped and gaped, staring into his eyes. "I can't believe it's you. But it is, it is." Mi Cha began to sob, tears streaking her wholesome face in torrents.

"Mi Cha, yes, it's me, Min Su," he beamed.

Everyone's attention was focused on the reunion of the two siblings. That distraction was all Joon needed to recover and secure his weapon. He aimed it at the group. He tried to unravel what had just happened. "Stop talking!" he shouted, raising his voice above the din.

Mi Cha stared at her husband with a confused expression. *Why is he pointing a gun at my brother?* She placed her arms around Kim, hugging him protectively.

Joon's face contorted in anger as he stepped forward and seized Mi Cha by the wrist. "You're coming with me!"

"No! He's my brother," she snapped. "Let go of me!"

Joon continued to grapple with her as she tried to get away. Kim reacted immediately. He ran three steps, grabbed Joon's left wrist and twisted it back, exerting pressure until Joon's fingers released the gun, which fell to the ground. Joon's response was fast, but he was already stumbling backward from Kim's palm punch to his jaw. Joon's head exploded in pain. Kim kicked into Joon's abdominal plexus and pounced on him when Joon landed on his back.

Mi Cha saw the futility of both men fighting. She grabbed the gun from the ground and said, "Stop! Stop or I'll shoot!"

Kim continued to pound Joon with the fury of thirty-two years of anguish, solitude, and loathing.

She fired the gun through the missing roof. Both Kim and Joon stopped fighting, got up, stood apart from each other and glared.

Joon was panting for air and pointing at Kim. "Kill him, kill him!"

Kim, who was just as desperate, shouted, "Shoot him, shoot him!"

Mi Cha's torment manifested into confusion and utterly disorientated her. She trained the gun back and forth between both men. Finally, exasperated, she shot the gun until it was empty. The earthen floor between them buckled with rounds, propelling soil in all directions. Both men relaxed in relief when Mi Cha dropped the gun on the ground in front of her. She fell to her knees, then laid her hands over her face and began to wail.

William ran past her, handcuffed Joon, and escorted him to the cube van.

Kim approached Mi Cha with slow, gentle steps, so as not to upset her further.

"Mi Cha, it really is me, Kim Mi Su," he said. "You're safe, now."

Her hands descended from her face and a curious smile grew visible. "I thought we would never see each other again."

"It's been a long time. Too long. I hardly recognized you, but for those bunny teeth."

"Oh, Kim, you still know how to tease me." She rose, brushing the dirt from her uniform.

They walked to each other and embraced. Both were weeping with happiness. An unforeseen joy neither had expected to be fulfilled, within the orbit of uncertainty.

Fifty-Six

Stay on Your Toes

William experienced a joy he seldom felt. He reveled in his friend's happiness. It was a miracle Kim found and saved his sister after so many years of worrying about what had happened to her. The elation displayed by Kim and Mi Cha became infectious as the group of friends rejoiced in their reunion. William's thoughts drifted toward Tracy. His joy, now mixed with sorrow, unsettled him. He knew he had to make amends with Tracy. He hoped soon.

William retrieved his notebook, sat back on the bench around the fire and began making entries in his case book. It had been a few days since he'd been in contact with René or Patrick. He envisioned their concern, wondering whether he was alive or not, but there was nothing he could do without exposing their position to the Chinese or the North Korean authorities. He was undercover and breaking every procedure and protocol. Everyone was in too deep to turn back. His determination and training set the stage for what came next. He needed to bring everyone out of the situation safe and sound.

Their circumstances warranted a quick departure. The gunfire would arouse curiosity and perhaps the police would arrive soon. William glanced at his Rolex submariner, making a quick calculation. He waved everyone over to him.

"It's time," said William. "We have to go now."

Out of earshot William said "Lim, Choi, secure these useless assholes and get them on the assault craft."

"My pleasure," said Lim.

William walked back to the van and opened the knapsack.

"Mi Cha, let's get you to your son," said William, holding up workers' clothes. "Get changed."

Once Mi Cha had changed, Kim placed a protective arm around her and escorted her to the passenger's front row.

Lim stepped out of the rubber boat. He fixed the tiller on the rubber raft. Its direction along the canal, if it stayed true, would merge with the Yalu River. The agents struggled to get free, and Lim and Choi smiled at their handy work.

"A bear couldn't get out of that," said Choi.

"I'll drive," said Bae, taking the wheel.

Kim and Mi Cha sat beside each other in the front row of the van while Lim, Sam and Choi took the rear bench. Joon was hog-tied and lying on his side in the cargo area of the van, the only signs of his presence were the occasional muffled grunts as he struggled against his restraints.

"Our destination is six hours south, to Danggang Harbor," said William, mounting the motorcycle and pulling on his helmet.

"We'll be fine if there are no checkpoints. Besides, I know the road like the back of my hand," said Bae, poking his head out the van's window.

"Good to know," replied William, his boot engaging the kickstart. He pulled out and the cube van followed, pacing him until they roared alongside eachother on the highway.

As they gained distance from their ordeal, Kim turned toward his sister and said, "I have so much to tell you." The only reply was the soft gentle murmur of Mi Cha's breathing, as her head slipped onto her brother's shoulders.

"Sleep, little sister," said Kim. "We can talk later."

***

Danggang was situated on the coast of the Yellow Sea, near the mouth of the Yalu River.

The estuary was entirely in North Korean territory. William and Kim knew that and planned to drive around it to the Chinese harbor, avoiding the trip down the river.

William pulled into the vacant dry dock facility. Kim had acquired a *sampan,* a boat with a large wooden cabin. The flat-bottomed wooden boat was tied up alongside the wharf.

"Everybody in," said Kim. William waved Bae onboard. "Coming with us?" he asked.

"No, I'll take my chances here. I don't want to start over," Bae said. "Kim, it was an honor to fight alongside you and your friends. I am glad you have found your sister," he added. Before Kim could reply, Bae had already turned and walked away.

"Time to get moving." William untied the lines and jumped on board. He moved over and made sure Joon's zip ties were secure.

"Where are we going?" asked Mi Cha, her inquiring eyes arching up.

"A bulk carrier called the *Princess Beatrice,*" said William.

"To South Korea?" said Mi Cha.

William said, "Yes."

Kim started the motor and leveraged the tiller in the direction of Korea Bay.

Mi Cha turned to her brother, making small talk. He listened like a lost schoolboy, mesmerized by the sight of his sister.

"The battle of the Yalu River happened here, September seventeenth, eighteen-ninety-four," said Mi Cha.

"Appa was always teaching us history," said Kim. "You remember what he taught us?"

"Yes, war between China and Japan over our nation. The Japanese won because of better training and more modern ships," said Mi Cha. She smiled at her amused brother and his loss of words.

"What happened to you?" said Kim.

"We crossed the border. The military arrested us," said Mi Cha.

"Did they hurt you?" said Kim.

"They interrogated us for months. Joon's uncle, under government pressure, arrived and claimed us," said Mi Cha. "The government indoctrinated us in their culture," she continued.

"How did you manage?" said Kim.

"Even now, I don't know how we survived the tough conditions, mental abuse, the food shortages. Then there was the killing of smugglers and starving people."

"I'm astounded at your survival."

"We persevered and made something of our lives. Despite Joon's brutality," she said. "How about you, my dear brother?"

"I became disillusioned with village life. The older I became the more I wanted to leave."

"What about our parents?"

"Both passed on early," said Kim. Mi Cha dabbed her eyes with a tissue and sighed.

"You left the house and the property?"

"There was a disagreeable woman who wanted to marry me. I left early one morning and traveled to Seoul. Without a trade, I signed up with the military. After my term, I joined the Korean police before getting married and then immigrating to Canada," said Kim, as he wiped the wetness from the corner of his eye.

"I look forward to meeting your wife."

"No, not possible," sighed Kim. "She died from breast cancer."

"Oh, Kim, I'm so sorry," she said. "You have been alone for so long."

"There's the ship," said Kim. He shifted the tiller until they came up alongside the enormous vessel. Sam attached the bow line to the gangway.

"Everyone, let's get on board," said William. "We need to get Joon out of sight as quickly as possible."

The water at the rear of the ship started to churn as the propellers' rotation thrusted the ship ever forward.

"Stay on your toes. We're not out of the woods yet," said William.

"Stay on our toes?" said Mi Cha, looking to her brother for direction.

"It's an expression," said Kim. "It means pay attention."

William climbed the stairs with Kim to the bridge to talk with the captain, the man with whom he had made a deal.

Fifty-Seven

There's No Time to Waste

The government of Pyongyang found themselves in a quandary. General Park Joon's Black Ops team, whatever was left of them, were found drifting, mid-river. The patrol boat's captain alerted the chief of staff's office. In the simplest of terms, the horse had bolted. Now every available resource came into play, even the Chinese Navy began searching on Pyongyang's behalf. The North Korean patrol boats blockaded the Danggang Harbor and boarded every boat around and near the Yellow River estuary.

Further afield, larger destroyers scanned with radar, crisscrossing Korea Bay. Coastal patrol craft with missile capability concerned William. The captain of the Princess Beatrice, aware of the dangerous position, demanded a new deal.

"Our arrangement is nonnegotiable," said William, his eyes glancing at the horizon. It was clear.

"I have a deadline: Bangkok in four days," said the captain.

"Our coordinates and time are set. Payment to commence with completion," said William, his eyes locking on the captain to make his point.

The captain flinched. Kim caught it, too, and grinned.

"No more than half an hour," replied the captain.

"That's all we need," said William.

"We have a long-range contact," said the radar man.

"Helmsman, keep our present heading," said the captain.

"How long before point of contact?" asked Kim.

"Anytime now. The sea is choppy, but the weather is reasonably good," said the captain and grunted as he sat down.

"This narrow area concerns me," said William scanning the horizon with marine binoculars. He let the binoculars hang around his neck.

The captain ran his finger over the map. "The cape here on the North Korean side near Monggumpi-ri juts out from the mainland. Opposite is China and the headland extends out to a town near Chenshan Corner. It's four hundred miles wide between both points," said the captain.

"Do you know if they'll try to blockade the gap?" said Kim.

"Without a doubt," replied the captain.

"Captain, multiple contacts on the radar display, sonar, and our GPS navigational chart," said the radar man.

"Navigator, hold course," said the captain, who frowned at William, hating his circumstances.

"I expect our communist friends are preparing a welcome committee," said William.

"On that, you can depend," said the captain, pacing the bridge, hands tucked behind him.

Kim touched William's shoulder. "Helicopter … no make that two."

William examined the horizon. A Chinese destroyer and a North Korean corvette began sea maneuvers, shadowing the South Korean helicopters playing cat and mouse.

"Now," said William.

The captain said, "Quarter speed." The massive bulk carrier eased to a slower pace.

William raised the binoculars and swept the starboard ocean surface. A froth of white-gray foam began to take form as the long black hulk of a submarine began to emerge.

The group assembled on the deck.

"Everyone get ready, our ride is here," said William.

"Move, there is no time to waste," said Kim.

Despite the fearsome swells, William encouraged all to descend along the gangway to the waiting, inflatable raft. He gave Joon a rough shove into the craft, then confirmed everyone was already onboard. They set off and made their way through the choppy waves to the KSS-III attack submarine.

The mariner piloted the raft across the narrow corridor between the container ship and the submarine and arrived safely. The group scampered on board and the submarine submerged. Its destination: South Korea, the naval base of the Republic of Korea. South Korea had informed Pyongyang that they had scheduled wargame maneuvers. It was an elaborate ruse to help William and his charges escape.

South Korean navy helicopters had orders to release smoke from their under-carriage canisters across the area, diminishing the enemy's visibility and allowing the destroyer and the submarine to escape. The choppers landed on the *Sejong the Great,* a KD-III class destroyer. The ship had remained south of the northern limit line. It was a demarcation line often disputed, but not today as the ship steamed through in its war game's role in the Yellow Sea.

After Joon was secured in the brig, William and his desperate company arranged themselves in the meeting room. Crew members from the kitchen arrived with coffee and sandwiches. Very little talk ensued while the hungry and exhausted group devoured their food.

After the meal, William hunched into the narrow corridor, snaking his way between crew members and arrived at the conning tower. The control room and the captain directed all functions and direction of the vessel.

"We appreciate your timely arrival," said William. "And your hospitality."

"I was under strict orders by the admiralty to bring you back safe," said the captain.

"When will we arrive at the Naval base?" said William.

The captain swiveled his head over his shoulder. "Helmsman, time of arrival?"

"Sir, one hundred and forty-five nautical miles at twenty-five knots. Five hours forty-eight minutes and forty-six seconds, sir."

"Thanks," said the captain. "You and your party have been through a lot. Why don't you get some rest?"

"Thank you, again," said William. He realized he was drained. Weariness dogged him as he ducked under every hatchway, a reminder that a thoughtless moment might be a painful moment. He returned to the meeting room and placed two paper cups into separate plastic evidence bags.

Approximately six hours later, the group arrived at the Second Fleet Republic of Korea Naval Base.

Fifty-Eight
You Must be Joking

The dock facilities were wet from a recent downfall. The air mingled with salt, fish, and the freshness that comes after a good rain. William took a deep breath as the cramped and stuffy submarine became a distant memory. Having disembarked from the submarine at the naval base, he knew his group would soon be subjected to never-ending interrogations.

National Intelligence Service Superintendent Kang was waiting with his entourage of agents to take Joon and Mi Cha into custody. They would be guests at the NIS for the foreseeable future.

"What will become of my sister?" said Kim, his eyes darting everywhere, and feeling completely helpless.

"Don't worry. You'll see her again soon," said William, putting his arm around his close friend.

Kim's eyes followed the agents as they separated into two groups; the first group escorted Joon to an official vehicle and the second took Mi Cha to another.

Kang approached William and Kim and said, "Mr. Kim, since you, Lim, Choi and Sam are civilians, my men will be taking you to a separate location for debriefing."

"Go, on, it'll be fine," reassured William. As Kim and his friends left with the officers, he turned to Kang and said, "I have a favor to ask."

William removed the two plastic bags, each containing a paper cup, from his knapsack and handed them to Kang. "Can you run these through? As fast as possible?"

"We'll have a report before you leave," said Kang.

William had completed his side of the bargain. Kang had agreed to the mission and had been keeping a watchful eye on him throughout the assignment. The NIS had their own network of agents in China and had been shadowing him and his group.

Kang's prize was two officers of the North. One ready to cooperate and another not yet. Mi Cha would go through a period of investigation and a debrief with the intelligence service. Park Joon, however, due to his murder spree in Seoul, where he killed Brian Pendergast and two Australian agents, faced the inevitable—capital punishment, or if he was lucky, incarceration. He was also responsible for the assassination of the North Korean Do Yun Cho in Canada. Despite protests from Amnesty International and people from religious, academic and legal circles, the death penalty remained part of South Korea's justice system.

William's statement and report would also be sent to RCMP headquarters in Ottawa, and to the attention of Superintendent René Bouchard of C Division.

***

William arrived at the US Embassy after making an appointment with the ambassador. Cleaned and suited up in a blue worsted wool suit, he swaggered into the meeting. His RCMP pin was prominently positioned on his left lapel.

"Pleased to meet you," said Albert Collymore, as he gestured for him to sit down.

"Likewise," said William, sliding into a cream leather swivel base chair.

"I take it you're sitting on something you want to share," said Albert, who came by his position by way of a political favor. He was around forty, of medium frame, with a pale complexion. William found himself gravitating toward the man's confidence and positive attitude.

"I delivered two North Koreans to the NIS," said William. "And I'm here to negotiate the terms of Park Ho Jin's release. I expect him to be transferred into the hands of the NIS."

Albert Collymore had a propensity to be too American, when it came to boundaries.

"You must be joking," said Albert.

William spent the next twenty minutes explaining the events in Montréal, Seoul, Dandong and the escape from China.

"Only General Park Joon is responsible for all the murders and all the failed missions."

"Is he willing to cooperate with the NIS?" said the ambassador.

"He has no choice. He's a dead man, if he doesn't," said William. "Considering they still have the death penalty here. If he agrees, they could be lenient."

"What about the trade secrets case the FBI have against Park Ho Jin?" asked Albert.

"I've explained why it makes more sense to implicate Johnny King for industrial espionage. He was the insider who complied and sent the initial schematics," said William.

"Agent Patrick Reilly isn't going to like this. He's a friend, isn't he?" said Albert.

"It's for the greater good. Park Ho Jin sees the good he can do providing information about the North Korean regime. A real advantage. It could save years of fruitless intelligence gathering," said William.

"If I agree, this cannot set a precedent," said the ambassador.

"Absolutely not. It's a one-time deal, but it benefits the Five Eyes and closes the investigation."

The ambassador tilted his head in thought. William rotated in his seat, feeling a little uncomfortable. It was a long pause.

"Okay, you sort this out with Special FBI Agent Patrick Reilly. I will pass on my recommendations to the Department of Justice (DOJ), director of the CIA and FBI," said Albert.

William rose from the designer chair and offered his hand. The ambassador stood up and reciprocated with a firm, vigorous handshake. The deal was sealed.

William's lips parted; his cheeks rose up as a broad smile cracked across his handsome features. His hand slipped across his face as he hid the relief from Ambassador Collymore. William strode out of the embassy, checking his watch.

William called Kang. "They've agreed to release Park Ho Jin into our custody."

"Excellent. By the way, I have just sent the NIS intelligence report to the US Embassy and copied your boss, René."

"Much appreciated."

He texted Patrick.

Meet me at Charlie H Bar.

William hailed a cab outside the embassy, and said, "Four Seasons Hotel."

Fifty-Nine
We Have Jurisdiction

The streets in Seoul became quieter as late June approached. The popular attractions were less attended with the monsoon season bringing heavy precipitation. The rain was periodic and predictable, generally peaking in July.

The American Embassy had its own storms to weather as the buzz from the latest NIS intelligence reports filtered through the intelligence center.

Deputy Chief of Mission, Jeff Boom, wore concern like his well-seasoned navy suit, a little loose and faded from too many dry cleanings.

RSO Daniel Levi approached the seated members of the intelligence team with the latest cyber security report. His lowered eyebrows and curled upper lip were enough to cause Oliver Briggs from the CIA to click his pen in nervous compulsion. Oliver, a fresh field operative just over from Washington, surveyed the faces around the table, and his eyes fell on Patrick Reilly. The Irishman with the strawberry red hair also looked quite concerned.

Patrick wore a fashionable desert sand suit and sensible brown shoes. He was tipping his chair back, holding the report at eye level. When he finished reading, he slid the report away from himself and spoke forcefully.

"We have sanctions and precautions and yet they managed to breach the two largest microchip manufactures in Seoul."

"The NIS discovered their capabilities are peerless. We were looking at malicious software, and the bastards snuck in the back way," said Jeff Bloom.

"We expected them to infiltrate the existing servers used for business documents," said Daniel.

Oliver tugged at the collar of his blue shirt. "Stealing product design and photographs of the plants is a total shit show," he said.

"I believe, as do the NIS, that Pyongyang is preparing to build its own semiconductor facilities," said Jeff.

Patrick leaned forward and the chair dropped to the carpeted floor. "Our friends from Canada have had a similar attack. A microchip engineer named Jim Graham was abducted by RGB agents right here in Seoul. My friend, RCMP Inspector William Fox, intervened and prevented the kidnapping," said Patrick.

"The South Korean semiconductor industry is an attractive target. My guess is the Chinese are helping the North Koreans," said Daniel. "They have also focused their sights on Taiwan."

"South Korea accounts for about sixteen percent of total micro chip exports. But Taiwan is a big player, and they have been hit by Chinese spying and ransomware attacks," said Oliver. He dropped his pen, bending over to retrieve it, flushing with embarrassment.

"We expect North Korea will always pose a threat to the south. We see enough border and cyberspace infractions," said Jeff.

"What group is responsible for this?" said Daniel.

"They are called Scar Craft," said Oliver.

"Have they surfaced recently?" said Patrick.

"Yes. They're targeting academics and experts in the south," said Oliver. "Oh, and the national news and media who report on Pyongyang's activities."

"Is there anything else to discuss?"

The room was quiet. "No, we're all good here," said Patrick.

"That about wraps it up here. Thanks everyone," said the Deputy Chief of Mission.

Eyes shifted toward an irregular tap on the door. An aide stepped in and handed a single page to RSO Daniel Levi and said, "This just came in from the NIS, sir."

Daniel snapped his fingers against the paper, ensuring it was a single sheet and not two stuck together. "The NIS managed to arrest two North Korean military officers," he said.

Jeff hand-gestured for the document. Daniel passed it over begrudgingly.

Jeff said, "Superintendent Kang headed up the investigation into their capture." He balled up the report and flung it across the room. "Damn it, how did the NIS secure these officers instead of our people?"

"Briggs, Reilly, get over to the NIS now. We need to secure those two officers for debriefing," said Jeff.

Both men pushed back their chairs and proceeded to leave.

"We have jurisdiction in this situation, but by all means be friendly," said Daniel.

"Oliver, I'll meet you over there. I've got something pressing," said Patrick, glancing down at the text he'd received from William.

Sixty

Pulling Strings

The Charles H. Bar at the Four Seasons was voted the best bar in South Korea. William had asked about the name and was told that a gentleman called Charles H Baker traveled the world in search of exotic food and drinks in the 1920s and 30s and wrote a book about it.

A suitable place to invite an old associate there to lessen the blow. A verbal southpaw, he prepared to deliver news that would be devastating to their once-cooperative friendship.

The lighting from the wall sconces gave off a muted quiet atmosphere. Few people were drinking this early in the afternoon. William undid his suit coat and slid into the buttoned leather chair beside the arched window. He sized-up the patrons in the room and focused on the door. The waiter had placed a flight of select scotches before him on the cocktail table.

"When my guest arrives, please bring him an absinthe cocktail," said William.

"Certainly, sir," said the server and departed in the respectful manner of Korean custom. William finished the dram of Talisker.

Patrick stepped through the door and strode across the knotted burlap carpet. William rose and they shook hands and sat down, giving each other level gazes. Patrick's lips pressed together; his light blue eyes betrayed his anger. The server arrived, placing the absinthe cocktail and bar napkin in front of Patrick.

"Good day so far?" asked William, sensing his friend's sour mood.

"Not so much," said Patrick and took a swallow of his drink.

"How is your drink?" said William, continuing the idle banter.

"That was you. You got those North Koreans out," said Reilly. "I'm ticked! You left me in the dark!"

"Superintendent Kang and I made an arrangement, so to speak," said William, staring into Patrick's eyes, looking for his reaction.

"Is this related to my case?" replied Patrick. He began to tap his foot in a nervous pattern. "Spit it out."

William downed the Glenlivet single malt, winced and cleared his throat. "As an FBI special agent, you are a servant of the Department of Justice," he said.

"You know it. My commitment is to the rule of law, ethics aside," said Patrick, "I repeat: is this about Ho Jin?"

Patrick's irritation externalized in a tight, drawn-in slumping of his shoulders. Lifting his drink, he said. "Is this appeasement for screwing up my case?"

"It was my turn to buy," said William. "Rule of law can be contested. It can be replaced by amicable resolution that results in meaningful sound justice." He wondered why his argument resembled a law professor edifying his students.

"I'm not having this debate. My job is to my government. My responsibility is to deliver Park Ho Jin, then present and point out the facts. The Department of Justice decides his future, not you!"

"The NIS is advocating for a clear approach of justice that centers on the instigator and not the victims," said William, as he sipped the next dram of single malt. "Park Ho Jin was the victim of his father's ambitions."

"Have you pulled some strings?" said Patrick.

William clenched his jaw and said nothing.

"They've given Park Ho Jin blanket immunity," said Patrick. "This is completely insane."

"Look at it this way. Park Joon and Johnny King will be prosecuted. Mi Cha and Ho Jin get re-educated and step into a new future. The Five Eyes benefit by way of intelligence, saving lives and resources," said William, finishing the final draught, a sixteen-year-old Lagavulin.

"Fuck you," said Patrick, as he abruptly stood up. "You can stick your platitudes up your arse." His Irish brogue bellowed through the bar, as he stomped out, shaking his head in disgust.

William understood Patrick's disappointment, but in his mind, he owed Kim. Years ago, in Seoul, when Kim was a metro cop he had come to his rescue. Teenagers at the time, William, Tracy and his brother were being mugged. Jamey was still in a wheelchair. If not for Officer Kim it could have been worse.

William repaid the favor, even though it had just cost him his friendship with Patrick. With his drinks finished, he signed the bill to his room and went up to the suite to think. He hadn't been this low since he had slept with Ava Ryan. *Things had better change* he thought, his conscience getting the better of him. He settled into a wing chair and debated, *More scotch or a hard workout?*

Sixty-One
The Sanctity of Freedom

Mr. Kim sat at the Incheon International Airport Café, drinking iced tea. His flight to Montréal would be departing soon. William was perched beside him on a stool, nursing a cold coffee.

"I have never been so moved," said Kim, swallowing his tea. "It was hard to say goodbye at the resettlement center."

It was the first time Kim had relaxed after liberating his sister. Moisture gathered at the corners of his eyes. William appreciated how his friend's emotion had gotten the better of him.

"There's nothing left to do but start over," said William, shifting forward on the stool to pat Kim on the back.

"I know."

"I bet your students already miss you."

"Waiting six months to see Mi Cha and Ho Jin will be unbearable," said Kim, rubbing the back of his neck in frustration.

"It won't be easy for them, but the consequences of culture shock are far worse. Besides, the resettlement program has been successful for so many."

"Thank you for helping. I expected too much from our friendship and I regret it."

"It's alright. You reunited with your old police buddies, and had one hell of an experience," replied William.

"How about you?" asked Kim as he crossed his arms. "When are you heading home?"

"There's a few matters to clear up and then I'll be back to my regular duties."

Kim stood up, grabbed the handle of his carry-on and turned to go, then thought better of it. He wiped his eyes with his thumb and forefinger, then pulled William in for a hug. He sniffled with joy and pulled away. William offered his hand and Kim clenched back.

"Have a good flight," said William.

Kim smiled, turned away and walked to the departure gate.

William drew in a deep breath, and calmly exhaled. *I'm glad it worked out for everyone.*

***

During debriefing by agents at the National Intelligence Service, Mi Cha and Ho Jin provided explosive information to help the South Korean government. Their explanation of their involvement in Bureau 39 raised a few eyebrows throughout the questioning period. The authorities became convinced they were not spies but legitimate asylum seekers and escorted them to the Hanawon Settlement Center. This was a prerequisite to integrate refugees into a society separated with fifty years of progress.

They settled into their seats for the first orientation class. Each faced their individual monitor screen, supported by a stand; note pads and pens were placed within reach. At the front of the class, beside the teacher, stood a larger screen.

The classroom's seven rows of desks were partially filled: only eleven people. Mi Cha suspected few people were escaping because of increased security at the border crossings. She surveyed the classroom again, fervently. Since human trafficking was so lucrative, most desks were occupied mainly by women. These women had escaped their restricted lives in North Korea, only to be sold off in China. Lonely Chinese men desperate for wives were the driving force behind the flourishing trade.

Today, the three-month program to re-educate them and help them integrate into society began, covering basic skills they would require to survive in a modern community.

"Welcome to Hanawon," said the teacher. "This will be our course outline," she said, pointing at the white screen behind her.

Mi Cha's eyes danced with delight and Ho Jin sat straight and alert, ready to learn. She placed her hand on his, grateful for a new beginning.

"This is the sanctity of freedom," she said.

"Mother, it's true. We'll be allowed to get on with our lives."

Ho Jin turned his attention to the front of the class. The screen displayed general principles of democracy, followed by human rights and finally, basic skills of life.

"Open your note pads and follow my instructions," said the teacher.

Mi Cha shook with excitement, energized by the program. Ho Jin was equally thrilled, opened his notepad and gripped his pen. The teacher started dictating as Ho Jin began to write on the lined paper. Mi Cha relaxed her shoulders in relief. There would be no more berating or beatings by Joon. Her hand glided the pen across the paper while the teacher spoke about how to open a bank account.

Sixty-Two

It's For the Best

William wrapped up all his loose ends before leaving for Montréal, ensuring he would be welcomed back to Seoul should the occasion ever arise. After what happened in Hong Kong he didn't want to be voluntarily escorted to the airport by police again for not following protocol.

Superintendent Kang was praised by the NIS director for his part in capturing a high profile North Korean agent. With strategic planning from William Fox and the South Korean Navy, they managed to free two refugees and arrest General Park Joon, the man responsible for killing Brian Pendergast and the Australian agents.

"Just to let you know, the CIA and FBI were here demanding to interview our North Korean guest," said Kang.

William's smile became stiff at the mention of the interference. "Briggs and Reilly?"

"Yes, I told them this matter falls under my jurisdiction."

"Did they try their intimidation tactics?"

"Yes, unfortunately. I had to ask security to escort them out."

"They are big boys. They can handle rejection," said William, his smile returning.

"You'll want to see this," said Kang, handing William the DNA report.

After perusing the results, William said, "This confirms it. They really are brother and sister." A wave of relief washed over him.

"Your instinct was well warranted," said Kang. "What if the North Koreans had slipped one of their own past us? They could have compromised all the defectors at the Hanawon Settlement Facility," said Kang.

"That would have ended your career, and many lives would have been lost," said William.

"Will you tell them?" said Kang. "About the DNA report?"

"No, let's both forget about this," said William. "If they found out, it would destroy Kim's trust in me. He's one of my oldest friends."

"It's for the best this way," said Kang, shaking William's hand. "The NIS thanks you for your insightful direction. I'd be honored to work with you anytime," he added.

"Likewise," said William.

***

William was upset he had stepped over the line and destroyed his relationship with Patrick Reilly. He sent an apology and a gift card for dinner at Charles H Bar and enclosed a congratulation note to Patrick on his new relationship with Nari Lee. William knew this was the beginning of a long process to repair a fractured friendship. Patrick remained at the US Embassy in Seoul and continued his duties. Johnny King from Trajectory Weapons Design would be held in jail pending the Department of Justice Indictment hearing.

Director Simmons was disappointed at losing Ho Jin, but pleased the Trajectory Weapons case would go to court. He still had his agents hunting for Amir Osman.

James and Fox Microchips were breaking ground and in the early stages of development in Kanata, outside Ottawa.

Arriving in Montréal, William reported to C Division for a meeting with Superintendent René Bouchard and the assistant commissioner of the National Security Criminal Investigations Program, who joined them via secure video conference from Ottawa.

William discussed the consequences of the case and his involvement with FBI Agent Patrick Reilly, including the interactions with Superintendent Kang of the NSI and Ava Ryan from the ASIS. Finally, he recounted helping his friend Mr. Kim to retrieve his sister from the North Koreans.

After his meeting with René and the assistant commissioner, he headed over to Boucherville to see Guy Allard, who had recovered from his knife wound. Over a lunch of *moules-frites*, a dish of mussels and French fries, they discussed how the case had concluded. Guy's expression had been serious. "You should know, I've been called as a witness for the prosecution in the trial of Chun Kwan. I expect they'll be calling you, too."

"Finally, Do Yun Cho will get justice," William had said, referring to the murdered North Korean messenger.

There was just one more thing on his list to do for that day. He checked the WestJet app and confirmed that Tracy would be arriving on time.

He mounted his Triumph Rocket and headed toward the airport to pick her up. Because of this case, they had not had enough time to talk about the loss of their baby. It was with a mixture of emotions that he headed to the Montréal-Pierre Elliott Trudeau International Airport: happy he would be seeing her but also concerned whether or not they still had a future together.

Sixty-Three

The Boat Ride

William awoke refreshed after sleeping in later than he thought. Tracy rolled over and moaned.

"Are you getting up?" she said.

"Coffee is ready. I'll get it," said William, scooching out of bed and slipping into his slippers.

"Bring me an English muffin, too!" Her coo resonated like a contented mourning dove.

On the way to the kitchen, William wondered if Anthony Fabergé, the teenager who had found the dead North Korean man, would still like to go for an outing on the *Midnight Fox*. He would call Anthony's parents, and they were in agreement, arrange for him to be dropped off at the marina.

William was going to take advantage of the day off. Remarkably, many people wouldn't appreciate the concept of a day off as it pertained to him, a cop driven to a strict work regimen. This morning, he slept in until eight thirty, setting a new personal record. After being snowed in during the winter of 2017, he'd slept in till eight, thinking he'd have a snow day. When the snowplows arrived, they'd awakened him, and he managed to get to his office by nine.

"Do you want it toasted?" He shouted from the kitchen.

"Yes, with butter and marmalade," she called out.

William reached into the cupboards, removed two cups and filled them from the carafe. He tore open two packets of Stevia and stirred in the sweetener, then placed the English muffin and coffee onto a tray and walked to the bedroom.

"You're a dear," she said.

"You know it."

Tracy crunched her English muffin and sipped her coffee.

"Have you considered what I said last night?" she asked. "The first time was unplanned ... have you thought about trying again?"

"Yes, but I need more time," said William. He changed the subject. "I was thinking of asking Anthony to spend the day on the water with us. What do you think? Just you, me and Anthony."

"The memorial for our baby is tomorrow," she said. "A day on the water would be a good diversion."

"This is such a painful time for us. The memorial will give us closure," said William.

"The minister told me that we should bring boots, because the ground is damp."

"I've arranged for a maple tree, and we can plant it together as part of the ceremony," said William.

"That's nice. I'grateful you arranged that."

"In the meantime, let's finish our coffee. Then I'll call Anthony's parents."

***

There was a light wind from the northeast as William and Tracy assembled on the dock with the Fabergé family. Some of the boat slips were empty. Sailboats and cruisers were on the water enjoying the day fishing or gracefully skimming the surface at full sail. William handed Tracy and Anthony lifejackets before slipping on his own and zipping it up.

"He will be safe with us today," said William.

"Don't get him overexcited," said Mrs. Fabergé.

"He'll be fine," said Tracy.

William started the launch while Tracy and Anthony boarded the watercraft. William guided the Midnight Fox out of the marina in the old port and past the Montréal Clock Tower into the river.

Anthony's parents waved goodbye from the dock. They had decided to stay at the marina and have brunch until the cruise was over.

William pointed at the tall clock tower and spoke to Anthony. "This tower is a Federal Heritage Building and is dedicated to the sailors from the First World War."

"I could write a story on that for history class," said Anthony.

"A lot of people don't know about the city's past," said Tracy.

"Maybe some of my classmates don't know either," said Anthony.

The wake of the Midnight Fox split the river water, and the boat bounced along the surface, shaking everyone like a wild carnival ride.

"This is fun," said Anthony.

After a while of joyriding, passing ocean freighters and motor craft, William adjusted the throttle and slowed down.

"Here take the wheel," he said to Anthony.

"I can?" said the youngster, his eyes dancing with excitement.

Anthony and William exchanged seats, and William avoided the temptation of patting his back. It took time to build trust.

"This is friggin' great!" exclaimed Anthony. "Wait till I tell the kids at school!"

"Keep your eyes on the horizon," said William.

"Okay."

William turned around and watched Tracy. She was looking at Anthony with fondness, a maternal smile playing on her lips. William's heart filled with hope. It would be nice to have a young man like Anthony to call his son.

Tracy and William glanced at each other. Their eyes met and they mouthed, "Let's try again."

The wind picked up and the waves rose in whitecaps, a sign of poor weather. Plus, Isle Charron was approaching in the distance. William intended to spare Anthony having to relive finding the dead body on the beach.

"Time to change seats, sport," said William. "And head back."

Anthony shifted over to the passenger seat.

"Who's hungry?" asked Tracy.

"I know a restaurant at the marina," said Anthony, stating the obvious and trying to be funny at the same time.

William took the helm shoved both throttles forward in the gate and the cruiser responded, leaning into the turn. William grinned like a kid as he pushed the cruiser to its limits.

"Hold on!"

Acknowledgements

No author is an island. It takes a team of dedicated people to make a book comprehensible. I am grateful to my wife, Angela Van Breemen, who encouraged me to develop the outline of Sanctity of Freedom. I respect her commitment and generosity for everything she tackles and with the love we both share.

She masterfully edited the first manuscript and added a perspective that smoothed out many of the rough edges. Her support and fresh viewpoint were immeasurable in shaping the qualities of my characters.

I'd also like to wholeheartedly thank Mike Madill, a well-renowned poet who edited the manuscript. He's a member of the League of Canadian Poets, the Ontario Poetry Society, Editors Canada, the South Simcoe Arts Council, and the New Tecumseth Public Library's Poetry Circle and Wordsmiths Writing Group. Mike put the final touches on the novel and added a polished follow through.

I'd like to thank my beta reader, Teri-Lyn Smethurst, a member of the Wordsmith Writing Group for her important contribution to the book.

And finally, I'd like to explain that any fault or inaccurate facts are solely my own and I take full responsibility, bearing in mind, the book is a work of fiction.

It was a great pleasure writing this book and I hope you enjoyed it. Reviews are very important to authors so I would be grateful if you would leave a review wherever you purchased the book.

If you purchased the book at an authors' book event or at a bricks-and-mortar store, please leave your review at:

https://www.goodreads.com/author/show/27863014.Peter_Thomas_Pontsa

Thank you,
Peter Thomas Pontsa

Author's Notes

Sanctity of Freedom is a book about people and how they interrelate despite their emotional limitations. All characters are fictitious, and a compilation of my ideas garnered over years of people watching and interacting with them. I consulted hundreds of articles, magazines and newspapers in researching elements and background to the novel. There are far too many to mention.

Hotels, restaurants and markets mentioned do exist, except for L'hôtel Expatrié. It may be a bit difficult to make dinner reservations or drop in for a drink at the Blue Velvet Bar and to mingle with the arms dealers since they don't exist.

Some other items for consideration are that former RCMP Cameron Ortis intelligence officer was found guilty of breaching secrets laws. The RCMP have stopped using thumb drives to transfer secret information as a result of Officer Ortis taking special operational information off site. Inspector William Fox does use a thumb drive however it's before these changes were implemented.

Retired RCMP officer Bill Majcher was charged with foreign interference. He used his extensive network in Canada to obtain intelligence and provided services to benefit the Peoples Republic of China to intimidate an individual unlawfully. He was investigated by the RCMP Integrated National Security Team (INSET), a multi-agency Canadian counter terrorist security force with teams scattered across Canada.

They investigate cases of national security, extremism, and terrorism. In my story, Inspector William Fox works with the National Security Information Network of which (INSET) is a branch.

Global Affairs Canada manages global network of over 175 missions in 110 countries. They find that gathering information reveals most significant national security threats, including terrorism and foreign interference. This includes weapons of mass destruction emanating from abroad or involving foreign networks or links. My character Brian Prendergrast was duly employed by Global Affairs Canada as a reporting officer.

I also mention (CSIS) Canadian Security Intelligence Service which obtains information from foreign partners' warranted intercepts and covert methods. Inspector William Fox calls upon them for information on the dead Korean Do Yun Cho. They operate in Canada, just like the National Security Agency in the United States. The same agency that FBI Director Peter Simmons asked to send Javelin, the fictional private military contractors to capture Amir Osman, and blow up the arms factory.

Throughout the diplomatic world, every embassy has an intelligence purpose, diplomats, agents and people attached to the embassy will take the pulse of the city to gauge what policy might be in the pipeline or how policy makers feel about a particular country or event. My use of the embassy's infrastructure in the story emphasizes the extent to which covert practices exist in the spy world. Since North Korea has few diplomatic ties and embassies it fills that void by obtaining intelligence through hacking into foreign government systems.

North Korea's oil smuggling ghost ships and complex transactions through shell companies and illegal banks have underworld associations. Triad networks have underground financing channels and sprawling family connections. I mention how Amir Osman will be paid by the

Houthis and North Koreans by using a complicated combination of mid-sea oil transfers and transactions in order to skirt NATO sanctions.

Furthermore, I read Yeonmi Park's In Order to Live. Her book is an eye-opening account of her journey to escape North Korea. Her interview on her defection was also on YouTube. I found the information she related very helpful to build a storyline.

RCMP International travel through Canada's national headquarters is part of a wide array of dedicated international policing activities. It includes international peace operations, deployments of Canadian police officers around the world with multinational organizations such as the UN, and NATO; in addition to diplomatic postings of RCMP liaison officers across the globe who are responsible for supporting investigations in their host countries. As Canada's INTERPOL National Central Bureau operator, the RCMP works with INTERPOL's 192 country bureaus, as well as the Europol network of agencies to combat transnational criminal activities.

While sophisticated criminal networks continue to evolve their techniques and international reach, RCMP Federal Policing also continues to advance its capabilities through the use of cutting-edge technology, innovation, and collaboration with international law enforcement partners while fulfilling its enduring commitment to protecting Canadians within and beyond its borders.

I also raised a question about why Canada does not have an organization such as the CIA in the US or MI6 in the UK. There are articles shown below which indicate there was interest at one point to protect our country with a separate spy agency.

- Article; Canada Ponders Entry into the World of Foreign Espionage. Author Jay Heisler, June 18, 2021

- The Case for Foreign Intelligence Agency in Canada, author Ryan Atkinson, posted February 25, 2017.

- I Spy; Does Canada Need a Foreign Intelligence Service, author Peter Jones, Alan R. Jones, and Laurie Storsater special to the Globe and Mail, June 11, 2021.

Kim Jong Un's regime continues to expand its nuclear capabilities and ballistic missiles and expects to have a spy satellite in a few years if not sooner. Bureau 39 continues to be the regime's slush fund and is in no peril of being closed down by outside influence.

My characters, Mi Cha and Ho Jin are in rehabilitation to learn how to enter the modern world with help from the Hanawon Settlement Support Center funded by the South Korean Ministry of Unification. I extend my personal thanks to the center for their vision and kindness integrating North Korean refugees into the community. Also, thanks to ELIM House from Crossroads, who also help the refugees adapt if they still have difficulty integrating into society.

About the author
Peter Thomas Pontsa

Sanctity of Freedom is Peter Thomas Pontsa's second book in the Inspector William Fox Series. He is a member of the Crime Writers of Canada and the Wordsmiths based out of Alliston, Ontario. An avid British sports car enthusiast, he has raced with Jagged Edge Motorsports, is a former president of the Headwaters British Car Club and a student of taekwondo with a second-degree blackbelt. A retired businessman, he lives in Loretto, Ontario, Canada, with his author wife Angela van Breemen, and their orange tabby, Mr. Tee.

You can connect with Peter on his website and social media:

https://peterthomaspontsa.com/

https://www.facebook.com/InspectorWilliamFoxAdventureSeries

https://www.instagram.com/peterthomaspontsa/

Also by Peter Thomas Pontsa

Outfoxed – An Inspector William Fox Adventure Series

Sometimes Inspector William Fox likes to go off-script like when chasing gangsters in his cigarette boat on the St. Lawrence River. For one case, the RCMP officer with a penchant for luxury fashion finds himself teamed up with FBI Special Agent Patrick Reilly, an Irish lad who prefers absinthe to Guinness. The pair travel overseas to track down members of a gang who have kidnapped Tracy Jordan, an American academic and archeologist with teenage ties to William.

In China, Tracy has been stealthily searching for evidence of Admiral Zheng He's 15th-century connections to the area that would later be known as Nova Scotia. It's here that Tracy and her team discover what might be Ming dynasty artifacts transported by Zheng He's "massive treasure ships" left behind on Mi'kmaq peoples' ancestral land. Outfoxed—a William Fox Story is a slick, globe-trotting adventure that involves the RCMP and FBI chasing the Foo Dog Triad operating in Hong Kong, mainland China, and New York City. Like Tracy and Kevin Steptoe, a Mi'kmaq lawyer, the gangsters are after the ancient Chinese treasures. Outfoxed is also a political thriller, diving deeply into the power struggles of the Communist Party of China and its shadowy operatives. It wades into the Fox family's political past in South Korea, where a tragedy took place that still haunts William years later.

Reviews

Thrilling, heart-pumping, and entertaining, author Peter Thomas Pontsa's "Outfoxed: An Inspector William Fox Adventure" is a must-read international mystery and suspense thriller filled with action, adventure, and romance. The twists and turns will keep the reader hanging onto the author's every word, and the author does a wonderful job of leaving just enough breadcrumbs or loose ends to allow room for more adventures for fans of the next great international action hero in the literary world. If you haven't yet, be sure to grab your copy today! Rating: 10/10.

ANTHONY AVINA, AUTHOR, JOURNALIST, BLOGGER

The premise of the story is fascinating. The age-old search for treasure is sure to catch the attention of many readers. Yet this book isn't just about seeking treasure. It's also a police procedural and political   thriller. Each of these three genres can be difficult to write. The story lines must be interesting, and the characters, descriptions, and facts portrayed in the stories must be realistic. This is difficult to maintain for each of these genres separately, but combined, this becomes much more difficult. Peter Thomas Pontsa does an admirable job in his novel.

ANDREA MARTIN

As a person of Chinese heritage, it was very exciting for me to read a book that spotlights Chinese history, an area I'm fairly familiar with. The novel's meticulous inclusion of elements from my culture resonated with my appreciation for the significance of Chinese history. Zheng He's portrayal, in particular, really stood out to me because of how his groundbreaking sea discoveries and historical importance are often sidelined in discussions due to cultural biases. Witnessing his prominence in the narrative was not only gratifying but also a poignant reminder of the importance of inclusive representation.

ANNE CLARENCE, THE READING LIFE

To order your copy of Outfoxed: https://peterthomaspontsa.comor visit amazon and other online retailers.